light skin gone to waste

Winner of the Flannery O'Connor Award for Short Fiction

light skin gone to waste

STORIES BY

toni ann johnson

The University of Georgia Press   *Athens*

Some of the stories in this collection were previously published: "Up That Hill," in *Xavier Review* 36, nos. 1 and 2 (2016); "Claiming Tobias," in *Emerson Review* 42 (2013); "Light Skin Gone to Waste," in *Soundings Review*, Spring/Summer 2014; "The Way We Fell Out of Touch," in *Callaloo* 40, no. 2 (2019); "Got to Be Real," in *Elohi Gadugi Journal: Narratives for a New World* 1 (2012–13); "Make a Space" as "Make a Space in the Lives That We've Planned," in *Hunger Mountain* 20 (Spring 2016); and "Time Travel," in *Phoenix Soul,* formerly *Sprout Magazine* online, Spring 2012; *Red Fez* journal online, 2014; *Arlijo Journal* online, 68 (2015); and *Gathering: A Women Who Submit Anthology*, November 2021. Lyrics to Buffy Sainte-Marie's "Until It's Time for You to Go" are reprinted with the permission of Kobalt Music Publishing America, Inc.

Published by the University of Georgia Press
Athens, Georgia 30602
www.ugapress.org
© 2022 by Toni Ann Johnson
All rights reserved
Designed by Erin Kirk
Set in 10.5 on 15 Minion Pro with Playfair Bold
Printed and bound by Sheridan Books
The paper in this book meets the guidelines for permanence and durability of the Committee on Production Guidelines for Book Longevity of the Council on Library Resources.

Most University of Georgia Press titles are available from popular e-book vendors.

Printed in the United States of America
26   25   24   23   22   P   5   4   3   2   1

Library of Congress Cataloging-in-Publication Data
Names: Johnson, Toni Ann, 1968– author.
Title: Light skin gone to waste / stories by Toni Ann Johnson.
Description: Athens : The University of Georgia Press, [2022] | Series: The Flannery O'Connor Award for Short Fiction | "Winner of the Flannery O'Connor Award for Short Fiction"—Page before title page.
Identifiers: LCCN 2022017996 | ISBN 9780820363066 (paperback) | ISBN 9780820363073 (ebook)
Subjects: LCGFT: Short stories.
Classification: LCC PS3610.O383636 L54 2022 | DDC 813/.6—dc23/eng/20220420
LC record available at https://lccn.loc.gov/2022017996

For Len

contents

light skin gone to waste

up that hill

Monroe, New York, 1962

Philip Arrington rounds a curve in his 1959 powder-blue Chrysler and finds himself unable to focus on the road. Walton Lake, a silver dollar in the sun, shimmers to his left. Flanked by lush woods, it's an impressionist painting brought to life, a dream he'd like to dive into and explore.

For the first time during his fifteen-minute ride from Goshen to Monroe, Phil's eyes have stopped scouring the road for Black drivers. He hoped to see at least one, but with this view it doesn't matter anymore. If being a lone pioneer is what it costs to enjoy this small-town beauty, he'll pay.

He turns off the road onto another, passing a convenience store and a sign for Walton Lake Estates. The car chugs up a hill beneath a canopy of maple trees. He inhales country air, refreshing, even with the oppressive heat.

Squinting out the window, he takes the second right, winding up a steep incline past single-story structures with decorative shutters. They seem fairly new, small—about twelve hundred square feet— and they all look alike.

Nearing a pale-yellow house with green shutters, Phil notices a lobster-colored man with a crew cut standing shirtless on the porch, facing the street. Two red-haired little girls run through a sprinkler in the front yard. He meets the man's eyes as he passes. Phil nods, smiles. No response. In the side mirror, he watches the man's eyes follow his car.

Farther up, Phil slows the Chrysler to a stop under an oak tree across from a white house with black shutters. The car is still now;

there's no breeze. It feels like he's driven into the mouth of a fire-breathing dragon, though all four windows are open and he's parked in the shade. With a handkerchief he dabs sweat from his forehead and upper lip.

The front porch is light gray. A carpet of grass and neatly trimmed shrubs line either side of the concrete walk leading to the porch.

Up ahead, the block rounds into a cul-de-sac. Two barking German shepherds chained to a pine tree jump at a blond boy riding a bike in circles. Next door, a teapot-shaped elderly lady in a straw hat prunes rose bushes.

A bird sings. Phil looks up at a red-bellied robin perched on a branch above the car. He imagines that at night there are crickets, fireflies, and an endless view of the stars.

He's eager for the respite from the Bronx—from the sirens and the trains thundering above White Plains Road, from his ex-wife and his mother.

His Timex says 5:40 p.m. Chest thumping, fingers trembling, he shoves the coil lighter in and eyes the pack of Benson & Hedges on the seat.

Looking in the rearview mirror, Phil runs a hand down his amber-colored face. He saw his barber on Sunday. The cut is short, kink tamed. He shaved again before leaving work as his *new* wife recommended. "Good grooming helps put White people at ease," Velma said.

He lights up and sucks in a few minutes of calm.

When he grabs the suit jacket off the back seat, he slips his fingers into the breast pocket to be sure the hundred-dollar bills are there. Polished Florsheims hit the blacktop gleaming. Sliding into the jacket, he feels sharp as a church lady's hatpin.

As he strides toward the little white house, a balding, lanky fellow in his late fifties emerges in dungarees and a white undershirt. The screen door bangs shut. The man descends the porch steps squinting at Phil through glasses. His pale feet in leather sandals are hairy and long.

"Dr. Arrington?" The man's voice is sandpaper on a cinder block. He clears his throat and coughs into a liver-spotted fist.

"Please, call me Phil. Are you Del?" Phil extends a hand. Del's mouth hangs open, momentarily mute. "Uh . . . yeah. I'm Delbert Matthews," he says. Looking at Phil's hand, he finally shakes it. "My nephew didn't mention . . . Ooh, boy." His smile is tobacco stained. "You don't look like I expected, *Doc*."

"Oh?" Phil says. "You don't like my suit, Del? I splurged just for you. Brooks Brothers. Custom-tailored, too."

Del chuckles. Crosses his arms. He leans back getting a better look at Phil. "Must be damn hot wearin' it. That's all I got to say." He glances up the street then back at Phil. "Jesus," he adds, shaking his head. "Well, all right. C'mon in."

Del's feet flap up the walkway.

In the living room, neatly stacked moving boxes line the walls. Del lights a cigarette and points to a burnt-orange vinyl sofa in front of a window with a view of the cul-de-sac. Phil tugs his slacks at the thighs as he sits. He eyes a painting on the wall behind the adjacent love seat where Del sits. It's a beautiful woman with long brown hair and doe eyes, wearing a coy smile and no top. Her large nipples are pink. Phil has the good sense to stop staring. He looks at Del and smiles as if caught with his hand in a forbidden cookie jar.

Del blows smoke through his nose. Winks. "Like that, huh?"

Phil feels sweat beading on his forehead. "It's a nice painting."

"Thanks. I painted it."

"Oh. That's impressive," Phil says. "You've got talent." He dabs his head with his handkerchief. "My wife, Velma, and I enjoy art. We were at the Frick just last Saturday."

"Ree-aa-lly?" Del places a hand on his stubbled cheek. "I love the Frick," he says. "You like museums?" He slides his glasses back on his nose.

"We collect art, too," Phil says. "Nothing of great value yet, but in time."

"No kidding." Del leans toward the coffee table, flicks his ashes. "Avery tells me you're a doctor, too?" He leans back, crosses his legs, and shakes his foot.

"A PhD, yes," Phil nods. "I'm chief psychologist at the mental health clinic where he and I work. Been commuting from the Bronx since the job started in April. The driving's too much, which is why I'm looking to rent closer."

"Yeah. Avery did tell me *that* part, Doc." He smiles sideways. "Where'd you get your PhD?"

"Yeshiva University."

"No kidding," Del says, his eyes brightening.

"You're familiar?"

Del nods. "Doug, my housemate, is Jewish. Some buddies of ours went there. Before your time. You part Jewish, Doc?"

Phil shakes his head.

"Too bad," Del says, stubbing out his cigarette. "You could almost pass. Me and Doug met in art school. Cooper Union."

"I know Cooper Union well," Phil says. "Almost applied for undergrad. Before psychology, I considered engineering."

"That right? Generous place." Del leans back, clasping his hands behind his head. "That full scholarship sure helps when you come from nothing. Bet *you* can appreciate that." His salt-and-pepper eyebrows bounce up as his chin drops to his chest. *Am I right?*

Phil forces a smile. Thank God Velma didn't come. He can shrug it off when people make assumptions. Velma tells folks right where to shove them. "So, you're an artist?" he asks.

"I work for IBM." Del's head hangs in mock shame. "Paint when I can." He smiles sadly. "Dougie stuck with it. *He's* an artist. You'd've met him today, but he's at our new digs. Gettin' things gussied up. We're outta here tomorrow."

"I see," Phil says. "Mind if I look at—"

"Avery mention Doug?"

"Uh . . . not that I remember."

"Oh, I think you'd remember." Del laughs until he coughs up phlegm.

Phil waits for the hacking to stop. "I like your work. Hope you find more time to paint. May I take a look at the other rooms?"

"Matter of fact, our new house has an art studio. We'll see." Del points behind him at the topless lady. "Dougie hates that piece."

"Huh. A competitive thing between artists?"

"Something like that." Del snorts. "You sure seem like a fine, articulate young man. Got more going for you than most of these country bumpkins around here. But listen, Doc," he says leaning forward, elbows on his thighs, "you and your Mrs.'d be the only couple like you in the neighborhood."

"We're used to it. Velma works for Central Hanover Bank downtown. I'm the only one at my job, too. And it was just me at Yeshiva. We've always managed to make friends."

"Yeah." Del smiles. "But, uh, these people are a whole other species from educated Jews and sophisticated city folks. He places two tobacco-stained fingers to his chest as he says, "*I've* got no problem with it. Ave says you're cool. You look respectable, and your landlord told me you pay on time. That's all I care about."

"Thank you."

"Just, don't expect the neighbors to welcome you with cakes or invite you to their barbecues."

A splat of gray-green bird crap on the hood greets Phil at the car. He lights a cigarette. The lease is signed, keys pocketed. He won't let this small thing rattle him. He has to pee. Del didn't offer so much as a glass of water; asking to use the toilet didn't seem wise. He could go behind the car, but there's probably some neighbor watching out the window.

He holds it, smokes behind the wheel, and forgets to enjoy the lake view as he drives out.

When he climbs the hardwood steps to the top of the two-family house they share on East 230th Street, Velma greets him at the door in a black lace bra and half-slip. He hands her his jacket and brushes past her into the bathroom.

Velma enters the open doorway behind him. He turns his head to look. Copper colored, with a chic bob, high cheekbones, and an hourglass figure, she's used to lots of compliments. Will she get them when they move?

"How'd it go?"

He turns back to the commode. "Check the pockets."

She does and finds the house keys. He sees her in the mirror, twirling them aloft while wiggling her hips—a celebration dance.

"My money was green, Vel," he says.

"Our money."

"That's all he cared about."

"Told you it'd be fine, honey."

He glances back at her. She smiles, a sexy slash of a smile.

"Hungry?" She's not asking about dinner. She drops the jacket, then the keys.

"Nah." He turns back to finish his business. "Late lunch," he says, teasing.

"What'd I tell you about spoiling your appetite?" She wraps her arms around him.

He laughs and sighs.

A fan hums in their bedroom window muffling a siren blocks away. Late-night news plays on the elderly couple's television downstairs. Phil sips watered-down scotch. Half-melted ice cubes clink against the glass as he places it back on the nightstand.

"The owner's a homosexual," he says.

Velma's cheek is moist against Phil's chest. Her perspiration smells sweet like the Chanel No. 5 she applies in layers—lotion, dusting powder, and eau de toilette.

"He told you that?"

Phil lights a cigarette. "Pretty much," he says.

"Why?" She fingers the curly hairs between his pectorals. "That's none of our business."

"Guess he wanted me to know he's different. Since we're different. He also said the neighbors are crackers."

"He said that?"

"Basically."

She rolls off his chest onto her back. With a shrug in her voice, she says, "They didn't lynch him. How bad can they be?" She kisses Phil's shoulder, reaches for his cigarette, and takes a puff.

Phil sits upright, against the wall. "He called his fella his *house-mate*. Doubt they held hands on their neighborhood strolls."

"You're worried?"

"Just telling you what he said, Vel."

"Well, I'm not worried. I survived Harlem. Country crackers don't scare me."

Saturday, Phil and Velma finish boxing their belongings. In the kitchen, Velma wraps dishes with last Sunday's *New York Times*. In the front room, Phil sits on the wood floor beside his rolltop desk, packing files. The front door opens. His mother appears on the threshold, her "key for emergencies" in hand.

She and Phil don't agree on what constitutes an emergency.

He stares up at her, stout, in a gingham housedress and white orthopedic shoes, her graying frizzy curls in a loose bun. She has his amber complexion and the same kink to her hair.

"Hello, Mother. May I have that key, please? I need to return it."

"You're going through with it, then?"

He gestures to the box he's packing.

"Terrible idea." She shakes her head.

"Is that what you walked over here to say?"

"Philip, they'll run you out of there."

His mother doesn't have his New York accent. She's lived forty years in the Bronx, but she was raised in Bermuda. Her accent isn't Bermudian either. The two have canceled each other out. She has no accent. What she has is an attitude, one he calls "anti-Phil."

"You said the same thing when I applied to graduate school. You also told me I'd never get a job, remember?" He lights a cigarette, continues packing his papers.

"Such a big shot, aren't you?" She closes the door behind her. "They may not mind you working beside them, but that doesn't mean they'll let you live beside them, too."

Massaging his eyebrows with one hand, Phil speaks with the cigarette clamped in his back teeth. "Thanks for stopping by, Mother. Your confidence in me is always comforting."

"And your smart mouth is always vexing."

"You blamed me for the pain of childbirth and you've been against me ever since!"

"Oh, stop with your foolishness. I'm worried. Don't wanna have to come up there and cut your big-shot britches down from a tree."

He returns his attention to the files. "Go home. And leave that key, please."

She steps deeper into the room. "Have you thought of Livia? After leaving her, now you want to expose that sad little girl to danger, too? Selfish big shot."

"Hello, Emily." Velma appears, her face smudged with newsprint.

Phil slides into a corner with his files. He watches Velma stare his mother down. His first wife, Dorothy, kissed up to his mother. Velma refuses; she's nobody's sycophant.

"Emily, we've got a lotta packing to do today," she says, patting perspiration from her cheeks with a dishtowel. "I've already boxed up the teapot. Dishes, too, so you'll have to excuse us. We have nothing to offer you."

"*Tsssssssssk*," Emily sucks her teeth.

Phil closes his eyes. He's dying for some scotch, but if he leaves this room, Velma's apt to call him a punk.

"I don't need your tea. Go back to your boxing. I'm having a conversation with my son."

Phil braces himself. These two . . .

Velma steps toward Emily. She drapes the dishtowel around her neck, tugging it at both ends like a fighter between rounds. "You're not senile yet, are you, Emily?"

"I beg your pardon?"

"You're in *my* house. You know that, right?"

Emily stands straighter. "I know I was speaking with my son."

"Stay calm, Velma," Phil says.

Velma flicks him a look before throwing Emily a death stare. "When you're in my house, you will respect me."

"*Aagh*," Emily scoffs. "I'm leaving." She pivots from the sight of Velma.

Velma crosses her arms. "It was nice to see you." She leans forward. "*Bye.*"

Emily flings a thumb sideways at Velma. "This one can take care of herself, but heaven help you if something happens to Livia. You hear me?" She turns and opens the door. "Heaven help you."

Phil stands. "I do need that key."

Emily walks back to Philip and puts the key into his palm. She takes his face in both hands, kisses his cheek, and says, "Be safe." Then she pads back out in her thick-soled shoes, leaving the door open. Her footsteps sound slow and careful as they clunk down the stairs.

Phil smiles weakly at his wife. "You didn't have to do that."

Velma's eyes roll without rolling. Her mouth tightens and turns up at the ends, yet she's not smiling. It's a round-the-way expression widely understood as: *Negro, please.* He watches her turn, lift her chin, and strut down the hall to a victory song only she can hear. What will White folks in Monroe make of his woman?

Later, the phone rings. "Dr. Arrington," he says, answering immediately.

"This the Arrington that's trying to move into Walton Lake Estates?"

Phil sits up, muscles tense. "Who's calling?"

"Jack Wilson. Y'know who I am?"

"Should I?"

"I sold Del Matthews the house he tried to rent you. That's not gonna work out."

"What are you talking about? I have a lease."

"He misunderstood."

"Misunderstood *what*? It's a binding agreement."

"Don't you raise your voice at me. I'm sure you'll be better off someplace else."

"Why's that?"

"'Cause you're not welcome here, that's *why.*"

Phil's pulse pounds in his neck. "The house belongs to Del, Mr. Wilson."

"You listen here. Walton Lake Estates is a family-oriented community and we're gonna keep it that way!"

"I hear you fine, but yelling doesn't give you legal standing. I put money down. Del is within his rights to rent out *his* property. And I'm renting it for my *family.*"

Velma appears in the doorway. "Who is that?"

Phil waves her away like a fly.

"Oh, you put money down, huh?" Wilson's voice continues. "If I was you, I'd pick it back up and find someplace else to live."

"You aren't me," Phil snaps and hangs up.

Velma stares at him. "Who was that, honey?"

He rubs his temples with his thumbs. "The guy who invested in the land and put the houses up—the developer." He reaches for his cigarettes on the floor. Sighs. "I was expecting some people might be unfriendly," he says. "But that man was hostile. You gonna be all right with that, Vel?"

"I am packed, Philip."

He lights a match. "Maybe my mother's right."

She looks straight into his eyes. "You think I've been helping to pay your school loans so I can live in the Bronx down the street from your fucking mother for the rest of my life? As long as we can afford it, we can move wherever we want. This is New York State, not the Jim Crow South."

They ride silently as Phil drives the powder-blue Chrysler out of the neighborhood, past tidy two-story houses with chain-link fences, ladies on the sidewalk in fancy hats, Bibles in their white-gloved hands, others in curlers, rolling carts up the hill toward White Plains Road. There are girls with pressed hair in ribbons, young men in suits, and fellas on the corner sipping beer for breakfast.

The car merges onto the Henry Hudson Parkway followed by a U-Haul truck with two guys from the neighborhood ferrying their belongings north. Phil holds the wheel with one hand, a cigarette with the other. Velma smokes, too. On the new Palisades Parkway, she stares out the window at freshly planted trees with young leaves.

When they reach the town of Monroe, Vel's eyes grow wide at the sight of large Victorian homes adorning grassy hills, like crowns. They round the curve and Walton Lake appears, dazzling, as sunrays dance upon its surface. She cranes her neck, staring back as they pass it. Phil caresses her cheek with his knuckles. How lucky he feels to have found someone moved by the beauty of what moves him, too. They pull into the driveway. Velma leaps from the car, crosses behind, and stands at the edge of the yard. She beams at the house and its vibrant grass, tidy shrubs, and sparkling-clean gray porch. She is glowing. In a white T-shirt and blue jeans, she looks more like a teenager than a thirty-year-old woman. She turns to see the maple, oak, and birch trees across the street and the way the sun pokes through their canopies. She looks up the block at how it rounds into the cul-de-sac. Then she turns to Phil. He's standing on the driveway watching her. She rests a manicured hand against the bare V of her chest and smiles from a deeper place than he's ever seen before. She nods, happy beyond words; it's a silence so sweet he hopes to remember it forever.

Inside, the first thing they see is the painting. Del has left the topless woman on the wall.

"What the hell is *that*?" Velma sets down the box of dishes she's carrying and marches toward it. A note taped on the wall says, "For your collection." She turns to Phil. "What fucking collection?"

"Calm down. I can explain." Frozen, in the middle of the floor, he holds a box of lamps.

"Oh, I *am*, calm. I'm calmly telling you: that shit needs to find another home."

"I didn't ask for it."

"Thought you said they were gay."

The husky movers, both in their twenties, enter carrying the bed frame. They stand near the door, eyes cast down, knowing better than to interrupt.

"I told Delbert we collect art," Phil says. "I think it was nice of him."

One of the movers cringes.

Velma stares at Phil for a moment in that Velma way of hers. She takes the topless woman down, turns her around, and leans the canvas against the wall. Then she picks up the box of dishes and moves into the kitchen.

As Phil directs the movers, Velma finishes unwrapping a set of glasses. She turns on the faucet to rinse them. Nothing comes out. She tries the hot water handle. None there either.

In the bathroom the yellow tiles sparkle. She tries both faucets. Still not a drop.

She moves to the bedroom threshold. Phil is helping the movers assemble the bed.

"Why isn't there any water, honey?" Velma asks.

Phil looks up at her. "What?"

"No water."

He walks to the bathroom. Tries the faucet. Velma watches from the doorway. She folds her arms. "I have to go to work tomorrow," she says.

"So do I. Don't worry. The main water valve is probably off. I'll find it."

Outside, Phil finds the valve near the hose spigot under a shrub beside the front porch. He moves the valve lever higher and turns on the hose. No water. He moves the lever down. Nothing. He drops his forehead into his hand.

Phil drives down the hill to the convenience store just outside the entrance to the development. There's a phone booth outside.

"Hey Del?"

"Yup." He exhales, as if blowing cigarette smoke. "Delbert Matthews, here."

A woman in a red sundress with her hair in a bun leaves the store, followed by two waddling toddlers licking pink Italian ices.

"It's Phil. Arrington. Did you have the water shut off for some reason?"

"Uh. No, Doc. I didn't."

The woman frowns at Phil through the booth's glass. She grabs the arms of the two chubby little boys and hurries through the parking lot past him.

"Well, there's none running," Phil explains.

"What's that?"

"We have no water."

Del is silent for a moment before he says, "Crap."

After buying several jugs of water in the convenience store, Phil drives back up the hill. He sees the woman with the kids, hiking up in flip-flops. She's slim, with a suntanned frame, her back and shoulders bare in the sundress. It would be no bother to offer a lift, but he knows better. He waves. The little boys wave back. The woman crinkles her peachy face like something stinks.

An hour later the movers are gone. Velma organizes the flatware drawer while they wait for Del. Phil drinks from one of the water jugs and watches Velma. Her face is sweaty, her lips set in a frown.

He's about to speak when he gasps instead. A fat brown spider crawls across the yellow countertop toward her.

"Vel," his voice quavers, "step back, honey." He grabs a piece of crumpled newspaper. Swallows. *God, that thing is huge.*

Velma looks at the spider, then at Phil, his hand holding the paper in the air, immobile. She slaps the spider dead with her bare hand.

"Christ!" Phil yells.

"What?" she shrugs. "I went to summer camp. Spiders don't scare me." She takes the crumpled paper from his hand and wipes the goop off. "*Now* would be a nice time to have some fucking water."

Phil bends over, hands on his knees, and exhales. "We need to put that painting back up."

Her head whips around.

"Just for now. The man painted it. He gave it to us and I don't wanna offend him, Vel."

"What about me? It offends *me*, dammit."

"I'm sorry." He moves behind her and massages her shoulders. "I'll take it down as soon as he leaves, but let's not argue about this now. Please."

Velma flips her hands up at the wrists. *Fine.*

Phil meets Del at the water valve in front of the house. Cigarette dangling from his mouth, Del moves the lever up and down like

Phil did earlier. He takes the blue baseball cap off his head and smoothes his thinning hair before putting it back.

"Jack did something shady's my guess. Threw a tantrum when he heard about you. Ah, brother." He drags on the cigarette and blows the smoke through his nose. "I'll call a plumber buddy a mine. Gotta use someone's phone, though." He heads toward the cul-de-sac, speaking over his shoulder. "Wanna meet Mrs. Lynch?"

Phil follows. "Is that really her name?"

Mrs. Lynch is the rotund lady he saw pruning roses the day he signed the lease. Standing in her kitchen with its dingy red-and-white-checkered floor and sink full of dishes, Del uses the telephone while Phil compliments her flowers. He mentions that his mother grows roses, too, in her backyard in the Bronx.

"My goodness, don't you speak nicely for a colored man," she coos, flashing her dentures. White hair hangs bluntly to her shoulders. "And I've got friends who suntan darker than you, dear. Your wife nice, like you?"

Phil bites his lip. He smiles and nods. He doesn't want to be there if Mrs. Lynch ever makes the mistake of telling Velma she's nice, or well spoken, for a colored woman. Those dentures may end up down her throat.

"Don't see what's so bad about you," she says. "Jack came by talking about some 'niggers'—oh," she taps her mouth with her fingers, "'Scuse me, dear, that's *his* word not mine. Said they'd ruin the neighborhood. But when I think of someone of that persuasion, a nice young man like you doesn't come to mind at all."

Phil hates himself for smiling again but he does. She smiles back.

Del finishes with the phone. "Plumber'll be over in an hour," he says.

Back at the house, Velma has changed into a sleeveless orange dress that shows off her small waist and shapely legs. Phil stares as she sets down a tray with bottles of Coke, saltine crackers, and Laughing Cow cheese wedges. She sits beside him on the antique loveseat she inherited from the old woman who took her in when her mother lost custody. Velma's natural scent mixed with the Chanel makes him delirious. He takes her hand.

"Thanks so much for the painting, Del," she says.

Del sits, smoking, in the bentwood rocker she found at a garage sale. He tilts his cap back and looks up, admiring his topless masterpiece.

Velma squeezes Phil's hand. "Owning original art is such a privilege. We're grateful to you."

"My pleasure." Del grins. "Glad she'll finally be appreciated."

Mario the plumber has the facial symmetry of a movie star, thick black hair, and a beer belly. He walks Del and Phil to a muddy spot at the edge of the yard where the grass has been dug up. They look down into a trench he's cleared with his tools.

"Here's where the water supply pipe's supposed to be. It connects the house to the water main. Yours ain't here."

"Come again?" Del says.

"Someone ripped it out," Mario says.

"Can you replace it?" Phil asks.

Mario folds his arms above his protruding stomach. "I dunno. If it's vandalism y'oughta report it."

"Jesus," Del says. "That son of a bitch. I . . . I'm sorry, Phil."

That night, after washing with bottled water heated on the stove, they lie supine in bed.

Phil turns his head and kisses Velma's neck. "Y'okay?" He worries about her. She doesn't like being psychoanalyzed and he tries not to push, but he knows her need for control and her toughness are connected to her childhood. Trauma makes things harder.

"I'll live, honey," she says. "Your White girl's in the closet, in case you're wondering."

He smiles and kisses her again, this time on the cheek. He can tell from her breathing that she's drifting off. Concerned about his wife, the water, and Jack Wilson, he doesn't sleep.

Early the next morning, Phil drives out of the development with Velma. A few other cars head out at the same time. While descending the hill, he sees the driver behind him, in the rearview mirror—a man in glasses and a suit jacket. He pays no attention to Phil and Velma.

They enjoy the lake view as they pass. Phil drops Velma at the station in Monroe, where she'll catch the train into the city.

When he gets to the Orange County Mental Health clinic in Goshen, he sits at his desk as Avery, his colleague, lumbers into his office lugging plastic jugs of water from the A & P. Phil moves a pile of papers and a pencil, clearing a spot. Avery sets the water on the metal desk.

"Six more in my car," he announces.

Avery is six foot four and solid. He has thick red hair and a full red beard. Aside from his white collared shirt and khakis, he looks more like a linebacker than someone with an MA in psychology from Columbia.

"That's nice of you, Ave. Thanks." Elbows on the desk, Phil holds the pencil between his thumbs and forefingers.

"Feel like I've gotta do *something*. My fault you're dealing with this bullshit."

"Not your fault people are bigots."

"Gimme the key to your trunk. I'll load the water."

"You don't have to do that."

"I want to. Listen, Uncle Del talked to Wilson. He confessed to pulling out the pipe, but he's refusing to put it back."

Phil's teeth clench. He snaps the pencil in two. "Okay." He exhales, collecting himself. "The confession's good news, though. Thanks."

"Good news?"

"A statement from Del that Wilson admitted to stealing the pipe is evidence he's violating my civil rights. I can handle that legally."

"You're a better man than I am." Avery's nostrils flare. "I'd just kick his ass."

Phil drops the pencil pieces into the trash. "If we were in the Bronx, and he was Black, maybe I could. But I'm not trying to end up in jail."

Phil picks Velma up from the station that evening. She climbs in, surprisingly fresh-faced for the day's end. She's quite lovely in a skirt suit she sewed herself using a Vogue pattern. He hadn't paid attention that morning. He takes her in now. Velma smiles back in a way that suggests she has an intriguing secret. She leans in and kisses him on the lips.

"Guess what?" he says. "Ben Gilman agreed to be my lawyer."

"*Our* lawyer," Velma says, settling into the seat. Gloved hands rest atop a designer bag in her lap. As he drives, she gazes out the window at Monroe's quaint, nineteenth- and early twentieth-century architecture.

"He used to work for the attorney general of New York State." Though Phil is upbeat, exhaustion dulls his voice.

"That's great, honey," Velma says, watching the buildings pass: a church, the town hall, Manufacturers Hanover Bank. "God, I stink," she says. "Like someone broke wind. I'd kill for a bubble bath."

"Gilman's getting a court order from a judge mandating that the water be restored."

Velma looks at him. "How long'll that take?"

"Could be a few days."

She sighs, turning back to the window. "Met a nice woman on the train. Her husband's a minister. She told me some things we can do with Livia when she's here. Oh quick, look there." She points. "See past that pond on the right, the airplane there? That's a playground. And down the road, she says there's a place to get ice cream custard. She also said there're a few Black people in town." She turns to Phil. "Including her *dentist*. Her dentist is Black. Can you believe that? And listen to this, he owns one of those enormous houses we pass on this road." Velma's eyes sparkle. Her hand covers her lips, as if to contain her glee. "If folks around here'll let a Black man stick his hands in their mouth, honey, your chances of building a private practice are even better than I thought. We can do this."

Phil squeezes her thigh.

As they approach the development, a group of people, five of them, stand at the edge of the convenience store parking lot at the bottom of the hill. Among them, the sunburned man with the crew cut Phil saw standing on his porch the other day.

The man points at Phil's car and runs toward it shaking a placard above his head that says: "NIGGERS GET OUT."

An egg cracks against the back window as Phil speeds past.

Velma yips and covers her head with her arms. In the rearview mirror, Phil sees the bun-headed woman with the sundress. Today she's in blue jeans, yelling, "Get out! Stay out!"

There's another woman and two more men, but Phil drives up the hill too fast to get a good look.

"Christ. You alright?"

"Del was right," she says. "They are crackers. I'm shooting their asses with my BB gun next time."

"*What*? No, you are *not*, Velma."

"Please. These White-trash bastards think they're gonna throw shit at *me*? I will put their motherfuckin' eyes out."

Phil gapes at her. She sounds even more combative than usual.

"Watch the road, honey," Velma says. "I know you don't like it when the Harlem in me comes out, but I'm telling you, somebody hits me with an egg, or any-damn-thing else, that's gonna be the last thing they *ever* do."

"Velma. I know you're upset. But we didn't move up here to go to war. Let me deal with it my way."

"Oh, you're gonna deal with it?"

"*Yes*," he insists, with a confidence he doesn't quite feel.

"Humph. If you say so," she says. "Don't dillydally."

Phil puts the car in the garage and wipes the egg off the back window with a rag and ammonia. He locks the garage door. He and Velma carry gallons of water, looking over their shoulder as they walk to the front of the house. The porch and the screen door are spackled with egg.

Velma pops Swanson TV dinners into the oven and then carries a gallon of water into the bathroom. Phil hears her use some to flush the toilet.

He pours a glass of scotch and sits at the red Formica table outside the kitchen. As thoughts of how much worse things could get arise, he drinks to drown them. Smokes, too. He focuses on what he sees. There's a mess of boxes, but also a mix of antique and contemporary furniture, oil paintings and signed lithographs waiting to be hung, potted plants, oscillating fans, candles on the coffee table, and drapes that frame a view of the trees and the cul-de-sac. Once they're unpacked this'll be a nice place.

Velma reenters wearing her lace slip. She slides into the chair across from him and takes his cigarette.

"Baby, look around," Phil says. "Except for the water business, eggs, and screaming neighbors, everything's just like I pictured."

Velma's eyes are dark and still as a lake. She blows smoke. "You're not funny, Philip."

"This is temporary," he says. Within a year we'll have enough to put down on a house, with an office. I *will* start my practice. Things'll be great." He takes her hand.

"I need to wash up," she says.

He watches her wipe her eyes as she walks away.

That night, though Phil can barely keep his eyelids open, he waits until dark, pulls Velma out of bed and leads her, barefooted, through the back door onto the cool grass.

"I don't wanna be outside right now," she groans.

It's too dark to see the tiny sliver of lake view between the trees. He tilts her head up. The starry sky is infinite. No city lights to diminish it. No sirens or trains causing distraction. Rapt, Velma softens, and lets the night drape around her like a glittering shawl.

The next day Phil pulls into the blacktopped parking lot outside the mental health clinic. Avery is waiting in the sun, leaning against his frost-blue Corvette with six jugs of water in the open trunk.

"I really appreciate this, Ave," Phil says, as they load the water into the Chrysler.

"Of course. How's it going?"

Phil puts the last gallon in and slams the trunk. "We've got a group of protesters now."

"What?"

"Protesters. They were there last night and a few were in the same spot this morning."

He scratches his head. "What do you mean, protesters?"

"Protesters, Avery," Phil says. "They have signs. 'No Niggers,' 'Niggers get out,' and they throw eggs and tomatoes and yell as we drive by." He points to the dried yolk on the back window.

Avery's bushy red brows meet. His hazel eyes narrow into slits. "You fucking kidding me? Oh, I'm coming over there."

"And do what, Ave? Fight? That's only gonna make them *more* aggressive."

Avery's fist taps his mouth. "You've gotta show them that you're armed. They'll back off."

Phil looks at him. "I'm *not* armed, Avery."

Avery folds his arms, tilts his head sideways, and looks at Phil, brows raised.

"Thanks, but no." Phil shakes his head. "That's asking for trouble I'm not equipped to deal with."

"Phil—"

"No, Avery! You trying to get me killed?" He widens his eyes and stares at him for several seconds. Then he walks off shaking his head.

At three o'clock Phil is finishing his notes on the last patient when he hears his colleagues clamoring down the hall, leaving early. The voices are cheerful. The next day is the Fourth of July and everyone is off. He keeps the door closed as he packs his briefcase. He's not in the mood to wish anyone a good holiday.

There's a knock. "You know how to reach me if you change your mind."

Phil opens the door. "I won't, Ave. But I do appreciate you. I do."

Avery nods. "Ring me if you need anything."

"Let's hope I can. The phone guy is supposed to come today. Would be nice if *that* worked, at least."

When Phil drives into the development, there's nobody waiting at the foot of the hill. Thankfully, it's too early.

The first phone call he makes after the serviceman leaves is to the lawyer.

"The injunction's been served," Gilman tells him. "And Wilson's been ordered to pay a penalty for each day you're without water."

"Fantastic," Phil says. "Thank you."

Before he hangs up he sees a white pickup through the window. It stops opposite the house. The door opens and a short, thick man in gray coveralls and a cap hops out. He has a ruddy face and looks to be in his late fifties. His quick movements seem tense. Muttering to himself he marches to the bed of the truck, reaches for the lever, and bangs it open. He grabs a long, thin pipe with both hands, hurries it to the edge of the yard and slams it to the ground. Phil steps closer to the window as the man stomps back to the truck and grabs a shovel.

Phil heads outside and approaches as the man digs. "Would you like some help?"

Wilson's brows are bricks of gray over blue eyes.

"Come out here to gloat, you bastard? You won this round, but the fight's not over."

Phil watches him shovel. "I don't wanna fight. Just trying to live my life."

Phil walks to the garage. Comes back with a shovel. As he reapproaches, Wilson flinches, his eyes large as plums.

"What the hell do you think you're doing?" He holds his shovel chest level.

"I'm going to help."

"Why?"

"Because I live here. And I'm gonna make sure you don't put anything in that pipe that'll poison my family."

Wilson looks at him. "Just because I don't want you here doesn't make me a monster. You think I carry poison around? I'll do this myself."

"Afraid I'm gonna whack you?" Phil smiles.

"Put the shovel down!"

"How do I know you won't try to whack *me*?"

Wilson grunts. Phil steps back and watches him dig.

"About these people you've got egging my car and—"

"Don't take it personally."

Phil gives him a Velma look.

"I got a responsibility to the people who bought these houses," Wilson says. "They trusted me and I gotta make sure the value of these properties grows. We let people like you get comfortable, more will start coming."

"People like me? You mean people with two masters degrees, a PhD, and a steady job?"

Wilson blinks.

"You don't have to worry about that," Phil says, "because people like me are gonna buy their own house within a year and move on. But if you and your friends keep harassing me, I'll get the NAACP involved."

"Oh, I'm shakin' over here," Wilson snorts. "Go to hell. And take your fancy degrees with you."

Thank God Velma was spending the night with her parents. Phil wouldn't be able to keep her from pelting this prick with BBs. He waits for the pipe to be replaced, the dirt filled in, and for Wilson's truck to disappear.

After washing egg off the porch, he fills metal ice trays with newly running water. He hooks up the Magnavox TV in the living room, preparing for Livia tomorrow. He smokes a few Benson & Hedges. Drinks too much Dewar's. He hurls the empty bottle into the trash so hard it shatters.

In the yellow-tiled bathroom, the showerhead is wider than the one in the Bronx and the water pressure is perfect. First shower in three days. The warm water running down his back is bliss.

He hears a tremendously loud *bang* as something heavy lands in the house with such force it shakes the walls.

He shuts the water off, his heart thumping in his throat. Completely still, he listens and then steps out of the shower into a robe. He yanks the chrome towel rack from its socket and holds it like a bat as he peeks into the hallway, looks both ways, and then walks to the living room. No one there. Not in the kitchen either. He sticks his head into the spare bedroom. There on the blue rug is a gray boulder the size of a football, and with it, the entire frame of the window screen.

This is the room his nine year old is supposed to sleep in tomorrow night.

Rage swells inside him, pulsing in the center of his body, spreading outward through his limbs, to the top of his head and to the edges of his skin. It bursts beyond the confines of his body and swirls around him.

He looks out the window but sees no one.

"Aaahhh," he yells, and bangs the towel rack against Livia's bed over and over until he rips a hole into the blanket.

The doorbell rings.

Breathless, Phil rushes to the door and peers out the peephole. There's a man and a woman, in their thirties, dressed in suits.

"What the hell do you want?" Phil shouts through the closed door.

The auburn-haired woman's head lurches back as if she's been smacked.

The man says, "Dr. Arrington?"

"Yes! What is it?"

"Sorry if we're disturbing you. I'm Minister Dorlander of the Methodist church. My wife told me about the way some people have been treating you, and we wanted to offer our support. You'd be more than welcome to worship with us if you care to."

Phil catches his breath and braces a hand against the door. He rubs his forehead with the other hand. "Sorry . . . a rock just came through my kid's window. Did you see anyone out there?"

Dorlander looks at his wife, then back at the door. He says, "Good gracious. I am so sorry to hear that. We didn't. Is anyone hurt?"

"No. But I can't entertain visitors right now." Phil takes a step back from the door and tightens his robe. "Thank you for stopping by." He stands there a moment, as his heart continues pounding in his ribcage like it wants to escape.

Back in Livia's room, Phil looks at the screen he'll have to replace. He closes and locks the window, glad it was open and not now shattered on the carpet. He pulls down the shade. What if those people weren't really from the church? Maybe *they* threw the rock. And if they didn't, who did? And what'll they do next?

Phil puts on dungarees and an Izod shirt and drives into the city the next morning to get Velma before picking up Livia from his ex-wife's place in the Bronx. He doesn't tell Velma about the rock. He tells her, "Avery's invited us to spend the weekend at his family's house."

"Why would we do that? I still have boxes to unpack."

"We're staying at Avery's, Velma!"

She eyes him. "I don't know who you think you're yelling at, but when you calm your ass down, I'd like you to tell me what the hell's going on. I'll take an apology with that, too."

He rests his hand on her bare knee. She allows him to leave it there, but they don't speak the rest of the way to the Bronx.

On the ride back to Monroe, Velma looks over the seat at her nine-year-old stepdaughter, who has bright eyes and curly black hair past her shoulders.

"And I hear the ice cream is *really* good," Velma says.

"Oh! Can we get some now?"

"Yes," she says. "They don't open till eleven, but there's a park nearby with swings and a slide and we'll go there first."

"Yay! What else do they have in Monroe?"

"There's a bowling alley."

Livia gasps. "I know how to bowl! Can we go there, too?"

"Sure. Maybe tomorrow."

Phil gives Velma an icy stare. She pretends not to notice.

Livia enjoys slipping down the slide built onto the silver and orange Korean War plane. Neither Phil nor Velma knows why it's there, so they can't explain it to her. Livia is okay with that, because it's fun. They stand a few feet away and keep an eye on her.

"You ready to tell me what's wrong?" Velma asks.

There's no one else in the park. Still, Phil's eyes dart around, vigilant for anything, or anyone that might come hurling at them.

"I'm ready for you to stop running your mouth," he says. "I told you we're going to Avery's. You can't even drive, Velma. Shut up and stop promising her things."

"I *know* you're not in your right mind, talking to me like that." Velma squints at him. "Like your mother always says: *heaven help you.*"

At the Three Bears custard stand, just north of the airplane park, Phil dutifully pays for three soft-serve cones at the window.

They sit at one of the picnic benches outside. Phil glances at the other families going about their business. No disapproving faces. No one says anything to them.

Livia happily chatters in between licks on her chocolate cone. Velma chatters, too. He watches them enjoy the experience. This glimpse of the life he wants for them makes his eyes water. When he thinks of driving back into Walton Lake Estates, it nauseates him.

In the back seat, Livia's curls fly around her head, breeze blown, as she meets Monroe through the open windows. Velma points out a waterfall, a movie theater, a library, and mallards on the pond in the center of town. Children in shorts throw chunks of bread into the water and the ducks gobble them up.

"Can we feed the ducks, too?"

"Not now, sweetie," Phil snaps.

"Okay, Daddy."

Livia looks out at the passing houses, green lawns, and trees. They approach Walton Lake. "*Ooo.* Can I swim there?"

"Not today, Liv. I want you to roll up the back windows," Phil says, closing his own, as they near the development.

"But it's hot, Daddy."

"Roll up the goddamn windows."

Livia's lip quivers. She does as she's told.

Velma closes hers, too. "Wanna play a game, Livia? Let's duck, so no one can see us." She bends down.

"That's not a game," Livia says. "That's silly."

Phil turns onto the street leading to the development. He looks toward the convenience store parking lot. A couple of people mill around smoking, eating. None of the usual protestors. A skinny teenager without a shirt, or shoes, gallops toward them. Phil speeds up. The kid flings his Italian ice at the car and misses.

Phil's stomach churns.

Livia looks out the back window as the teenaged boy ends up in the center of the road behind them.

"Why's that guy yelling at us?" she asks.

Velma sits up.

"Some White people don't like Black people," Phil says. "But that's only *some* people. You know that."

"Yeah. I know," Livia says, sighing.

When they get to the house, Velma goes into the bedroom to pack. Livia wants to look around.

"No honey," Phil says. "You stay here with Daddy." Livia sits at the red table with him while he smokes.

There's an extremely loud *pop* outside.

Phil drops his cigarette. He lurches out of his chair and pulls Livia onto the floor with him. "Stay down!"

Livia laughs and shakes her Keds in the air. Velma runs into the room.

"Get down, Velma."

Livia squeals with amusement. Velma crouches down.

"Daddy's so funny."

"Funny?" Phil is incredulous.

"It's firecrackers, Daddy, not a shootout."

Velma looks out the window and smoothes her dress. "Yup. Boys up the street." She looks at Phil, shakes her head.

There's another loud *pop*. Livia stands. "May I see my room now?"

Climbing to his feet, Phil reaches for his cigarette. "Later, baby."

"Phil, why can't she—"

Phil stops Velma with a scowl. She throws up her hands and walks down the hall.

They hear loud guitar music. Then Bo Diddley singing. Phil looks out to see Avery's Corvette pass the house, the radio blasting. He rounds the cul-de-sac then pulls up in front. The music stops.

Phil opens the front door with Livia on his heels. Avery emerges wearing overalls, combat boots, and a white undershirt. There's a tattoo of a pirate on his left bicep.

Livia huddles close to Phil, grabbing his leg. "Who's that big man, Daddy?"

Phil chuckles. "This is my friend Dr. Matthews."

Avery hops onto the porch. "Not a doctor yet," he says. "You can call me Avery." He shakes Livia's hand.

She looks up at him, "You look like Paul Bunyan."

He laughs. "So I've been told. Phil, can I speak with you by the car for a sec?"

"Livia, go inside and sit with Vel," Phil says. "Tell her I'll be back in twenty minutes and we'll leave."

"Where are you going?"

"I'm gonna take a walk with Avery."

Livia bounces on the balls of her feet. "I wanna go for a walk. Can I come, too, Daddy?"

"No. Stay here. Tell Velma what I said."

Livia crosses her arms and pouts. Phil opens the door and gently pushes her back inside.

When Avery opens his trunk, Phil sees two rifles. He doesn't know what kind and he doesn't ask.

"This is what we'll do," Avery says. "We're gonna—"

"I know what the hell to do," Phil shouts. "I'm gonna walk up and down this block and all around the goddamn neighborhood with this thing so these sons of bitches know they need to stop fucking with me."

Avery smiles. "All right, then. Glad to see you do have a Y chromosome."

Phil blinks a couple of times. "Not that I'm planning to actually use it, but is there more to it than aiming and pulling the trigger?"

"That's basically it," Avery says, handing him one. He aims his at the oak tree across the street.

Phil mimics the move. Avery lowers the gun and hangs it over his shoulder, strap to the back, barrel up. Phil does the same.

"Ready?"

Phil nods.

Strapped, they walk side by side toward the cul-de-sac.

Two barefoot, blond boys in shorts squat in the center of the circle, lighting a firecracker. Seeing Phil and Avery approach, the boys back away, then run inside a house.

Avery does an about-face a few yards from the center and walks back the other way. Phil follows. The firecracker explodes behind them. Phil resists the urge to cover his ears. He moves through the shower of sparks raining down and through the sulfuric smell of smoke.

"You alright?" Avery asks.

Phil nods.

As they head in the direction of the house, he sees his daughter's curly head in the window. Velma's head appears in the window, too. *Christ.*

He doesn't look at them. He stares straight ahead and marches like a soldier.

"Sorry, man. Shit. What're you gonna tell them?" Avery asks.

Phil shakes his head. He doesn't know. He's not even sure he'll make it down this hill. Neighbors have begun showing up in their windows. A few step outside onto front porches.

Avery whispers, "It's working."

Phil doesn't answer. He doesn't want to talk. What he wants is to wake from this nightmare, this battle born by his audacity to start a life.

Through the trees, Walton Lake glimmers below—nature's masterpiece. If he *does* make it down, he plans to dive into that beauty and let it drown everything that smolders inside him.

claiming tobias

Monroe, New York, 1968

If you're born Black in Monroe, New York, in the 1960s, it doesn't matter if your daddy gets rich, if your mom is good-looking, or even if you're almost light enough to pass. You're an alien, always, even if this is your hometown.

You're born in the same hospital and brought directly to the same neighborhood on the opposite side of the street as Tobias Milton. Your father sees patients downstairs in the four-bedroom colonial your parents own, which is larger than the one Tobias's blue-collar parents lease.

When you're three years old and it's summertime, you and Tobias run squealing together, potbellied, through the sprinkler in the front yard. With your wild curls tamed into two tight braids and his hair as long as yours, you hold chubby hands as thin streams of water lift in unison up-up-up, then delicately down-down-down, drenching and delighting both of you. Your mother and his across the street keep an eye on you through windows that face each other.

You're four before the summer's end and so is he. Wading in the pink kiddie pool, you notice each other's private parts. Different, but not alarming, because no one has explained to either of you why private parts are private.

He eats cakes from your Easy-Bake Oven. Your brunette Barbie dates his G.I. Joe.

He says, "I'm going to marry you when I grow up."

And you agree.

At five, you're equally graceless at badminton, the rackets too bulky for your pudgy little hands. Instead, you try playing catch with the birdie. When it bops you hard in the eye, he soothes the eyelid with his lips and says, "Magic kisses. Your hurt has disappeared."

You stop crying and pretend the magic has worked, even though it hasn't, because knowing that he wants it to is almost enough.

After badminton in the yard, his barefooted mom, wearing braids and a peace-sign necklace, comes and walks you both across the street and down the small hill to his yard, where you sit at the wooden picnic table while she hangs white linens on the line to dry.

Your mother has given you each a foil-wrapped Yodel, which you eat the same way: biting off the ends, nibbling away the chocolate candy coating, then unrolling the dense, dark cake with your tongues and lapping up the cream filling inside the way you've watched his gray cat Lucy drink milk from her dish.

After your snack, you remain at the table to draw pictures of yourselves and each other on large sketchpads with crayons from a box of Crayolas. You agree that he's "peach" and you're "tan."

When he asks, "How come you *always* have a tan, Maddie?" you shrug and say, "That's how I was made."

Your father is a tan crayon, too, but your mother, darker, is "raw sienna," which you can't read yet, or pronounce correctly. Tobias's mother remarks that your parents are attractive *colored* people, like the movie stars Harry Belafonte and Dorothy Dandridge, but you don't know who they are and you don't understand what she means by "colored." In your five-year-old mind, *everyone* can be "colored" with a Crayola crayon.

The summer you turn six, your mother, sick of being a housewife, has begun a weekend business selling antiques, and before your father hires a nanny, she thinks he should babysit. He should stay home with his daughter, she says, instead of carousing at the tennis club down the hill with those ladies in their short skirts. He goes to play tennis anyway, with Tobias's father, so you and Tobias get dragged along. You've both been going there since you were tiny and neither of you is too fond of the place. There are four red clay courts with a high chain-link fence around them and an empty barnlike clubhouse facing the courts. It's unfinished inside, mostly beams and bare wood frames of rooms, except for a bathroom that's always out of toilet paper. Sometimes adults stand inside and talk, but there's nothing for kids to do, and your fathers foolishly expect you to sit quietly on the benches in front of the clubhouse and watch them play tennis. It makes you uncomfortable to see Tobias's father play, but you'll never say that to Tobias, because it would hurt his feelings. He's sensitive about the silver leg braces his father wears because he had polio as a boy. The Ferrell kids, who live on the block below Tobias's house, have teased him about this and made him cry. You hate seeing Tobias cry.

Two giggly ladies in shorts skirts with suntanned legs join your fathers and the four begin to play doubles. Even though you're only six, you know your mother will disapprove, because she's asked you to tell her if your father plays with ladies, and when he does, she gets mad. You and Tobias try to sit still and wait for your fathers to finish playing, like they've told you to. You try to block out the squeak and rattle the leg braces make as Tobias's father runs. You listen to the ball bounce on the clay court, *clokt*, then bounce off the rackets, *ting*. *Clokt—ting—clokt—ting* . . . But you're bored, and you're six, and sitting still is just not possible.

There's a creek in a wooded area behind the clubhouse. It's slimy and foul smelling and grown-ups at the club say it isn't a real creek at all, just sewage flowing to wherever it flows. There are frogs and toads in it, which makes it real enough to occupy you and Tobias.

Because you're on the chunky side, you both wear husky-sized Toughskins from Sears. The Ferrell boys, the neighborhood terrorists, call them fake jeans for fat kids and make fun of you. You've rolled yours up, and you step from rock to rock, looking for creatures, trying not to get your sneakers wet in the fetid slime. You sing your favorite song not knowing that it's "soul" music or that the group, the Foundations, is "integrated." You don't even know what integrated means. You just like how it sounds to sing the words to Tobias. The song is "Baby, Now That I've Found You." You sing it loudly and Tobias huffs.

"Maddie," he protests, "you're gonna scare the frogs away."

You lower your voice, but Tobias isn't the boss of you, and you'll sing if you want to.

Bobby and Kevin, the meanest of the Ferrell clan, show up on the hill on the other side of the creek. They squint down at you, their arms folded, contemplating which particular mode of torture to inflict this afternoon. Bobby, nine, is lanky and athletic with clear blue eyes and wavy blond hair. Your mother says he's a beautiful child, but you don't share that opinion. Snot-faced Kevin, who's seven, has stick-straight dirty blond bangs that half cover his beady brown eyes. Like Tobias, he has allergies and his nose runs. Tobias's parents wipe his nose several times a day, but Kevin's parents let the snot pool and crust up above his upper lip and it makes your stomach queasy to look at him. Mr. Ferrell, who has a crew cut and wears a black-and-blue uniform when he comes back from New York City every day, doesn't play tennis, but there's a path through the woods behind the Ferrell's house that leads down to the creek. Your mother and Tobias's have told you to forgive the Ferrell boys if they're mean to you, because their sister, Elizabeth, who's your age, is very sick and often in the hospital. The family is sad, you've been told. You don't understand why being sad makes them mean.

"This is our creek," Bobby declares. "You're on our property." Kevin's head bobs up and down, Bobby's little yes man. Then he breathes in sharply through his nose, trying to suck up the dripping snot, but he gives up, sticks out his tongue, and licks it off. You screw up your face, and look away, down the creek.

"What you makin' faces about, trespasser?" Bobby hisses at you. "You little *trespasser!*"

Tobias's head sinks into his shoulders. "Leave us alone, Bobby," he pleads.

There are no grown-ups in sight and you fear the Ferrells will push you both into the green, smelly slime like they've done before. As you look for an escape, you see something moving on the rocks. From where you are, it looks like a big brown rock itself, but it's crawling. You point and say, "Look."

Kevin turns. "Oh shit. A turtle!" he yells. Then he sniffles.

The brothers hop down the rocks toward it, and away from you, thank God. You grab Tobias's hand and run squealing back toward the boring but safe bench.

The next afternoon, Tobias is over, and you both sit on the edge of the concrete patio sucking on fudge pops. It's Monday and your father is with a lady patient downstairs in his office. Your mother is in a bad mood, because earlier that day she argued with him. Your sister, Livia, who used to visit from Friday to Sunday and babysit you sometimes while your mother sold her dusty old furniture, has stopped coming. She's mad at your mother, and your father has refused to watch you on weekends any longer, since you can't sit still like you're told. You and Tobias turn to see your mother stomp outside wearing a frown. She's got Brutus, your father's Great Dane, on a leash. They're on their way for a walk up the path through the woods behind your house. Brutus is big. He yanks away from your mother, his leash escaping her hand, and he dashes toward Tobias's fudge pop, which disappears in an instant. Tobias squawks and throws his arms in the air like you've seen him do when he plays cops and robbers.

"Bad dog!" your mother scolds. Brutus growls at her. Your mother's normally pretty face squinches into a scowl, and she whacks Brutus hard on his long snout. He immediately bites her on her lower arm and she screams.

You drop your pop onto the grass. Then you start to cry. Tobias grabs you by the belt loop of your Toughskins and pulls you backward toward the house to lean with him against the wall. He's shaking as you sniffle. Brutus, knowing he's in big trouble, crouches and hangs his head low.

"Don't you move!" your mother snarls at you and Tobias. She picks up the end of Brutus's leash, pulls him off the patio into the back yard, and ties him to a maple tree. She eyes you two, daring you to disobey, and she goes inside the house. A few minutes later, she comes back out with Bactine and a Band-Aid. You and Tobias have not budged an inch, because you're terrified of your mother.

"Let Tobias kiss it, Mommy," you say. "It'll make the hurt disappear."

Tobias looks at you like you're crazy and you can tell he wants to do no such thing.

"I'm okay," your mother says, smiling a little, as she cleans, then bandages her wound. You and Tobias breathe easier for a moment until, to your horror, you see her step off the patio, pick up rocks from around the yard and begin hurling them, full force, at Brutus.

"You *ever* bite me again," she shrieks, "I'll fucking kill you! You understand me?"

She misses sometimes, but mostly she doesn't, and the dog yelps every time a rock strikes. You and Tobias are both crying now. Your mother has gone bananas.

"What are you doing, Mrs. Arrington?"

She whips around, her eyes wild, to find a red kickball rolling into the yard followed by all four Ferrell kids: Bobby; Kevin; their six-year-old bald sister, Elizabeth; and their older brother, Jack, eleven. Jack is a handsomer, snot-free version of Kevin and the only one brave enough to speak to your mother.

"Why are you throwing rocks at your dog?" Jack asks, sounding understandably judgmental.

Bobby picks up the ball and the siblings stand there, staring.

"Get outta here!" your mother roars, loud enough to make you and Tobias cover your ears. She draws her hand back holding a rock the size of her fist. She doesn't throw it, but the Ferrell kids dash out of your yard. Elizabeth turns to look at you as she goes.

You don't know her very well, because she's had cancer for a few years and she's rarely seen outside. You think it's sad that her head looks like a ball of Silly Putty. Your mother has told you to keep that thought to yourself.

When Tobias's father, to your delight, hangs a tire swing from the tall pine tree in their yard, you *do* see Elizabeth outside. The huge tire comes from a tractor. It's big enough to seat the backsides of several children, and he hangs it, horizontally, with gigantic silver chains. The first day you see it from your bedroom window is the day the Haitian nanny, Martine, arrives and you find out she's going to live with you. Your parents want you to stay home and play with Martine so you can get to know her, but you throw a fit and they let the nanny walk you across the street to ride the swing with Tobias, Elizabeth, Bobby, Kevin, and Jack. As she stands off to the side, the kids gape at your nanny like they've never seen anything like her. They're quiet, perhaps disturbed by her presence, but you're more interested in playing than you are in Miss Martine, because you can look at her later. You sit between Tobias and Elizabeth, and Tobias's dad tells you all how to kick your legs in unison to keep the swing moving.

"That's your babysitter?" Elizabeth asks, as the swing rises then falls. Her voice says she thinks this is unfortunate for you. She shakes her head and her lips turn downward and even though she has no hair where her eyebrows should be she squeezes them together and says, "She's *ugly*."

Her brothers snicker in a mean way.

Martine is very dark brown and her hair is black and spongy and shaped like a football helmet, but she's not ugly, in your opinion, just different. You've seen people who look like her when you've visited relatives in New York City. You like how Martine's white uniform dress fits her slender shape and you think her smooth, high cheeks and bright white teeth are pretty. Elizabeth, with her Silly Putty head, is ugly, but you don't say that.

You say, "That's not nice, Elizabeth."

"But it's true," she says, smiling.

"Yeah," Tobias adds, giggling. "We'll have to color her with the *ugly* crayon."

Your lip sticks out and it quivers. Tobias has never mocked you before, or taken a Ferrell's side over yours.

As it turns out, you and Martine don't hit it off. She doesn't speak English and you don't speak French. You don't realize that her refusal to speak your language has been negotiated by your parents, who hope you'll have some sense and learn hers. And you naively assume she doesn't understand a word you say.

Your parents leave the house the day you have a slight cold, and your mother has told you not to go outside. She especially doesn't want you playing with Elizabeth while you're sick, because her illness makes her more susceptible to everything.

While Martine is cooking downstairs, you see from your bedroom window that Tobias and Elizabeth are riding the tire swing. Just the two of them. Elizabeth has on a red jumper and a red scarf around her head, and even though she's bald as a balloon, she looks good that day.

You run out the front door, Martine on your heels, wagging her long, skinny index finger, like Brutus's tail, and yelling, "*Arrêtez! Arrêtez!*"

You know she's telling you not to go anywhere and you know damn well you're not allowed to say shut up. *Shut up* is as bad as a bad word, but you say it anyway.

"Oh, shut up, Miss Martine! Just shut up!" And you keep going on your chunky little legs, in your husky fake jeans, because you think Martine doesn't know what *shut up* means anyway, and no way are you going to be left out of a fun time on the swing. Tobias is *your* best friend and you're gonna see that it stays that way.

You cross the street by yourself, but you figure Martine can't tell on you, because she can't even speak English, so you're not worried. When you get to the swing, Tobias's mom waves from the picnic table and you forget how jealous you are that Elizabeth is there in her cute red outfit with Tobias, because Tobias is glad to see you, and he cheers, "Maddie! Maddie! Maddie!"

You hop on the swing and kick your legs. Elizabeth teaches you all the words to "Miss Mary Mack-Mack-Mack, all dressed in black-black-black, with silver buttons-buttons-buttons all down her back-back-back," and she shows you the arm movements and the claps. She doesn't want to show Tobias because, she insists, "It's only for girls."

When Tobias starts kicking his legs really hard to make the swing go higher and faster, you can't do the arm movements anymore, because you have to hold onto the chains so you don't fall off. You know he's pissed, so you drop "Miss Mary Mack" and start singing the song by the Foundations to him. You sing about building your world around him and you mean every word. He sings back that he needs you, even if you don't need him. You smile inside and out.

"All right, all right," Elizabeth says louder than either of you. "I'll teach him, too. Fine."

She begins showing the song to Tobias and then you're left out, but it's okay, because it's his turn and you don't mind sharing Elizabeth. You sing and swing along with them for what seems like forever until you hear your mother screaming from across the street.

"Madeline! You better get your butt down off that swing!" And you see her flying toward you as if she's on a motorized broom. The terror begins in your trembling thighs, moves up into your belly and onward to your forehead, where you begin to sweat. You're really in for it now. You start to slide off the swing, but you don't make it. She snatches you off by the waist and sets you down, hard, on your feet. She whacks your backside several times in front of your friends, before grabbing your wrist and yanking you out of the yard, up the hill, and across the street without even letting you say goodbye. She doesn't say another word to you until you're in the house with the door closed. She backs you up against the refrigerator and you can see Martine behind her at the stove. Your mother is wearing makeup and she looks pretty with her red lips and long lashes, but her eyes have that frenzied look they get when she's so mad she doesn't know what she's doing.

"I told you to stay inside, Maddie!"

She slaps you in the face and it hurts and scares you. Martine looks over at you from the stove. Her perfectly round head tops her crisp, white collar and you think she looks like a Milk Dud with eyes, on top of a vanilla-frosted cupcake.

"You crossed the street *by yourself*?" Smack!

Your face stings again and you're humiliated and terrified, because you don't know if she'll ever stop and you're sad that your mother doesn't love you anymore.

"And you told Miss Martine to shut up?" Smack! "Don't you *ever* talk to her that way again. You understand me?"

You stare at Martine. Her hands cover her mouth and her eyes look like she thinks someone's about to hit *her*. You know now that she tricked you. She was only pretending not to understand English and you hate her ugly, lying guts.

Sometime later, your cold is better, you've survived your beating, and you and Tobias ride the swing again. Just the two of you. You sit across from each other, holding onto the chains and kicking your legs.

"You look sad," Tobias says.

You nod.

"Why?" he asks.

You look down at the ground passing by as you swing. It makes you dizzy. "My mom and dad have been fighting and my mom's always mad at me."

You want to tell him he hurt your feelings the other day, but Elizabeth walks into the yard and you don't get the chance. She has on a yellow sundress and a short, sandy-blond wig that's crooked on her head.

"We're barbecuing hot dogs. Want some?"

You and Tobias aren't ones to pass up hot dogs. You both hop off and follow her. The street between their houses isn't a main road like the one between yours and Tobias's house. It's a private dirt road for residents, so you're allowed to cross it without an adult if you're careful. As you and Tobias follow Elizabeth down the Ferrells' stone driveway, Elizabeth stops when Jack, Bobby, and Kevin appear at the other end, close to the garage. They look in your direction. They don't smile or seem the least bit welcoming. Jack is the first to pick up a few stones. He stares at you, his eyes lifeless. You sense that he's about to throw them at you, but part of you can't believe it. He hurls one. Then another. Bobby and Kevin gather up stones and soon do the same. You're struck in the lower leg and the arm, and it hurts, but you don't have time to feel it. They're chasing you and you've turned to run. You think they're throwing the stones at both of you and so does Tobias. He runs with you, back toward his house.

"Stop, Tobias," Bobby yells as he grabs up more rocks.

But Tobias keeps running and you and he make it to his yard and duck behind the swing. Soon a shower of rocks pelts the tire until they've run out, and the three boys stop at the edge of Tobias's yard.

"Maddie," Jack yells, "stay away from our sister. We don't want her playing with niggers."

Tobias's eyes are wide as he looks at you and whispers, "You're a nigger?"

You're out of breath and your heart is pounding. You're not sure what a nigger is. You think it might be someone who plays with kids with cancer when they're not supposed to, because they have a cold.

"Stay out of our yard, Maddie," Bobby shouts. "Tobias, you can come."

You watch as Jack, Bobby, and Kevin turn and walk back toward Elizabeth, who's still across the street standing in her yard. Her wig is sliding sideways off her head and hanging almost to her shoulder as she faces her brothers, who move toward her. Jack reaches her first, straightens out her wig, puts his arm around her, and walks her to the back of their house. Kevin and Bobby follow. You're still unable to move, but you breathe easier as they disappear. You and Tobias remain crouched behind the swing for a few more moments. You look at him, but he won't look you in the eye, and it's just as well, because you don't know what you'd say if he did. You see that on your arm, just above your elbow, a red welt is forming.

He finally stands up straight and says, "Thought all niggers look like your babysitter. Are you one, too? Is *that* why you always have a tan?"

If Miss Martine is one, you think you might be one, too, but you don't want to admit it, so you say, "I don't know."

"I'm gonna ask my mother." He leaves you at the swing and runs into his house.

Your arm hurts as does your leg where the rocks have hit you. You ache to go home, but you're not allowed to cross the street by yourself. You climb to the top edge of Tobias's yard.

"Miss Martine! Miss Martine!" You scream until she looks out the window and sees you.

When she collects you, you squeeze her hand so tight it makes her wince. After you cross the street, she lifts you up and carries you the rest of the way.

At your insistence, Miss Martine walks you over to Tobias's house a couple of days later after dinner, but he won't come outside. You stand on the back porch and see him inside watching an old movie on TV, *The Wizard of Oz.* You've watched it together before. His mother is at the open door and she calls him, but he will not turn around.

"Tobias, that's rude, son. Maddie came to see you. Now go on outside and play." Tobias shakes his head without turning around.

"Can I come in and watch with you?"

He shakes his head again. His mother looks at you, "I'm sorry, honey. I'll talk to him," she says. "Try back later."

Your father tells you to leave Tobias alone for a while. "I talked to his dad," he explains, kneeling in front of you, as you play alone with the Barbies in your room. "And he says Tobias is afraid of being bullied and he needs some time to learn how to stand up for himself."

"He doesn't want to be my friend anymore?"

"I'm sure he does, Madeline. But boys go through stages, and maybe right now he wants to play with boys instead of girls."

"Is it because I'm a nigger?" you ask.

Your father's clean-shaven cheeks burn red and his lips turn inward and disappear leaving a mustache with no mouth. His eyes drift away from your face, up toward the ceiling, and you can see that they're getting watery. He doesn't say anything for a few moments. When he finally speaks, you have to strain to hear him.

"Don't say that word, baby. That's not what you are." He looks at you again and blows air out of his mouth. "You're an Afro-American. Some people won't want to play with you because of that, but if they don't, you don't need them for friends. You don't need them."

You wish that something, some magic, maybe the Wizard in *The Wizard of Oz*, could change you from being Afro-American into whatever Tobias is.

When school starts in the fall, Tobias doesn't talk to you at the bus stop. He talks with the Ferrells, who become even meaner after Elizabeth dies at the end of September. You're sad about Elizabeth, too, but they don't know that. Sometimes when they call you mean things, Tobias does, too. You can tell his heart isn't in it, though.

Once in a while, you bring a Yodel to the bus stop and eat it in front of him, the way you two used to, biting off the ends, nibbling away the chocolate candy coating, unrolling the dense dark cake with your tongue, and then lapping up the cream filling. You think he must remember, but if he does, he doesn't let on. You imagine him giving you a magic kiss, and you wait for the hurt to disappear.

lucky

West Africa, 1971

Phil, Velma, and Maddie have been enjoying a sweet, air-conditioned hotel with clean white sheets, hardly any bugs, room service, a TV, and a view of a sparkling azure pool, where Maddie, who's just turned eight, has finally mastered the doggy paddle. As she moves through the water toward her dad, she uses a word he taught her during their flight: "This trip's going *swimmingly* for me."

And it is.

Or it does, until her mother gets the idea that as Black Americans visiting West Africa, they should have a uniquely African experience. It's not enough that the African airlines they flew from New York to Dakar lost Velma's luggage. The suitcase traveled without them to Paris, she's been told, instead of arriving in Senegal, where they are. If it had been Maddie's suitcase and she were the one washing out her underpants in the sink and wearing the same dress for three days, that would be enough uniqueness to last the entire vacation.

In a plant-filled leasing office, Phil and Velma hold hands and discuss rental terms with a tall Senegalese man. He refers to the huts as "boongahlohz." Maddie is charmed by his French-African accent, and she's curious about the green-and-gold tunic that hangs to his knees over matching pants. She leans against the carved wood counter and stares up at him. When he smiles at her, she says, "Sir, may I ask why you're wearing a dress as a shirt?"

Velma side-eyes Maddie, reaches out, and pinches the skin on the back of her neck, hard, until she yelps.

Well.

When the gentleman doesn't answer and Phil's whiskey-colored face flushes rosé *and* "I'm sorry, monsieur" flies out of his mouth like a cuckoo bird out of a clock, Maddie gathers that her parents understand something she doesn't. She's still learning the nuances of manners.

Hands on hips that have recently narrowed due to ballet classes and cutting down on snack cakes, she peers out the leasing office window at the colony of tiny structures. "Those things are *huts*, not bungalows."

Phil's head drops to his chest. Velma's claw comes at her for another pinch. Maddie dodges it and throws a tough-girl frown she's learned from her cousin Suzy. Her mother called them huts herself. *Why should I take a pinch for agreeing with her?* Maddie thinks. Her mother had said, "I'd like to stay in one of those huts on the beach."

Maddie knows what a bungalow is, and what it isn't. In Monroe there's a place called Rosmarin's that rents bungalows to summer tourists. Those little things they're looking at through the window: *huts*. Straight outta *National Geographic*.

Her father finishes signing the agreement. Maddie hates to leave the office because it's comfortably cool and smells like mint tea, but it's not up to her.

She drags her feet through hot sand behind her arm-in-arm parents, as they follow the towering Senegalese man from the office. He carries Maddie's bag and her dad's across a stretch of beach to their tiny quarters.

"This'll be an adventure, right, honey?" Velma says.

"We'll see," Phil says.

As they approach the hut, Maddie looks up at the thatched roof. It isn't attached to the stuccoed walls. There's a gap. "Oooh," she groans. "Why did we leave our nice hotel, for *this*?"

Her mother glares back at her. "Stop whining."

Maddie is truly trying to make sense of it. She figures this must be like one of those other things they make her do that she doesn't enjoy, that are ostensibly good for her, like going to a million museums, sitting through a boring opera, or watching Walter Cronkite on the news.

"But look at that space up there." She points. "Can't bugs and things get in that crack?"

"Madeline." Her father bares his teeth the way her grandparents' cat does when she hisses. "*Not another word.*"

They follow the man inside. He sets the bags on the tile floor and turns to Phil, who places money into his outstretched palm. The man squats to Maddie's eye level and grins. His skin is dark and lustrous as polished coal. His chalk-white teeth have a space between the front two about as wide as the one between the ceiling and the wall. She can't take her eyes off it.

"In dze night," he says, his deep voice elevating in pitch, "dze wall will riiiise to kiss dze roof." He winks. As he stands again, his long legs unfold like collapsible stilts. He strides out of the hut with a full-bodied cackle that reminds Maddie of the uncola man from the 7UP commercials.

She plants her feet near the door and surveys the small room.

"Don't put people on the spot like you did about that man's clothes," Velma scolds. "Be polite and respect that we've brought you to a place where things are different. He was wearing a tunic, not a dress. It's a common style here. Haven't you noticed that?"

Yak-yak-yak. Normally her mother's tone would irk her. Maddie can't stand the constant fussing, but she feels sorry for Velma. Her mother's sleeveless beige dress is as sweaty and wrinkled as a used paper towel and the poor thing has nothing else to wear. As Velma moves toward the double bed, a vaguely musty smell hangs in the air.

"Don't expect things to be the way they are at home," she says. "They wanna call this thing a bungalow, let 'em. No one needs your smart-ass corrections." She glances over at Maddie. "Understand?"

Maddie nods. She rolls her eyes when Velma isn't looking.

"Stop complaining and embrace the experience." Velma presses the mattress with one hand. The rickety bed creaks. Sounds old as dust.

There's a lousy cot a few feet from the bed. *Pour moi*, Maddie realizes. The cot and the bed are covered with what looks like pieces of burlap, but au contraire; she's learned it's called "mud cloth." A bronze floor lamp with a dingy shade stands across the small room beside a green plastic beach chair and a matching footrest. Her mother turns the floor lamp on and off. Her dad sits a few feet away at a tiny wooden desk, where he lights a Benson & Hedges cigarette and loads film into his rangefinder.

"You have no idea how lucky you are," her mother says. She eyes Phil, tinkering with his camera. Then she turns toward the bathroom.

Maddie follows.

As her mother walks, she smooths her dark-haired bob away from her face with both hands, securing it in a bun. "When I was your age, I hadn't been to any of the places we've taken you. I'd hardly been out of Harlem."

"But Mommy, you told me Grandpa took you to Cuba, Jamaica, *and* Canada."

"Don't contradict me," Velma snarls. She sticks a bobby pin in her mouth and steps into the bathroom.

Maddie isn't purposely being annoying. She wants things to make sense. How is she supposed to understand anything if true and false are blurred?

Her mother finds the light switch and stands over the small porcelain sink in front of the mirror to finish tidying her hairdo. She had her hair relaxed and trimmed at a Black beauty parlor in her childhood neighborhood before they left the States, but without the curling iron and electric adapter (lost with her luggage), she can't do much except pin it back. This makes her even crabbier than she typically is.

There's a chrome showerhead sticking out of the brown tiled wall and a rusted drain in the floor. No shower curtain. No tub. A few towels, small and threadbare, and they don't match. Could be worse, Maddie thinks. At least there's an indoor toilet. And there's a small green creature perched atop the plastic seat. She bends closer to it, but not too close. "Is this real?" She hopes it isn't.

Her mother sucks in a breath and clutches her own neck. A few seconds pass before she squeals, "Honey. Help!" She scoots from the room. "There's a . . . a Godzilla thing on the toilet."

Not anymore. Maddie hops back as the tiny Godzilla scurries to the floor and disappears behind the trash basket.

"He's so little," she says. "Don't hurt him."

"Shut up, Madeline," her mother yells from the other room.

"Velma, relax," her dad says. "It'll leave on its own. Probably be gone by the time we get back. Let's skedaddle."

"Phil. What if it crawls into our bed?"

The film is loaded and he heads out the door.

He's rented a car so they can drive down the coast. While her parents marvel at the loveliness of the landscape and how the soft blue-gray of the sky almost matches the color of the water and blends seamlessly with the tan-gray of the sand (you'd think they'd never seen a beach before), Maddie's digging her outfit: a groovy red-and-white-checkered midriff top, denim short shorts, and brown leather sandals. She thinks it's too bad the sandals are Buster Browns; those aren't cool, but they're *almost* big-girl cute. She's grown a couple of inches in the last year. Ballet has toned her muscles. Her skin is bronze from the African sun and her curly pigtails brush her shoulders. Unfortunately, she has her dad's Howdy Doody ears. And her knees are scarred from the time her sister, Livia, dragged her up their driveway. Those flaws aside, she thinks she looks pretty good.

Before they left New York, she visited her cousin Suzy on Long Island and Suzy told her that Colin, the boy next door, said she was "fine." Maddie didn't understand. Fine? Where she lives, *fine* is what you say when someone asks, "How are you?"

Suzy said, "He thinks you're *pretty*, stupid."

Maddie likes boys. And she wants them to like *her*. Since Livia went to college and never stays with them on weekends anymore, there are no Black kids besides her in their neighborhood. The White boys call her a few things. Pretty isn't one of them. In her cute outfit, she hopes African boys will think she's fine, too.

Phil slows the car as they approach a fishing village. Through the window, Maddie sees a group of children, her age, older and younger, helping some men pull two small boats ashore with ropes. The kids are lined up along each rope, like a game of tug-of-war.

As they get out of the car, the breeze lifts Maddie's pigtails in the air and musses her mother's bun. They walk across the road to the beach and see that a giant net hangs between the two boats. As the boats slide onto the sand, the net is dragged along with them. Phil says it's called a seine. As the seine becomes more visible Maddie sees that it's filled with wriggling skinny fish, black on top and silvery white on the bottom. The children begin scooping them up and loading them into metal buckets.

"See how *lucky* you are?" Her mother pokes a finger in the air. "Those kids have to work."

Maddie watches them chatting and laughing. Seems like they're having fun. She wants to have fun, too, and she wants to see what the fish feel like in her hands. She starts toward them.

Her mother grabs her arm. "Wait."

Wait for what? Doesn't she want her to "embrace the experience"?

Maddie watches. The kids are beautiful. There are about twenty of them. "Look," she says, "they're all the color of black olives."

Her mother exhales. "Don't say that to anyone, please. It's not polite to share every observation."

Maddie continues to observe without comment. The boys' haircuts range from shaved heads to short, spongy Afros. The girls have Afros, too. A few have cornrows in zigzag patterns. Others have puffy hair parted into sections. Some boys are topless. A couple wear American-style T-shirts in bright yellow and orange. Most of the kids wear tops made of patterned African textiles in different colors. Every one of them appears to be healthy, clean, and well cared for. Happy, too. Nothing like the images she's seen on TV and in magazines of naked, starving African children with flies on their faces, distended stomachs, covered in sores.

Her mom thinks *she's* lucky? When does she ever get to hang out with a community of kids like her? Her only sibling is ten years older, has a different mom, and hardly visits anymore. Her own cousins aren't like her. They live far away in neighborhoods where people look and act different from where she lives. These kids have each other. *Bet they never have their butts kicked at the bus stop because they're not White.* Back home, kids think Maddie's parents are nuts for taking her to Africa.

"Why the hell would anyone wanna go *there*?" Lisa Megna, her redheaded next-door neighbor asked. "Haven't they ever heard of Disneyland?" And Lisa's brothers made *gobble gobble* sounds after Maddie's parents took her and Livia to Turkey. The Megnas had never heard of the place. Lisa didn't think it was nuts when Maddie's parents took her to France and Italy, though. She said it was groovy. And Lisa and her brothers even said it was cool that Maddie's father goes skiing in Switzerland every winter. But, for some reason, Africa's not cool to kids back home.

The kids and the fishermen begin looking in their direction. One of the men, two boys, and two pretty girls, one with dimples in her cheeks and another with a missing front tooth, walk toward them with curious expressions.

"*Bonjour,*" Maddie's father says. "We're American." He offers his hand to the muscular man wearing a striped T-shirt over puffy white pants that remind Maddie of *I Dream of Jeannie.*

"English, no good," the man says, shaking Phil's hand. He raises his eyebrows. "Français?"

Phil hangs his head, and shakes it. "*Un peu, seulement.* Sorry." He holds up the camera. "Okay if I take some pictures?"

The man understands. He gives a nod. With jumbo-sized grins, the kids huddle and face the camera. Maddie wonders if they meet tourists all the time.

"Stand with them, Maddie," her father says, directing with his chin.

She feels shy. And phony, because she doesn't know them and they don't know her. A *real* picture would be of them without her. She doesn't belong.

The taller of the two boys beams at Maddie. His white teeth are breathtaking. Happiness seems to swirl in his eyes. He's about ten, she guesses, and so cute it unnerves her. He wears bright green shorts without a top. He has muscles, too.

"Omar," he announces, tapping his chest. "*Allo.*" He stresses the first syllable of *allo*, as if imitating an amorous grown-up he's seen in a movie.

"I'm Maddie," she says, and laughs through her nose a little.

She appreciates his attention, though it renders her so bashful she wedges herself under her mother's arm.

"Oh, Maddie," Velma says. "Stand next to the boy, he's not gonna eat you." She lifts her arm and bumps Maddie away with her hip.

She stumbles. *How embarrassing.* She hopes Omar doesn't understand that much English.

Omar motions for her to stand by him. What else can she do? He smells a little fishy, but not too bad. The smaller boy and the two girls huddle close to her. She touches Omar's shoulder with her own. He leans away slightly, so they aren't touching, but still close enough that she can feel the heat coming from his skin. Somehow, the proximity makes it seem like she knows him better than she does. On her other side, the girl with a missing tooth strokes one of Maddie's pigtails with the backs of her fingers the way one might touch a baby's cheek. A pair of little hands pat her shoulders from behind. The kids are welcoming her. It's a sweet feeling. Her father takes their picture and she's glad. She wants to remember this always.

Then something pierces the second toe on her left foot, like a huge needle plunging into a pincushion.

"Yee-ow!" Maddie yells.

The children back away. She lifts her sandaled foot to her hand and bends her head to look. She sees nothing. Omar dips down to the sand and rises again with his arm held high dangling what looks like the biggest cockroach she's ever seen. He grips it by the back of its wings. The damn thing is the size of a bird. It begins flapping and slips from Omar's grasp. They watch it land several feet away on the sand.

She looks at her mother. Velma widens her eyes. Her mouth hangs open. Maddie starts to cry.

Her father slaps his palm to his forehead. "Is it dangerous?" He looks at the man with the striped T-shirt and then kneels down to examine her foot.

The man crouches beside him and waves a hand back and forth from the wrist. "*Non. N'est pas dangereux.*"

Maddie realizes she'll live. She watches the man jog back over to the other fishermen and to the kids who are still working on the net.

"Only hurt," Omar says. He points at her foot and then scratches his hand furiously while scrunching up his face. "How you say?"

"Itch," Maddie says.

"Itch." He nods. "Big itch."

"I have something for that," her father says. "It'll be okay, kiddo."

Her mother shakes her head. "It's always something with you, Madeline."

"You're the one who told me to stand there!"

Maddie knows her mother thinks she's a walking calamity. She says Maddie expects the worst and usually gets it.

The man with the striped shirt returns with three fish in a coffee can. They're stinky and floppy and still a bit alive. He hands them to Maddie.

"Oh, no, no, no." Her mother waves her finger from side to side like a windshield wiper. "She can't take that." She grabs the can and hands it back to the man.

"Velma." Her father turns to her mother. "Let her take the fish."

"You crazy? It'll stink up the car."

He steadies his gaze on her. "Give her the fish."

Velma clicks her tongue and hands Maddie the can.

"Say thank you," Phil says.

Maddie doesn't want the smelly fish any more than her mother wants her to have them, but *this* she understands—it's impolite to refuse. "*Merci, monsieur.*"

The man smiles. He gestures for her to come with him, and he heads across the road near where they've parked. He waves for Phil and Velma to follow. Up the road, there are some ladies outside a red-clay colored building, cooking over a fire built into the ground. They fry the fish and serve it to them with rice and vegetables.

Maddie wonders if her mother feels foolish for thinking they'd give them some dying fish in a can and send them on their way, but she knows not to ask.

She and Velma take about three bites between them. Maddie thinks fish, no matter the kind, is nasty, and Velma isn't keen on eating something prepared by the side of the road. Phil makes up for it by finishing his plate, and a hefty portion of each of theirs.

They find out that the man in the striped shirt is named Idrissa, and Omar is his son. Idrissa's wife is slim and elegant. She wears a head wrap and carries a baby on her back in a swath of fabric that matches her long, textile pattern dress. She cuts a rag with a knife to make a strip of cloth for Maddie that she dips in salt water and wraps around her toe. It's beginning to swell.

While their parents sputter attempts at conversation, Omar and Maddie have a chat, too. He speaks French, a little English, and a native language called Wolof.

"How you say?" he points to her shoes.

"Sandals," she says.

"Sandals," he says.

"How do you say that?" she asks, pointing to his shorts.

"Short," he says.

She tilts her head and crinkles her brows. That can't be true.

He grins. "*Tubéy*, in my language."

She nods and points to her shirt. "How do you say this?"

"*Chemise*," he says. Then he winks, and adds, "*Jolie*."

She knows it's a compliment. Her face feels warm.

"Do no worry. I will no eat you," he says with a giggle.

Maddie squeezes her knees to her chest and hides her eyes in them. Her mother and her big mouth.

Omar falls back onto the sand, hysterical, a flopping mass of laughter.

She has to smile. It's impossible not to be happy around Omar, even though her toe has started to itch like crazy. She scratches and laughs.

Maddie wants to hug Omar when it's time to leave, but as she leans toward him, he steps back, and waves.

She senses he doesn't *mean* to hurt her feelings, because his eyes linger on hers, and he keeps waving for a long time, even as they drive away.

In the car, her dad explains that a lack of physical contact between males and females is something called a "cultural difference." Maddie repeats the words and tries to make sense of them.

She's so tired when they get back to the hut that she nestles into the cot before it's dark out. The sound of waves lapping at the shore right outside is soothing as a lullaby. She thinks maybe her parents aren't so bad for moving them to a hut on the beach after all.

She wakes up hours later, sopping with sweat, and realizes she's clawing at her toe. She's been scratching in her sleep. The room is suffocatingly humid, and it smells like farts.

She sees her mother across from her, crouched in the green plastic chair next to the floor lamp. Velma's wearing one of Phil's Fruit of the Loom undershirts and a pair of his boxers. Breathing heavily, she's cowering as if fearful of something. She holds one of Phil's sandals in both hands, like a bat. All at once, she screams, stands straight up in the chair, and slams the wall with the shoe.

A giant cockroach, like the one that bit Maddie, plummets to the tile floor with a clatter.

Her father moans from the bathroom. The door is open. There's a massive explosion of flatulence and then what sounds like liquid pelting the bowl. The stench intensifies.

Eeew, Maddie thinks. *Why do I have to have a dad who leaves the door open when he has the runs?*

Face up on the cot, she covers her nose with the sheet. She spots something at the top of the wall: an *army* of humongous bugs is lined up along the rim under the roof. They look like a troop of York Peppermint Patties. With legs. Most of them seem to be gathered in the light above the lamp. A couple begin to march down the wall in unison. Her mother whimpers and bashes one with the shoe. The other begins flying around the room. Velma squeals, climbs off the chair, and ducks.

Maddie covers her head with the sheet.

"Honey," her mother cries, "can you *please* help me in here?"

For a moment, Phil only moans. Then he creaks out, "Can't you hear what my situation is? Don't ask me anymore stupid questions."

"You're the fool who ate all that fish!"

Maddie feels something land on her stomach, outside the sheet. She's too scared to peek. She feels prickly feet crawling toward her belly button. Her body freezes.

"Mommy! Heeeelp!"

The prickling continues toward Maddie's privates.

She hears nothing to indicate that her mother is coming to her rescue. She uncovers her head, grabs the top of the sheet with both hands, and shakes it, to make it billow. She thinks the motion will fling the bug off, but the thin cot isn't heavy enough to hold the sheet secure at the bottom. All she does is pull it off of her legs.

The giant roach falls onto her bare thigh. Maddie shrieks as she bats it off with the back of her hand.

Despite her scream, Velma doesn't so much as glance in her direction. Maddie watches her mother standing there wincing at the gooey carcass of the bug she's squashed. It remains stuck to the wall, and she trembles and whimpers like a little girl. Her mother is more concerned about being attacked herself than she is about her daughter.

Something moving on the floor catches Maddie's eye: the little green lizard. It skitters across the tiles toward her mother's bare feet. Maddie has to pee, but there's no getting into the bathroom. She tucks the sheet back under the useless mattress and though the room feels hot enough to cook humans, she pulls the mud cloth completely over her head, too. Seconds later, her mother screams, "Godzilla thing!" and she topples into the chair with a traumatized howl.

The three of them are packed and out of there by the time the sun rises.

When they leave Senegal, they fly to Ivory Coast. Hôtel Ivoire in Abidjan is as spectacular to Maddie as the hut on the beach was a dump. It's gigantic. It's new. It has air-conditioning, comfy beds, plush towels, and crisp sheets. It has a skating rink, a bowling alley, a casino, shops, restaurants, and a pool the size of a lake. This is no exaggeration. It *is* a manmade lake. The water temperature is perfect. They can just walk right in. It's paradise in West Africa to Maddie.

On the second day they take a drive into the rain forest. It's lush with spectacular trees and plants. They visit a farm where mongooses are raised. Maddie gets to hold a baby. He's furry and soft and he tickles her fingers when he hides his little face between them.

Her toe is still itching, and it's swollen fat as a pickle, but Ivory Coast is magical. She forgives her feckless parents for the hut on the beach.

She wakes in the cushy room at Hôtel Ivoire to the sound of her mother's hushed voice saying she can't do . . . *something*. Maddie's unable to make out what. She's annoyed at having been woken from a fun dream of playing with the baby mongoose. As she stretches and feels the smoothness of the cool cotton sheets against her calves, she realizes she has to go to the bathroom.

Her father stands at the foot of her parents' bed, two feet from Maddie's, in front of the TV. Its volume is low. Light flickers from the screen. He's smoking a cigarette.

And he's completely naked.

She really has to go. But how is she going to do that without dealing with *this*? He moves into the gap between their beds to use an ashtray on the nightstand. He sits with his back to her mother, facing Maddie's bed. Before she squeezes her eyes shut, she sees all his dangling stuff.

Ew. Big ew.

She's seen a drawing of a man's private parts in a book her father keeps in his office, but she certainly doesn't want to see her own *daddy's* ding-a-ling. In all her eight years, Maddie has never heard of any kids seeing their father naked.

She makes some noise—yawns and stretches again—hoping her stirring will make him cover up. She hears him suck his teeth and exhale, like it annoys him to have to do it, but he *finally* gets under the covers. And she gets up to pee.

The next morning when she wakes up and gets ready to go down to breakfast, her parents won't get out of bed. It's 9:00 a.m., the time they've been going, but they stay under the covers.

"What's going on?" Maddie asks.

Her father peers over the sheet. His unshaved face is spotted with stubble. "Go down and buy the paper for Daddy. By the time you get back, we'll be ready."

She stands at the foot of their bed and looks at them, both staring back at her, their limbs entwined into a single log under the covers. They think she's clueless. But Maddie has a feeling something *grown-up* is going on here. And she gets it, they've been on this vacation for a week and she's always around. Every minute of every day. There's no sending her to her room or going to theirs. But what do they expect bringing her on the trip without her big sister? The last time they traveled, she and Livia had a separate room from them. Her parents' grown-up stuff isn't her problem, and no way is she going to wander around alone in a place as huge as Hôtel Ivoire. Even at her age she knows that's some bullshit.

"That's all right." She sits down on her bed. "I'll wait."

"Madeline. Do as Daddy says. Go down to the gift shop and buy the paper."

"We can get the paper when we all go together, like we've *been* doing."

Her mother blows air through her lips. "Maddie, your father needs some privacy."

"Okay. Get up and come with me so he can have it."

"I need to help him with something."

"With what?"

Velma sits up. "With *none of your business*. Go get the paper. Make it an adventure. You're a big girl."

"I'm not that big. I could get kidnapped."

"We should be so lucky," her father says.

Just mean. Maddie crosses her arms over her chest.

"Don't be such a baby," her mother says. "When I was your age, I was taking the city bus to school by myself."

Her father points to the table. "Take that change," he says, gritting his teeth, "and do what I said. Or you won't get to go in the pool for the rest of the trip."

Maddie hangs her head and leaves.

She trudges almost all the way down to the elevator bank at the end of the hall and realizes the money to buy the paper is still in the room. *Good*, she thinks. *Why should I have to get their stupid paper, anyway?*

She plods back down the hall and sits outside their door on the sea of green carpet. A few used breakfast trays dot the quiet hallway. Knees to her chest, she rocks on her backside. She wants to tell someone about her parents' transgressions.

A stout, graying man in black slacks and a white jacket walks down the hall and approaches the door. His tan skin is the peanut-buttery color of Mary Jane candies, lighter than most Africans she's seen. There are French people in Abidjan, White ones, and Black Africans, too. She thinks maybe he's a mixture of both. His nametag says, "Xavier."

"*Bonjour, mademoiselle.*" He eyes her as if he has a question.

"*Bonjour, monsieur.*" Embarrassed to be sitting out here, she can't look at him. She stares down at her fat toe squeezed into the Buster Browns.

"This is the room belonging to Dr. Arrington?"

She nods. She likes how his *this* and *the* sound like *zis* and *ze* in his French accent.

"There is a message from the airlines about the luggage."

She looks up to see the slip of paper in his hands. "Want me to give it to them?"

"They are inside?"

Maddie nods and scratches her toe.

"Er, what is wrong with your foot?" he asks.

"Bug bite."

"Tsk, tsk. Allergic reaction. You have seen the doctor?"

"No."

A crease appears between his bushy brows. "You are out here all by yourself? *Pourquoi?*"

She thumbs at the door like a hitchhiker. "Ask them."

Xavier clucks his tongue and knocks.

"Goddamn it, Maddie," her father yells. "You haven't been gone five minutes. Just wait!"

Xavier steps back and puts a hand to his chest. He looks at Maddie, his eyelids pulled up like window shades. She shrugs.

He knocks again. "Er, begging your pardon for troubling you," he says, sounding the opposite of sincere. "I have come from the front desk with a message." He clears his throat.

"Oh. Okay," Phil says, his tone softening. "Just one moment, please."

Xavier humphs, looks at the ceiling, and mutters something Maddie doesn't catch.

When the door opens, Phil is bare chested in a pair of brown slacks. He smiles. Xavier is stone-faced. He stretches his arm with a flourish, presenting the note as if it's a royal edict.

"It is about the lost luggage. All the information is there."

"All right, thank you." Phil takes the note. He notices Maddie, and growls under his breath.

"Pardon me, sir," Xavier says. "I am obliged to tell you that we have a policy: children twelve and younger *must* have adult supervision at all times. The hotel cannot be responsible."

Phil's eyes darken. He nods.

Xavier winks at Maddie and walks away.

Phil doesn't ask about the newspaper. He walks back into the room. Maddie steps inside and closes the door.

Velma is in the bathroom fluffing her hair in the mirror. She had a wash and set in the hotel beauty parlor the day before. She wears a new bra and panties she's bought in one of the boutiques downstairs.

Phil slaps the note on the marble counter. "They found your luggage."

"What?" She gapes at him in the mirror.

"Told you not to go buying all that stuff." He moves to the closet and flings the door open.

"The thing was insured, Phil. I expected to get reimbursed."

"You only get reimbursed if they don't find it."

"What was I supposed to do? Wear the same clothes the entire trip?" She steps into the doorway. "I wanted to look nice for you."

"You could've done that with a lot less." He pulls an Izod shirt over his head.

"Thanks, *I guess*." She turns back into the bathroom and snaps the door shut.

Phil grabs his cigarettes and leaves the room.

Maddie's parents aren't speaking much when they drive through Abidjan after breakfast. Phil wants to visit the American embassy. Velma is sullen and she doesn't comment as he points things out through the window.

Maddie is quiet, too. From the back seat of their rented car, she watches a Frenchman, White, in a military police uniform, use a club to beat a Black African man on the ground. It shocks and scares her. Her parents drive by with no mention of it. Though the image sears itself into her mind, Maddie doesn't say a word. She doesn't know what to say. She notices that most of the French men and women on the streets are nicely dressed, while many of the Africans' clothes are shabby. She sees another Frenchman shout at an old Black woman, who holds out her hands, begging.

At home, she's seen Black people beaten on the news. White kids have thrown stones and called her names. But it surprises and saddens her to see that this kind of unfairness takes place even in Côte d'Ivoire, *in Africa*, where Black people came from.

They park near the American embassy and arrive to find a young marine guarding the entrance. He has baby blue eyes and scorched skin peeling on his nose. He looks overheated in long army fatigues.

"Good afternoon." Phil nods and smiles. "How're you doing?" His voice sounds too friendly. After what Maddie's seen in the streets, she doesn't want her father sucking up to this young man.

"Fine, thank you." The marine is stoic. Not rude, and not gracious either.

"Good. Uh . . . I'm here from the States—New York. And I wonder if I could meet any of the Americans working here?"

The marine squints and leans forward. "Y'all got an appointment?"

"No," Phil says. "But I was told that tourists could come by the embassy and sometimes meet Americans living here."

"Who told you that?" He looks behind Maddie's father to where she and her mother are standing.

Maddie gives him the look she learned from Cousin Suzy—narrowed eyes, crinkled nose, pinched mouth. He doesn't seem to notice.

Her father glances back at them. She can see he's getting annoyed, but he doesn't let irritation appear in his voice. "I did some work for the Peace Corps recently in Ankara, Turkey, and I heard it then."

"Never heard anything like that here," the marine says.

"I see. Would you mind asking, please?"

The marine stares at him.

"We've done the tourist activities. I'd love to speak with people who actually live here—get a better idea of what life is really like. How long have *you* been here?"

Finally, the marine smiles. He scoffs at the same time. "*Too* long," he says. "All right, wait here a minute, please."

He disappears inside the gate.

Phil lets out a breath. Velma stares at him. She pats her hair as if she wants a compliment. He lights a cigarette, turns away, and drops the match on the driveway.

This seems inappropriate to Maddie. There's no other dirt or trash there. She picks the match up and sticks it in the back pocket of her shorts. She doesn't want her dad to get in trouble.

The marine returns. "No one's available to come out. What ya might wanna do is *call ahead* next time and make an appointment."

"May I make an appointment now? Since I'm here?" Phil asks.

"Person who does that's not here right now. Call later."

Phil's jaw tightens. "Thank you."

They drive away. Maddie doesn't know where they're going. She hopes back to the hotel to swim.

"Cracker," her mother says.

"Velma," her father says.

"He *was*."

"Please. Not now." Phil eyes Maddie in the rearview mirror.

"What's a cracker?" she asks.

Both parents are silent.

Her father glares at her mother. "Well? Why don't you tell her?"

Velma exhales. "It's a bad word, Maddie. I shouldn't have said it. And don't you say it." She turns to look at her. "I'm sorry. Mommy shouldn't say bad words around you."

"But what does it mean?"

"It doesn't matter what it means, because you can't say it, so don't worry about it."

Pas de respect.

A boxy beige Peugeot pulls alongside them at a traffic light. The driver, a Black man wearing a suit, motions for Velma to roll down her window.

"Are you the folks who were just at the embassy?" He sounds American and looks about her dad's age, late thirties.

"Yes," Phil says.

"Alan Reese, secretary to the ambassador. I'm on my way to host a luncheon at my home. If you're free, you're welcome to follow me."

"Oh, yes. We'd love that. Thank you."

Mr. Reese's house has a small green backyard. And the best thing about it, in Maddie's opinion, is a floppy-eared, Labrador retriever puppy named Othello. She loves puppies. He licks her all over the face and nibbles her fingers with his pointy teeth. They run together, trampling the grass. She's worn out and panting for a break when her mom calls her inside.

They sit around a long table with a wicker ceiling fan overhead. There are tall palm plants around the room, artwork, and African masks on the walls. Maddie learns that Mr. and Mrs. Reese are from Washington, D.C. They have no kids. He's light brown and over-weight, with ingrown hair bumps on his cheeks. His wife is copper brown with short curly hair, and she looks fit in a sleeveless navy blue dress. An African lady in a gray uniform serves the lunch.

There are a number of guests, men and women of different races, who seem fancy to Maddie. Sophisticated. Her mother whispers that they're diplomats from around the world. She guesses that *diplomat* means important person, since that's how they appear to her. The conversations are over her eight-year-old head. There are no kids and she isn't hungry, so she goes back outside to play with the puppy.

Mr. Reese follows. He sits on the patio steps. Othello and Maddie roll around in the grass. Each time she looks up, Mr. Reese is smiling at her. She gets the feeling he thinks she's younger than she is, because he pats his thigh, inviting her to sit on his lap. *Who does he think he is, Santa Claus?* Maddie doesn't know him. No way she's going to sit on his lap.

She looks through the sliding glass doors to see where her parents are. Not checking for her, that's where they are. They're probably glad to have adults to talk to after being stuck with no one but her and each other for a few days. She wonders if Mr. Reese wants to hang out with her because he doesn't have kids of his own. Maybe he doesn't like diplomats. Maddie wishes he'd go back inside. Othello turns over onto his back, and she scratches his belly.

"It's time for him to eat. Would you like to help feed him?" Mr. Reese asks.

She has to think about that. "I have to ask my mother." She knows her mother won't care, but she doesn't think he knows that. She isn't sure what feeding the dog will entail. Will she have to be alone with Mr. Reese? Will she have to sit on his lap?

He laughs and stands up. "*Othello, prêt à manger?*"

The dog ditches Maddie like she has cooties. He runs to the patio's sliding door. Mr. Reese waves for her to follow.

He stops by the table where her parents sit. They're each chatting separately with the person beside them, smiles on their faces, cocktails in their hands.

Mr. Reese taps her mother's bare shoulder. "Excuse me, your little girl says she needs permission to feed Othello. That okay with you?"

Velma glances at him quickly. "What?" She laughs. "Of course." She goes back to her conversation without even looking at Maddie.

Othello is already waiting in the kitchen when they get there. He's whining, and his nails click on the tile as he dances a jig around the metal bowl on the floor. Mr. Reese picks up the bowl and gives it to

Maddie. He turns to the sack of dog food sitting on the counter. He unfolds the bag and hands her a scooper from inside.

"Reach in and fill that up, sweetie," he says.

As she does, Othello jumps up. One of his back paws lands on her inflamed toe. Excruciating. Still, she manages to pour the food into the bowl. Othello is so excited, he jumps on her again as she leans over to set it down. This time he knocks her off balance. The bowl falls with her. Pellets scatter everywhere and Othello busies himself gobbling them up.

"You okay, pretty girl?"

She is. Embarrassed, but fine. The way Mr. Reese lifts her up from under her arms doesn't bother her, though she doesn't think it's necessary. But then he starts dusting off her behind. *That*, she minds.

Maddie's mother has told her she must never let anyone touch her private parts. Mr. Reese brushes her butt repeatedly. She wants to tell him to stop, but would that be rude? If it is, and he tells, she'll be in trouble.

"Looks like you have a burn mark on your *derrière*," he says. "Sorry. I thought it was something from the floor."

She forgot she put the match at the embassy into her pocket. There'll be a scolding, maybe even a spanking, if she shows her mother a burn on her clothes. She isn't going to say anything about it. She leaves the kitchen without a word and goes back to her parents. She sits on her father's thigh.

When Mr. Reese returns to the table, he tells her parents that there's a black-tie party at the ambassador's house the next night, with dinner and dancing. He says he'd be delighted if they'd attend as his guests.

A light sparks in Phil's eyes. "We'd love to." He grins.

In the car, Velma says, "We can't bring her to a formal, nighttime event. Why did you say yes without even asking me?"

"You don't want to go?"

"Of course I do, but—"

"The hotel has babysitting services, Velma. Relax."

In the back seat, Maddie leans toward Phil. "I don't wanna stay with a hotel babysitter."

Her mother turns to look at her. "Do you realize how lucky you are to be staying in a hotel nice enough to *have* babysitters?"

"But what if I don't like her? What if she's mean?"

"Madeline." Her father eyes her in the rearview mirror. "Mommy and Daddy need a break."

"A break? From what? You're on vacation."

"Listen, kiddo," he says. "I'll take you swimming tomorrow, but *only* if you don't make another sound."

"But—"

"Ah, ah. You wanna go swimming?"

The next day, Maddie's mother goes to the beauty parlor and her father keeps his word. He stands in the manmade lake where the water reaches his hips and he watches as she does handstands and underwater flips and doggy paddles in circles around him. He cheers halfheartedly, says that her swimming has improved, she's like a mermaid, and if she keeps it up, she could be in the Olympics one day. They both know he's full of it, but the attention makes her smile.

She stops swimming and stands with her toes touching the bottom. The water is at her chin. "Daddy," she asks, "if you and Mommy wanted to go out and do things without me, why'd you bring me?"

"What choice did we have? Leave you home alone?"

Not the answer she was hoping for. Weren't parents supposed to *want* their kids to be with them?

"No one else would take you for three weeks. We love you, but you don't seem to realize that the world doesn't revolve around you."

"Maybe you and Mommy would like the world more without me? Maybe you shouldn't have had me."

He exhales. "Stop it. Let your parents have a night out without the drama. Okay?" He leans down and kisses the top of her head.

Phil is already annoyed with Velma for overspending on clothes. That hasn't stopped her from buying *another* new dress in one of the hotel's boutiques. Though her luggage has been located, it hasn't yet arrived, and she needed something special. It is. Long, tight, and red, with a plunging neckline. It shows off her round hips, small waist, and ample bosom. Her hair is in soft dark curls around her face. She douses herself in Chanel No. 5, filling the room with a perfume fog. As she stands in front of the mirror on the dresser and lines her eyelids in black, Maddie stands beside her and watches.

"Why does the ambassador want you and Daddy to come to his party?"

"I don't really know. Maybe because Daddy worked with the Peace Corps. I think the Reeses were happy to see another Black American couple and wanted our company."

"I don't like Mr. Reese. He talks to me like I'm a baby."

"Go put your pajamas on, please."

Finished with her eyes, Velma applies red lipstick.

"It's not even six o'clock," Maddie whines.

"I want you ready for bed when the sitter comes."

"Why?"

Velma turns to Maddie. "Do what I said."

Her father is still in the shower, but she changes quickly, in case he comes out. He might like walking around naked but she doesn't want him seeing her that way. Her pajamas are light blue with a button-down top. She likes them even though they aren't girly or pretty.

There's a loud knock. Maddie's stomach drops like an elevator falling. Her forehead begins to perspire. *Will she be nice? Will she speak English? Will she play cards and let me stay up late?*

Her mother checks her face in the mirror and smiles. She knows she looks good. Maddie watches her glide across the room with her shoulders back and her chin up, as if modeling on a runway. She opens the door.

A young Ivorian man stands there. He might be a teenager. He's wearing a white kufi hat that resembles a bowl upside down and a long white tunic (which Maddie won't mistakenly call a dress) over matching pants. His eyes bulge at the sight of Velma.

"Jacques." He smiles and bows his head.

He's handsome—broad shoulders, smooth dark skin, straight white teeth, high cheekbones. *Fine*, as they'd say in Suzy's hood. Maddie wonders why he's here. To deliver the lost luggage? She doesn't see it, but it is supposed to arrive today.

"Hello," her mother says. "Can I help you?"

"Yes," he dips his head again. "For dze bey-bey." His accent is thick as a jungle. He obviously doesn't speak much English.

She hesitates. "Uh, *you're* . . . the sitter?"

"Sittah. *Oui.*" He nods.

Maddie is behind her mother and can't see her face. She's silent. Is she shocked? Maddie sure is.

"Uh . . ." Velma swallows. "Okay. Come in."

"No," Maddie whines. "It's *not* okay."

"Calm down, Madeline."

Jacques steps past her and her mother and sits across the room at the table where her father's cigarettes are. Maddie eyes him. Terror twitters in her stomach as she watches him place his hands on his thighs. He keeps his long fingers stuck together. They remind Maddie of Kit Kat bars. Then his legs begin shaking, bouncing his candy bar hands up and down.

Phil comes out of the bathroom, dressed in his black suit.

"Daddy, the sitter is a man!" Maddie wraps her arms around him and buries her face in his jacket. "I don't want to stay with him."

"Uh. I see." Her father looks at Jacques. "I apologize. She's upset, because she was expecting a lady sitter." He pets Maddie's head.

Jacques stands. "Sittah. *Oui.* For dze bey-bey." He holds out his hand.

"Oh boy," Phil says, leaving Maddie to cross and shake Jacques's hand. "No English?"

"Anglais, no. Français."

Phil looks at Velma. "I asked them if there was someone who spoke English and they said yes."

"Did you ask for a woman?"

"I said it was for my daughter, I assumed—"

"Call the front desk, Phil."

The phone rings as he moves toward it.

Maddie nuzzles next to her mother.

"That's probably them," Velma says. "They know they made a mistake." She puts an arm around Maddie.

"Yes," Phil says, as he answers. "Oh. I see . . . Wow. Really? . . . All right, yes. We'll be right down." He hangs up and turns from the nightstand toward Velma. "The ambassador's Rolls-Royce is here. We have to go."

"Nooo." Maddie whimpers.

"Phil. What's wrong with you? Call the concierge." Velma says. "She's shaking."

"I—the car is here, Velma."

"They can wait. Call back and tell them to send a woman."

He turns and dials the desk.

"*Relax*," Velma mocks. "*They have babysitting services.*" She shakes her head.

Maddie sees Jacques standing by the table, smiling at her mother with his bulging eyes.

"Yes, hi, this is Dr. Arrington again . . . I know, we'll be down shortly, but wait, no, no, don't put me on hold! Hello? . . . Yes, I'm calling about something else. The child-care service sent a young man to look after our daughter and we need a woman . . . What? . . . Ah. I see. Okay. When? . . . Are you sure?" He exhales. "Thank you . . . Yes, yes. We'll be there directly." He hangs up.

"What's going on?" Velma asks.

"It *is* going to be a woman. She's running late, so they sent him, but she's on her way."

"How long?"

"They said five minutes."

"Humph," Velma says. "How long is that in African time?"

His face reddens. "Why don't you wait with her? I'll take the car, you take a cab and meet me."

Velma frowns. "Why don't we both take a cab when she gets here?"

"Velma. I . . . Because they sent a chauffeured Rolls-Royce and it's bad form to refuse it."

"Bad form?" Velma scoffs. "And what do you call *this*?" She gestures from Maddie to Jacques.

"Then stay here," he yells.

"*You* stay! You're the one who messed this up."

Phil angrily spins toward the door to leave. Then he keeps turning, making a full circle until he's facing them again. He exhales. "The lady will be here in five minutes. Okay, Maddie?"

"No." She hides her face in Velma's waist.

Velma leans down and kisses Maddie on the forehead.

Her father steps toward them. "Madeline," he says, taking Velma by the arm, "Mommy and Daddy have to go." He tugs Velma away from Maddie and pulls her toward the door.

"No!" Maddie follows.

Jacques decides his work has begun. He moves to Maddie and tries to pick her up. She swats at his Kit Kat hands. "I'm not a baby. I don't want to be picked up." She looks at Phil and Velma. "Don't leave me!"

"She'll be here any minute," Velma says. "And we won't be gone that long." She reaches out and rubs Maddie's cheek. "He's not going to eat you. Just watch TV until the lady gets here."

Maddie leaps onto her father's shoes, smudging them with her bare feet. She latches onto his leg. Tears make wet splotches on his pants.

"Madeline, please. Be a big girl and calm down." He pries her off, wriggles free and out the door, with Velma on his heels.

Maddie chases them into the hallway. They dash toward the elevator. She follows, until Jacques grabs her and scoops her up.

He carries her back inside and kicks the door closed. His firm grasp makes her feel like a small animal locked in a trap. She wails.

He brings her to the bed and sits down without letting her go. She's cradled in his lap. She tries twisting to squirm away. He squeezes tighter. At fifty-three pounds she's no match for him.

When she held the tiny mongoose in her hands, he trembled at first. Then he calmed down. Maybe this is like that, she thinks. Maybe she should relax. She can't stop crying.

Jacques peers down at her and without easing his grip he stretches a long thumb to wipe her forehead. He's removing her mom's lipstick, she guesses. He smells of woodsy cologne and a little BO.

"*Ne pleure pas*," he says, caressing her face. He smiles. "Shh shh, bey-bey. *Ne pleure pas, ne pleure pas*." His voice is gentle, as if it means to be soothing. He leans down and kisses her forehead, then her eyelids, and then her wet cheeks. This scares her even more. *Why's he kissing me?* Then he lifts her out of his lap, stands up, and sits her on the edge of the bed. Her heart is thumping double time. He kneels in front of her and kisses her cheeks again.

Ewww, she thinks. She pulls her knees up and rests her forehead on them. She wants to move away, but she stays still. What if he's really trying to comfort her? She remembers her mom saying: *Be polite and respect that we've brought you to a place where things are different.* What if he doesn't mean to be creepy?

He uses a finger to tickle her hip. Her body recoils. He hugs her and kisses her face again. Maddie knows she's too old to be cuddled and kissed by a stranger this way. But is this one of those cultural differences?

With Omar, he preferred not to touch. That was Senegal. In Ivory Coast, is this normal? How's she supposed to know?

He unfolds her body, pushing her knees down, away from her torso. He begins to unbutton her pajama top. One button . . . two . . . three.

Maddie shudders. Dread thrums in her chest and stomach. Tears drip down to her lips and into her mouth. *Where is the lady?*

"Nooo," he coos softly. His eyes widen as if surprised by her fear. "*Ne pleure pas*, shh shh." He smiles, cups her face in his hands, and kisses both cheeks. Then his hands slide down the sides of her neck, under the pajama top and onto her shoulders. He leans in and kisses the center of her bare chest. "Shh shh," he purrs. He moves the pajama top off her shoulders and begins kissing her small nipples.

Panic spreads from her chest and stomach down to her thighs. They tremble. This is very bad and getting worse. No one's supposed to do what he's doing. If they were in America, he would know it's not allowed.

"Don't do that," she says. "I don't like that."

"Shhh, shh," he says. He swirls his tongue around her little, flat breast.

She pushes his face away and crosses her arms over her chest. "Don't you know *any* English?"

His eyes are on hers, his expression inscrutable.

"I know a French song," she says. "It has your name in it. '*Frère Jacques, frère Jacques, dormez-vous, dormez-vous.*'"

He smiles and takes her hands in his, kisses each palm, and then holds them away from her body. With his tongue out, he leans back into her chest.

There is no lady, Maddie thinks. Her mother says she always expects the worst and gets it. She's quiet now. What's the use in screaming? She could be alone with this monster for hours.

Jacques nudges her onto her back. His chin feels sharp, an arrow digging into her bare chest, as his fingers fumble with the drawstring on her pajama bottoms. She closes her eyes. Tears drizzle sideways and pool in her ears. Terror rises like water around her. She would drown if she could, so she wouldn't have to remember what happens next.

She'll try to forget. She won't tell anyone, not even Livia when she says she's hurt that their father took Maddie on the trip and not her.

While Jacques does things she won't speak of for decades, she imagines being elsewhere—in Hôtel Ivoire's lake, doggy paddling, clumsy at first, then slowly becoming graceful, as her legs fuse and smooth, and scales appear to cover them. Fins form where feet had been. She swims down to the deepest part of the lake where nothing can catch her.

There's a rap on the door.

Her eyes open. Her wet lashes are clumpy. She makes a noise and the monster covers her mouth with his hand. She can't breathe through her nose. It's clogged from crying. She blows out as hard as she can. Snot flies onto his knuckles. He presses his palm into her lips.

The door opens. Maddie hears heavy footsteps. She lies on her back, facing away from the door, yet she can see upside down that it's not a lady. It's Xavier, the man who brought the note about her mother's suitcase. She squeals.

Xavier gasps and drops the blue Samsonite into the center of the floor. The thud shakes the bed.

"Pardon! I did not know there was anyone here."

Jacques stands. His white tunic cascades down his body.

Xavier looks at him askance. "Jacques?"

Maddie pulls her pajamas bottoms up over her hips and jumps off the bed. She runs to Xavier and stands behind him. "Don't leave me with him. Please."

"Where are your parents?"

"At the ambassador's party."

"And they left you? Alone? With *this* idiot?"

She buttons her pajama top.

Xavier shakes his head. "Put on your shoes and come with me."

Jacques says something in French and Xavier shouts at him in French. He shouts the way Maddie doesn't like seeing the French treat Africans. Like they don't matter. Jacques deserves it. He touched her private parts. She'd thwack him with a club herself if she could. She stares at the floor while Jacques walks past her and out of the room.

Maddie exhales. She sticks her feet into her sandals. Xavier holds out his hand and she takes it. He squeezes her fingers and he's silent for a moment. He looks down at her foot.

"Your toe is still swollen, I see." He speaks in a whisper. "I will take you to the medical suite. They will take care of you."

As they walk toward the door, Maddie looks back at the suitcase. She can hear her mother's voice in her head. *Do you know how lucky you are?*

wings made of rocks

The Bronx, New York, 1942 / Monroe, New York, 1971

Early on a Friday morning, Phil's father rose from his bed in his long nightshirt, stretched his arms aloft, and collapsed to the floor. He stopped breathing before the ambulance arrived. Phil was ten.

A few days later, before his father was buried in a prepaid plot in Woodlawn Cemetery, Phil lay awake in bed as his brother snored on the other side of the room.

Sounds of their mother down in the kitchen with her niece, their older cousin, May, were a brief comfort. The kettle whistled, stopped, and teacups clinked on saucers. His parents were fond of having tea together at that hour most days, early, before the sun came up. He'd wake and fall back to sleep, soothed by the predictability of their routine. This particular day, his mind tricked him and all was well. Then his father's voice wasn't there, and Phil remembered.

He climbed out of bed and sat at the top of the stairs in his pajamas to listen. No one had explained what killed his father. Maybe he'd hear them talk about it.

A yellow glow spilled into the hallway from the kitchen. His mother's voice flowed into it and ascended toward Phil like a disembodied spirit.

"Of course, I'm sad, May," she said. "And I'm angry, in equal measure. He expected me to give him children and I did. He wasn't supposed to . . . He should be here for them."

"I'm sure he meant to be, Auntie."

"I almost went first, y'know?" his mother said. "I could have. And I didn't. Nearly died in labor with Philip. The pain was so much worse than with the first one. You could've heard me yowl all the way back in Bermuda. Instead of coming out, the baby was going back the other way. It was fighting me. And it felt like it *meant* to, to cause me harm. It was the most unbearable agony. My heart slowed and threatened to stop. *If it would just die,* I thought, *I'll be all right.* Makes me lightheaded even to think of it. As I prayed to God to help me, the doctor said he had to move the baby. Then he reached inside me with his whole hand, just like that. It was awful, May, everything about it. But I didn't want to die and leave my family, so I forced myself to keep breathing. I fought to stay. Tell me why their father couldn't have done the same? He could have kept breathing… When the devil inside me was finally out, and he was alive, and I was too, I was astonished."

"Auntie. He wasn't a devil. He was a breech baby, that's all."

His mother was quiet for a moment. "He intended to kill me, May. I could feel it."

As Phil sat on the stairs, tears came, and he tried not to make a sound. She really *didn't* love him. And now he understood her abiding indifference. She believed her story and held it against him. This was why his father gave him extra love. There were many hugs. And his father *really* listened to him. When Phil spoke, his father looked him in the eyes and smiled. He told Phil he was Daddy's beloved boy. He told him he believed in him and that he could grow up to achieve impossible dreams. Yes. *Impossible* dreams. He would hold onto these words forever.

Phil waited for his brother to wake that day and then he followed him down to the kitchen. Their mother was standing at the stove, her back to them. She turned, brushed curls from her eyes, wiped tears with her palms, and then looked at Phil's brother with bedazzled eyes, as if she were basking in the presence of magnificence.

"Lawrence, you're the man of the house now, darling. I'll need you to be your best."

His tall, skinny, brown body straightened like a knife. "I will, Mother," he squeaked.

Man of the house? Phil thought. *He's only two years older than me.* Round-faced Cousin May, who was twenty, sat with her tea and biscuits at the table. Her eyes connected with Phil's. May was fair skinned like him and his mother, and she flushed crimson as she smiled wide with her mouth closed. She seemed to find Lawrence's sudden ascension as preposterous as he did.

Phil told himself he'd heard his mother incorrectly that morning. He'd misjudged her tone; she was only being facetious.

Over the next several years his mother and brother conferred during mealtimes like life partners. They spoke of Lawrence's studies, the kinds of government jobs he'd pursue, his plans to have a family. If Phil's mother ever asked what he wanted to do or be or have, he couldn't remember it.

His subconscious returned his father to him in dreams. Typically, he only recalled how he felt in them. On occasion, he remembered his words. Once he told Phil not to be discouraged by his mother. Another time he said to develop his intellect. Phil's father was more than two decades older than his mother, and unlike her, he'd been an independent thinker with a propensity for interests not typically ascribed to their race. Phil's grandfather was the first man of color to buy property in the Bronx, and Phil's father, having inherited the spirit of a pioneer, bought his own house as a young man, too. He exercised whatever freedoms were available to him. During the day he worked as a customs inspector. At night in the living room while Phil's mother read the Bible, his father sat in his platform rocker poring over books on history, politics, and philosophy, occasionally novels and poetry, too. On weekends he took the family to see movies. Sometimes they saw theater. He brought them to the library and to museums downtown. He introduced his sons to jazz and to symphonies. Their father strove to remain unshackled by the limits the White world meant to place on him.

His voice became Phil's inner voice. In his father's absence he used it to encourage himself.

As Phil was nearing the end of high school, Lawrence was home on leave from his military training. The khaki uniform he wore puffed him up a bit. They sat down for breakfast with their mother in the kitchen. After she said grace, Phil drew the courage to announce his plan. "I'm going to college to study psychology."

There was silence, and then uproarious laughter.

"Negroes don't go to psychologists, you fool," his brother said.

"And White people certainly won't go to a colored one," his mother said.

Their heads shook at his stupidity. They eyed each other, gleeful in their self-proclaimed superiority.

All that he'd accomplish would be to prove them wrong.

Phil stayed in the house his father left them far longer than he meant to. When he was nineteen and in college, he got a girl pregnant and had to marry her. They lived with his mother, and his brother and his brother's wife, because Phil couldn't afford a place of his own. He loved and adored his beautiful daughter, Livia. Her mother, however, was much like *his* mother, someone who felt life had been unfair to her. Phil's wife blamed him for her unhappiness, which he could make no more sense of than his mother blaming him for a difficult birth.

The first time he fell in love, he was twenty-five and earning a second master's degree at City College. To pay the bills, he worked for the Welfare Department, checking up on recipients. He and his wife and daughter were still living at his mother's. When Phil's beloved, a graduate school classmate, broke up with him, he grieved the loss for months.

The day he finally packed up to move out of his mother's house and leave his wife, Mother stood in the doorway watching him. Her thin floral dress was faded. Her curls, peppered with gray, were pinned back from her face.

"God help you, Philip," she said. "Now you have nothing."

He saw his reflection in the wall mirror beside her. They had the same full lips, slim nose, and angular chin. His dark eyes were framed by heavy brows like hers. But Phil's face had no frown lines. And the thrill of life still shone in his eyes. "Oh, I have plenty, Mother," he said. "I have my mind."

He became a psychologist and remarried. The time between marriages, less than two years, was the only time he lived alone. He savored it like good scotch. The company of women was nice; even nicer was having no one to criticize him, no one making her happiness his responsibility.

The next time Phil fell in love was with his second wife. Velma had a difficult early childhood with a financially unstable mother who left her alone for days on end. She was placed in foster care and adopted by a good family, but the bumpy beginning left its marks. Still, she was gutsy and beautiful and a supportive companion. Curious about the world, she was willing to travel with him to places no Black person she knew had ever been, like Moscow and Istanbul. And she didn't blink at leaving the known world of the Bronx for uncharted territory in Upstate New York. Her fearlessness inspired him.

Then they had Madeline.

Phil heard them together one afternoon while she was giving Maddie a bath. The child was four and going through what Freud called the phallic stage of development.

"Mommy, why did you say not to touch myself while we were at the store?"

"Because we don't touch ourselves in public, Maddie. It's not allowed."

"But, Mommy, it's *my*-self." She said this as if it were the final word on the matter.

"Listen, I catch you touching yourself at the A & P again, I'm gonna pop you, you understand?"

Madeline was quiet for a moment. "Why can't other people see our private parts?" she asked.

Velma scoffed. "Because we use them to do private things. Stop talking. Mommy doesn't want to talk."

"Why don't you want to talk, Mommy?"

"Because I don't. Be quiet."

"I want to get out now."

"Sit down, goddammit," Velma yelled.

Phil heard a splash.

"Ow, Mommy, that hurts!"

"Shut up."

There was a slap. Phil ran down the hall and into the bathroom. Velma was in striped short shorts, kneeling on the bathmat. Small, dark-eyed Madeline, with long curls and cheeks that puffed out like she had a pear in each one, was sitting in the tub.

"What's that?" he asked, pointing to a strawberry-colored mark on her face, a face that resembled his own.

"She stood up and grazed her cheek on the faucet," Velma said.

Madeline looked at her mother with eyes the size of saucers. The lie stunned her. Her little shoulders slumped and her chin dropped to her chest. Phil recognized those hurt feelings, the frustration of being small when someone grown behaves unfairly. It reminded him of his mother. Not the hitting, Mother wasn't like that. It was the ease with which she was cruel to her young child.

With a steady gaze on Velma, he shamed her until she looked away. She knew he knew what she'd done. It was a jolt that left a crack in their foundation.

His first wife was neglectful. Mothering wasn't of interest to her. Phil recognized his pattern: drawn, unconsciously, to what he'd meant to escape.

After finishing a PhD in clinical psychology, he earned a post-doctoral diploma in psychoanalysis. During training, undergoing analysis himself was mandatory. He explored how losing his father and being emotionally rejected by his mother affected his unconscious and manifested in his behavior. Once training was complete, treatment ended.

He'd planned to get back to it when he had more money. When he made more money, he thought he'd do it when he had more time.

Monogamy never appealed to Phil. He realized it was what most women hoped for, but it didn't seem reasonable or even possible. Girlfriends provided the excitement of newness and relief when a wife's sex drive wasn't in sync with his own.

Abby Goldberg was an artist from an adjacent town. She'd been a patient at Phil's home office in Monroe. Once their mutual attraction was clear, they terminated the professional relationship. Abby began making trips to Phil's Manhattan office, which was a rented one-bedroom on lower Fifth Avenue. He saw patients there three days a week and often spent the night. Their affair inspired her to paint a biomorph, a magnificent, multicolored abstract, from which shimmering rays seemed to project, with vague shapes of two bodies entwined, one golden and one pearl white. She told him it was a representation of them—their souls—during the act. Together, they hung the painting in his office. Looking at it never failed to make Phil's entire body smile.

Phil noticed that Madeline seemed depressed when they came back from their summer vacation in West Africa. She was sleeping more than usual. She never wanted to get out of bed. At first, they thought it was jetlag. Then it went on for weeks. She asked to stay home from school. She quit her ballet class. And she began acting out in odd ways. For example, she decided not to wear the pajamas she'd worn on vacation anymore. Phil thought that was fine—she was asserting her independence—but one night Velma made her put them on. The next morning, as had become typical, Madeline wouldn't get up. He went in to wake her and found shreds of light blue pajama fabric in a heap on the floor beside her bed. She'd cut them up with scissors.

She was sleeping on her stomach, with one arm over her teddy bear. Phil touched her on the back and she shook awake with a whimper. When he tried to embrace her, she cried.

Their Great Dane galloped up the stairs and into her room to see what was going on.

"Look who came to see you," Phil said. "See, you're okay, Brutus won't let anything hurt you." The dog sniffed at her head.

When Phil touched her again, she wriggled away and covered herself to her chin with the blankets. She avoided eye contact. Phil was puzzled as he sat where she'd been and watched her tear-stained face. "Did you have a bad dream, baby?"

She didn't answer. He asked again.

She sniffled. "I don't remember, Daddy."

"Okay. But if you do and you want to tell me about it, you can."

She said nothing more.

When Phil told Velma about the pajamas, the two of them were down in the kitchen. Her jaw clenched. She turned and banged through the swinging door marching toward Madeline. He followed and caught her by the arm.

"You're *not* spanking her. She's upset about something. Why don't you try to understand her, instead of shaming her constantly?"

"I'm trying to train her, Phil." She yanked her arm away, tightened the belt on her bathrobe, and patted at the curlers on her head. "She's gonna have to wear things and *do* things she doesn't want to. That's life. She's not gonna be able to chop up the shitty parts of it she doesn't like."

"Leave her alone."

Velma's lips moved over clenched teeth. "You think I don't want to hack up the things in my life *I* don't like?" She thrust her face up toward him and cocked her head. "If I could take an axe to the crap I hate, I would. But I can't, can I? Well, neither can she. She has to learn to suffer through bullshit like the rest of us."

"Keep your hands off my daughter, Velma."

"Bring your ass home from Manhattan after work, *Phil*."

"Velma—"

"I'm a single parent while you're down there fallin' up a bitch's pussy. You don't like how I'm parenting? Come the fuck home at night and do it yourself."

She was nothing if not direct.

On a Saturday, while Velma was at her shop, Phil stayed at the house with Madeline and had her come into his office and play with the therapy dollhouse he used with children.

"Show Daddy something that happens in our house."

She sat cross-legged on the checkered linoleum floor in her stretch pants and stared at the dollhouse for a while.

"It's only one floor," she said. "It's not like our house."

"Can you pretend?"

Her hair was in two braids and she scratched her head in the middle. "Okay. It can be the upstairs." She looked at the "daddy" doll.

It was small (a few inches tall), malleable, like Gumby, and its flesh was white. "These dolls don't look like our family."

"Pretend, Madeline."

"Okay." She set the daddy doll aside and said, "He's not here." She put the "little girl" doll (herself) in her bedroom, alone, playing, and her "mother" at the other end of the house in Mommy and Daddy's room. She said, "Mommy's in front of the mirror putting on makeup." Then she had the mommy doll come to her room. "I'm going to the antiques auction," Mommy-doll said. "'The babysitter's going to stay with you.'"

"'I don't want to stay with the babysitter, Mommy. Can I please come with you?'"

"'You know you don't like being in that dusty place with those dusty old things and dusty old people. No.'"

"'I'll be quiet. I promise.'"

"'You will not, Maddie, and you know it. You have to stay home.'"

She walked the mommy doll out of the house and slid her away across the black-and-white floor. Then she stared at her doll-self in the bedroom.

"Where's the babysitter?" Phil asked.

She tapped her thumb on her bottom lip.

"What are you thinking, Madeline?"

"I don't want to play this anymore."

"You don't like staying with the babysitter?"

She turned to look up at him. "Some are nice. Sometimes, I don't know them, and I'm scared."

He nodded. "I remember you were scared of the babysitter in Ivory Coast."

She looked down at the floor and traced one of the black linoleum squares with her finger.

"What's to be scared of?" Phil leaned toward her in his chair.

"They could hurt me."

"They wouldn't hurt you," he said.

Her eyes bored into his with the force of a shove. "Daddy, you don't know what happens when you're not there."

His heart lurched. "Did the babysitter hurt you?"

She eyed the floor again.

"Madeline, did that babysitter do something to you?"

"I don't know."

"What you do mean, you don't know? Either he hurt you or he didn't. Tell me what happened!"

She lifted her head. Her shoulders tensed. "Are you mad at me, Daddy?" Her voice quivered.

"No." He opened his arms. She rose and came into them. "If you want to tell me, it's okay. I won't be angry with you. Daddy loves you."

She didn't want to talk or play anymore. Phil didn't push her.

He drank more than his usual two glasses of scotch that day, and the days after. Something may have happened to his daughter because he left her. He tried to sip away thoughts of what someone might do to an eight year old, where he might touch her, and how. He drank and reminded himself of the time Cousin May made him go to his room without dinner because he sassed her. He wanted to get her into trouble so he told his father she locked him in the closet. She'd done no such thing. He drank to reassure himself that what happened to Maddie couldn't possibly be as bad as his worst fears. Maybe, because she didn't want to be left with the babysitter, Maddie made up a bad story in her mind. When he was sober, the fears came forward again.

He planned to tell Velma. Then he imagined the conversation; it led to hysteria and blaming him. It didn't help any of them. Phil's own mother's voice squawked in his head like an annoying crow: *Look at you, Philip. There you go, failing your family yet again.*

He began coming home on Wednesday nights, instead of early Thursday mornings. Occasionally he returned on Friday nights, too. While he couldn't say it made Velma happy, she seemed less angry.

Abby still met Phil in the city sometimes. One evening they were fooling around on the sofa bed when the buzzer rang. He lifted his head from between her legs and turned toward the outer room.

"You're *not* thinking of getting that."

"Uh . . ."

"Babe, are you kidding me?"

"Just let me see who it is."

He walked, bare-assed, to the intercom, which was in the waiting room, near the front door.

"Daddy, it's Livia," the voice on the intercom said. "I came down for an event in Washington Square Park. Thought I'd say hi and introduce you to Brett."

"Okay, give me a minute," he said, and buzzed them through the street entrance.

Abby stomped into the waiting room. "You're a putz, Phil." Her breasts pointed at him like fists.

"I haven't seen her since I took her to school." He pushed past Abby, into the bathroom, and washed his face.

She stood on the threshold. "You expect me to hide? I have to catch my bus soon."

"No, you can meet her." Phil moved around her and into the bedroom to pull on his pants.

"Why would you want us to meet? That's insane."

"Stop bitching and get dressed, Abby." He put his button-down shirt on and left it untucked.

"Could've stayed home with my husband if I wanted kids interrupting my happy hour."

"Hurry up," he said.

She made a noise, like she was sucking food from between her teeth.

He threw his socks and shoes on. Didn't bother to fold up the bed. There wasn't time. The bell rang as Abby pulled her short dress over her head.

"Close this door when you come out," he whispered. "And please put your tights on. And your shoes, too."

"Why would you subject your kid to this?"

"I'm welcoming her, Abby. So she knows I'm always happy to see her."

"She doesn't want to know what's going on here."

"Then don't tell her."

Livia's Afro greeted Phil at the door. It was new, and it was *big*.

Beach ball big. She was in a black leather jacket, bell-bottom jeans, and platform shoes, which made her tall frame Watusi-like. Beside her was a handsome, brown-skinned young man also in bell-bottoms. His Afro was wide and high, and he was long and lanky like she was. With their skinny bodies and Hula-Hoop-sized hair, they resembled two dandelions that had gone to seed.

"Hi Daddy." She smiled with all her gleaming teeth.

Phil and Livia hugged. "Hello, my sweet," he said. "What a fantastic surprise. And when did you do *that*?" He grinned at the hair. "In September it was smooth, straight, and past your shoulders."

"Like it?"

"You look beautiful. I'm thinking of an Afro myself. A bit shorter, though."

She introduced Phil to Brett, who said Livia talked about him all the time, which made him smile. He ducked into the kitchen to get drinks. Then he heard Livia.

"Oh. I didn't know you had company." Her warm tone turned to shade.

Phil hurried back into the room with ginger ale. Livia stood there, staring at Abby, who was perched on one of the black loveseats. She'd put on her go-go boots. Her bare legs were crossed. They each said hello.

"This is my friend Abby," he said.

Livia turned to him with darkened eyes. "Your friend, Dad?" She took a seat beside the boyfriend on the sofa opposite Abby and Phil.

Brett patted her thigh as if to soothe her. "Um, hey, so, uh, Livia tells me you're a psychologist and psychoanalyst. That's fascinating. And, she's uh, immensely proud. Right, Liv? My dad's a doctor, too, actually. A cardiologist," he babbled.

Livia continued to stare. "And, how do you know each other?"

"I'm from Sterling Forest," Abby said. "That's near Monroe."

"I know where it is."

"Groovy. Your father's been to my studio and bought some of my paintings." She ran her fingers through the top of her dark hair.

"Livia's an artist, too," Phil told Abby. "She draws and paints marvelously well."

"Oh, I'll attest to that," Brett said, squeezing her thigh. With his other hand he unzipped his jacket. He'd begun to sweat.

"Right on," Abby said. "I take an art class at the New School on Fridays. Sometimes I meet your father for a drink before I catch my bus back upstate."

Livia stared at her. "Really," she said. "Well, excuse the interruption. We're not staying."

"It's fine, darling," Phil said. "You don't have to rush off. I'm glad to see you."

Abby's foot began to bounce up and down in her boot as she bobbed her crossed leg. Phil had to resist the urge to grab it and hold it still.

"You're busy," Livia said. "Just wanted you to meet Brett."

"We're going to the peace concert," he said with a chipper lilt. Perspiration beaded on his brown cheeks. "Richie Havens is playing."

Livia's eyes slid from Phil to Abby's moving foot and back to Phil. "We stopped in Monroe and saw Maddie and Velma on the way here."

"Yeah?" he said.

"What's wrong with Maddie?"

"What do you mean?"

"She's acting weird."

"How so?" Phil felt the sensation of his innards keeling off a roof.

"She saw me coming up the driveway, and she sailed out the door, running toward me, yelling, 'Livia! Livia!' with her arms open to hug me. Then when she got closer her eyes went wide like she was terrified and she screamed, 'Liv-i-AAAAHHH!' She threw her hands over her head, turned, and flew back into the house."

Brett covered his mouth and closed his eyes. His chest bounced as he tried to suppress laughter. "Sorry," he said. "I'm sorry."

Livia flicked a look at him before eyeing Phil again. "I thought it was funny, too. At first. Then she hid behind Velma and wouldn't talk to me the whole time I was there. Wouldn't say hi to Brett. That's not like her. She's usually turning pirouettes, or cartwheels, and demanding attention. She seemed scared."

Phil rubbed the space between his eyebrows with two fingers and took a breath. His head hurt. "Maybe she's not used to those huge Afros, Livia."

"Oh, c'mon, Dad. She's seen Afros before. Maddie's not unsophisticated. I mean, *she's* been to Africa, right? *I* wouldn't know, because *I* wasn't invited, but I'm assuming she saw all kinds of things. She's never been scared or antisocial like that. Maybe something's going *on* that's upsetting her?" She stared at him. "Kids are intuitive."

"She's okay," he said. "Kids go through different developmental stages."

"She seemed strange to me."

Christ, Phil thought.

The boyfriend began blathering again, this time about his plan to take Livia to Martha's Vineyard to see his family's vacation house in Oak Bluffs. He went on about all the Black professionals who "summer" at "the Vineyard" and that he was surprised to hear Phil had never been.

"Nope. Never have," he said. "I *summer* around the world, Brett. Did Livia tell you *that*? Last summer it was West Africa."

"Yes, the *family* trip without *me*," she said. "He knows about that."

"The year before it was England and Scotland (with *no* kids)," he said looking at her. "And before that, it was Paris, Rome, and then Greece and Turkey for eight weeks with my both my daughters. Right, Livia?"

Her eyes drifted to the ceiling.

"Next summer it might be Japan. I'm not a spend my summer in the same place with the same people every year kind of guy, Brett. Self-segregation isn't something I aspire to."

"Dad." Livia stood. "Okay, we're leaving."

Brett got up, too. He took Livia's hand. "Guess we should get down to the park. Very nice meeting you, both."

"Yes, you, too." Phil followed them to the door. "Good to see you, darling. The hair looks great. Love you."

When they were gone, Abby was on her feet. Her eyes were wide and seemed bewildered.

"What?" Phil said.

"That was . . . You're one of the most unusual people I've ever met."

"Good. I prefer that to ordinary."

"It wasn't a compliment."

"Those Black elite snobs he was talking about didn't give me the time of day when I was coming up, because I didn't come from professional parents."

"Black elite?"

The skepticism in her voice irritated him. "Yes, Abby. Educated, well-to-do, Black professionals, and *that's* why I'm not part of that crowd, because you don't even know they exist! White people don't know, and they don't care. If I'm going to network, I'll do it in the crowd that matters."

"I don't think that kid gave a stinking fart where you 'summer.' He was trying to survive the excruciating awkwardness. Your daughter was . . . You shouldn't have invited them in."

"My children are always welcome around me."

"Yeah?" She gathered her leather bag and her art portfolio. "Well, *I* didn't feel welcome. And you invited me here, Phil. Wasted my bus fare and my night."

He folded his arms. "Abby. It was a one-time thing. And don't tell me how to handle my kids. Livia needs to know she's important to me."

"You think you showed that by introducing her to *me*?" Abby laughed, and pulled her long coat from the brass rack near the door. "A girl wants to admire her father, Phil. You don't need a damned degree in psychology to know that." She opened the door and was gone.

Her rose scent lingered like an echo. He inhaled deeply and held it as long as he could.

Madeline came into the city with Phil to meet Yumi Miyoshi, a child psychologist he knew through NYU. They were both adjunct clinical professors in the doctoral program. She had an excellent reputation and an elegant office at One Fifth Avenue. It smelled of jasmine. He settled into her waiting room, which with its view of the Washington Square arch, chrome-and-white-leather furniture, and collection of woodblock prints made his look shabby.

Later, he went into the office while Madeline waited. She'd told Dr. Miyoshi things that were bothering her—bullies at school and in the neighborhood, and that her mother yelled at her too much—but she wouldn't tell Miyoshi any more about what happened with the babysitter in Ivory Coast than she'd told him.

The doctor leaned across her desk and touched Phil's hand with warm fingers. He found her strikingly attractive. "I understand your anxiety, Philip. Not knowing can be worse than knowing."

He nodded, struggling unsuccessfully to avoid being distracted by her touch, her glossy hair, slim figure, and impossibly poreless skin. The looks were only enhanced by her intelligence, as well as a husky voice he found interesting in its contrast with the rest of her.

"The good news is, whatever happened, it's done," she said. "And we know it hasn't happened again. Sometimes, when a child suffers a one-time event and then never sees the offender again, the effects of the trauma might manifest for a period of time and then resolve without intervention."

Phil struggled to concentrate on Madeline and her well-being while Dr. Miyoshi was drawing all his attention. He had to repeat her words in his head to register and retain them.

"We can hope for that." She squeezed his hand and then mercifully let go. "Or you can keep bringing her to see me. Though, there's no guarantee when or if she'll talk about it. You could also monitor her for the next several weeks, see if there's an improvement, and if not, we can try another session."

Madeline promptly told her mother about the pretty lady doctor with the straight black hair. Velma didn't bother to ask why he'd brought her before she announced, "If you take Madeline there again, I'm coming, too."

Livia went to her mother's on Christmas Day. She'd stopped spending it in Monroe with Phil when she was thirteen and in the middle of the night three-year-old Madeline opened every gift under the tree, including all of Livia's.

She visited a few days after the holiday before going back to Cambridge. He didn't see patients that week. Velma was at her shop, and Phil took the girls skiing nearby in Sterling Forest. Abby lived near the ski center. He hoped he might run into her there. They were still out of touch.

On the way in the car, Livia sat up front next to him, and Madeline in the back, singing quietly. She wasn't herself yet. Still wary of strangers, not as talkative as usual, and sleeping too much, though she did seem a bit less depressed. She was elated to be off from school.

Phil asked Livia about her classes, and about her boyfriend, and she gave one-word answers. When he asked why so terse, she turned and made a face—furrowed brows, and a sneer that pulled her lip sideways. Reminded Phil of the looks opponents gave when he boxed in the Bronx as a teenager. He smiled at her ridiculousness.

At the slopes, he kept an eye out but didn't see Abby. Madeline saw some school friends, and their mothers invited her to ski with them on the bunny hill. Livia and Phil took the lift up a bigger slope.

"Stop being so surly," he chided. "If you want to say something, say it."

Her face pointed down at the naked trees and snowy white path below. The fabric of her hood fluttered from the force of the wind.

"You know, kiddo, I give you much more affection and support than I ever had as a kid. I'm not without faults, but I'm always here for you, aren't I?"

She tapped her ski pole on the chairlift's footrest. "You never worry about how your actions affect other people. You did it to my mother, too. And I *knew*. You behave however you want and you expect to be appreciated for what you think and feel as if no one's hurt by what you say and do."

The wind snarled and shook the chair.

"Livia, do you realize that since I was just twenty years old, less than two years older than you are now, I've had the responsibility of supporting you, your mother, my mother, and then Velma and your sister? *I* had to work while going to school. There was no chance to enjoy the college experience. I never got to live in a dorm. Or go to an elite university like you. I couldn't afford it. I didn't have a father to go to for advice or get an allowance from. And in all these years of taking care of you women and girls, you think I've had emotional support from any of you? No. You all constantly want, want, want. And I provide. Is that all I'm good for? Do I get to want anything?"

Livia scoffed in an obnoxious teenager way. Someone else might have wanted to smack her, but she was his adored child. It pained Phil to see her unhappy, even if he was the cause.

"You may not understand this yet," he said, "but adult lives and relationships are complicated. Your father isn't perfect. I know. Despite my shortcomings, I've always tried to show my love."

She remained quiet. They sat with their thoughts as the lift pulled them through the wind and higher up the mountain.

On a frigid Thursday in early February, after a few months of not being able to reach Abby, Phil was leaving the next day for his annual solo trip to the Alps. The thought of not seeing her before he left was unbearable, and so he got in his car and soon found himself banging his gloved knuckles on her studio door. She'd cut her hair short and chic, and she'd been practicing yoga. Her body was sleek. Sexier than ever. She was still angry and it didn't help that he showed up while she was in the middle of a commissioned piece and there was a deadline. Nonetheless, she locked the door, closed the blinds, and by the way she kissed him, Phil knew she'd missed him, too.

He noticed two large paintings on her walls similar to the one she'd made of the two of them. They disrobed and landed together on the canvas sofa where she sometimes napped. Bodies entwined and pulsing with energy, they resembled the paintings.

When they were getting dressed, she said, "Phil, I know you're not going to like this, but I think I should tell you something. It's about Maddie."

His stomach plunged. He braced himself, breathed in the turpentine fumes of the studio, and tied his tie.

"My friend Sharon's daughter Elsa is in Maddie's class," Abby said as she zipped her blue jeans.

"Why is your friend telling you something about my kid? You talk about me to your friends?"

Abby was quiet for a moment. She stared directly at him. "I broke up with you, remember? It was over. And she's my best friend. You're in no position to make rules for me."

Phil felt his face turning hot. He wished he could've told her to shut her face. He couldn't because he did want to hear this.

"Sharon said Elsa told her that every day, when the kids line up to go to lunch, a boy calls Maddie a nigger."

"Every day?"

"That's what Elsa said."

"I don't believe that. She would tell the teacher."

"Sharon said he's been picking on Maddie for a while now. Elsa was upset by it. The same boy picks on some of the Jewish kids, too. Their teacher knows. Elsa said the teacher told Maddie to ignore the boy. It hasn't stopped. Sharon debated calling your wife. But according to her, your wife has a bad temper."

"What are you trying to say, Abby?"

"I'm not *trying* to say anything." She moved to her easel. "I told you what happened."

"And what do you think I'm supposed to do? I could talk to the teacher, complain to the school about the kid, but this is where we live. A lot of these people are simpleminded. Am I supposed to take her out of the school because kids say racist things? Where's she going to go?"

"I didn't say any of that, Phil. What you do or don't do about it is up to you."

"When she's upset by this stuff, she tells us, and she hasn't said anything. Madeline may not *enjoy* being the only Black child in her class, but that's all she's known. And she's been taught that if someone calls her that word, it only says something about that person. It doesn't define her."

Abby turned from her canvas and stared at Phil as if searching for something in his face.

"What's that look?" he asked.

"You think a little girl stops to remember all that when she's being bullied? Are you delusional? My daughter gets picked on in private school. Sometimes she's the only Jewish kid in her class. It's hard being different. But at least she has her friends at Hebrew School. Does Maddie have anything like that? A place where she fits in?"

A feeling swelled in Phil's heart. It kept growing until it reached his throat and he couldn't answer.

"You dismissed what that kid said about Martha's Vineyard. Maybe they *summer* there so their families have a place where they're not different? Jews socialize together. Call it self-segregating if you want to, but I don't feel any worse off for it."

"Abby, you're constantly condescending and telling me what to do. You know why? Because you feel superior. Your privilege is talking. Be quiet. Madeline's being raised with White people so she doesn't fear them, or feel inferior to them. Can you fathom that I might love my children, and that I've thought carefully about their upbringing?" He walked out.

Fucking Abby was a pleasure. Having to defend himself with her was too goddamn much like marriage.

Madeline didn't mention the bully. To Phil's relief, she appeared to be less depressed, more like herself as the year continued. She was playing again with Lisa, the Megnas' daughter next door, after she hadn't for weeks. And Velma had hired Gertie, a soft-spoken, middle-aged White woman, who cleaned and also kept Maddie company for a couple of days a week after school. Maddie liked Gertie, and their connection seemed to perk her up a bit. Some of her spunk returned.

On the Saturday before Easter, Phil and Maddie sat at their dining table with his mother, Emily, while Velma stayed away at her shop. The house was impeccably clean, not a streak, smudge, or fleck of dust, thanks to Gertie. Emily, who typically had some negative critique of Velma's housekeeping, was uncharacteristically without complaint. The three of them had tea and English shortbread biscuits Emily had brought. Phil was miserable with hay fever, sneezing and blowing his nose. Emily eyed a cluster of family photos across the room perched on top of an antique piano Velma had recently acquired at an auction.

"Livia was such a beauty when she was your age, Madeline. She had such shiny hair and the loveliest smile," Emily prattled on. "Neighbors used to stop us on the street to tell me how pretty and sweet my little darling was."

Madeline sipped her tea and tapped a foot against her chair.

Phil was certain she had no idea that his mother was making a dig at *him*. Livia and his ex-wife lived with her when Livia was that age. And Phil didn't. A dream from around that time had stuck with him. His father showed up at the tennis court in Monroe and sat beside him on a bench. Phil stared at him, astonished by his presence. His father touched Phil's thigh and said, "Don't worry, son. In the end, she'll be glad you were her father." And Phil believed him. He saw Livia regularly then, and though she was nearly an adult now, his mother continued to chastise him for missing her childhood.

He sneezed.

"Bless you, Daddy."

"Thanks, kiddo. Mother, why don't you ask Maddie something about herself?"

"If she wants to tell me about herself no one's stopping her." Emily brushed crumbs from her lips with a finger. They landed on the lace collar of her Sunday sweater.

A familiar fury toward his mother rose from his gut and slammed up into his sinuses. He blew his nose, hard, as if he could rid himself of it. Of *her*. Maddie was doing better. He did not want this nasty old woman's nonsense compromising her mental health.

Maddie looked at her grandmother.

"All right, tell me, Madeline," Emily said. "What subjects are your favorites in school?"

"I love reading, spelling, and vocabulary. And music class. We have a choir and we're rehearsing a song called 'School Days.' It's fantastic. I sing alto."

"What about arithmetic?"

Maddie huffed out a breath. "I don't like that as much."

"Oh? And why's that?"

She looked down at the table. "I'm not as good at it."

"Really. Your sister excelled in arithmetic when she was in the third grade. She was an absolute whiz at it."

Christ, Phil thought. Time to stop making his kid suffer these awful obligatory visits.

Madeline cradled her chin in her hand while staring up at her grandmother with the evilest eye Phil had ever seen her give. She looked like Velma.

"Livia was a whiz at everything," Emily continued. "She excelled in reading, spelling, and vocabulary, too."

"Grandma, why don't you just shut up?"

Phil choked on his tea, as shocked as his mother was.

Emily's face was nearly purple as she turned to him and shouted, "Aren't you going to reprimand her?"

Both sets of eyes looked at him as if he were a referee. He thought about it. Sneezed. And shook his head. "Mother, you did the same damn thing to me. You'd go on and on letting me know you thought more of Lawrence than you thought of me. I didn't appreciate it and Madeline doesn't either. If your feelings are hurt, it serves you right."

He watched his mother's tears drizzle down as if on cue. "I was only making conversation," she said, sniffling. "I'm a guest in your home and I should feel welcome. I let you live in my house all those years."

"My father left that house to the three of us. And I paid rent."

"When I'm with Lawrence's family I'm treated with respect!"

"If you want to go there, Mother, no one's stopping you."

Madeline said, "You try to make me feel jealous on purpose, Grandma Emily, and that's not nice."

Emily dabbed her eyes with a napkin and pushed away from the table. "I'm going to lie down."

Velma ran downstairs into Phil's office late one night in May while he was on the phone. She ripped it out of the wall and threw it at him, slamming his chest. It woke Brutus. He jumped up, barking.

"Shut up!" she yelled at the dog, and then at Phil, "Don't think you're gonna go off and leave me to raise a kid like you did your first wife. I'll be delivering her to wherever you and whoever you're screwing end up."

"You're going to pay for that phone, Velma."

"Make me, motherfucker."

Brutus growled, and she yelled some more before stomping, barefooted, out of the room. He went to close the door and saw that Madeline was sitting on the steps outside his office in her footie pajamas and her hair in pigtails. She looked so little. She stared up at him, her brown eyes big as chestnuts. "Are you going somewhere, Daddy?" Her little forehead was tense.

"No, honey." He picked her up and carried her into the office. When he tried to set her into the reclining chair, she held onto him with her arms around his neck and legs around his waist.

"I don't want you to leave me," she said.

That startled him.

Phil had said precisely the same words to his father in dreams.

"I won't, baby. I won't." When he put her down, he had to turn his head so she wouldn't see his eyes.

"I'm not giving you a divorce," Velma said. "It's not something I believe in. My parents have had their problems, but they've stayed together."

It was early June and she'd just brought him breakfast in bed on a tray. Eggs, toast, and orange juice. They hadn't talked, really, since the night she broke his phone.

Phil sat up. "Okay. I don't want to pull our lives or Madeline's apart either. But . . ."

"But what?" She stood over him, pretty, in her simple white dress, hair and makeup done.

"I'm not capable of fidelity, Velma. It's not for me."

"What?" She leaned back and squinted as if she were staring into the sun.

"I'm just being honest. I can commit to staying together if it's an open marriage," he said. "There's a new book about it. It explains a lot. My needs are not abnormal."

Velma closed her eyes and then opened them again. When she spoke, her voice was low and guttural. "*You* proposed, Philip. I didn't force you. My life was successful. *You* were in debt." She drew in a breath and placed the heel of her hand between her eyebrows. When she lowered it again she was shaking. "I moved to this hick town for *you*. Drained my fucking savings to help buy this house." As her rage crescendoed, she began to scream, "Then you made me leave the bank, and stay home, while you screwed around as much as you pleased. And after nine years you want what? *Permission*? To humiliate me?" Tears puddled in her eyes. She was quiet for a moment, staring at him sadly. "I've been a good wife."

Phil looked down at the tray she'd prepared. He didn't disagree. Nor did he feel the shame she hoped to elicit.

"You've got some big balls to treat me like this," she said.

He looked up at her again.

Velma's face began to change before his eyes, the sadness reconfiguring into something sharp and hot. "You keep it up," she said, her voice cutting like a laser. "And I just might puncture those motherfuckers." She turned for the door.

"Oh, really?" Phil said. "You just want to throw threats? You're not mature enough to even consider the lifestyle, or discuss it?"

Velma stopped still. "It's not like you're giving me a choice, you sociopath. What the fuck is there to discuss?" She continued out of the room without looking at him.

They decided they'd travel to Japan for the summer, Tokyo, Mount Fuji, and Kyoto. Velma seemed upbeat about the idea of being away for a few weeks. Phil wondered if she figured that was time he couldn't be with his girlfriend.

He and Velma told Madeline about the trip at dinner while they sat at the round oak kitchen table.

Instantly red bumps appeared and swept across Maddie's face and arms. And there were tears. "I don't want to go. Let me stay home."

"That's just stupid," Velma said. "Don't you realize how lucky you are to see the world?"

Madeline dropped an ear of corn to her plate. "But I don't *want* to see it," she cried. "I don't like it."

Across the room, Brutus's head popped up from his bed.

"She's not stupid, Velma. She has a right to her feelings. Tell Daddy why you don't want to go, Madeline."

"You'll leave me with a hotel babysitter!" she screamed and ran from the table.

Phil watched her bang open the swinging door. He and Velma looked at each other across the table.

"That girl has no idea what a privileged life she has," Velma said. She picked at her salad. "When I was her age, I was happy to have ten cents to go to the movies. And she's turning up her nose at a chance to see Asia?"

"Did you hear what she said?" Phil took a cigarette from his jacket pocket. He was still dressed for work, with three more patients to see that night. "She had a bad experience with that sitter in Ivory Coast."

"What? She told you that?"

"No. But—"

"Oh, please. Maddie doesn't like strangers. She's spoiled."

He lit up and drew the smoke deeply into his lungs before blowing it out. "You pick on her out of spite for me, and she doesn't deserve it. I'm telling you, as a professional, she suffered some kind of trauma. If you were at all attuned to her, you'd've noticed. *That's* why I took her to my colleague in New York."

"And you didn't think to tell me?" Velma stared at him through the smoke.

"You didn't even ask why I took her. You didn't seem to care."

She leaned toward him. "Just because you have an opinion about me, Philip, doesn't make it true. And *you* were the one who wanted to leave her with that boy, because you were so goddamned eager to ride in that Rolls-Royce and hobnob with the ambassador."

"Velma—"

"Weren't you? Social climber."

Phil promised Madeline they wouldn't leave her with any babysitters in Japan.

In early July, a few weeks before they were supposed to leave, the malaise she'd been suffering became significantly worse. She stopped following Gertie around while she cleaned. She seemed fatigued and didn't want to get up, not even to eat or watch TV. She wasn't in school, so there was no reason for her to fake it. Phil suspected her depression was deepening.

Then she developed other symptoms: a fever, stiff neck, body aches. She was vomiting and having diarrhea.

Her pediatrician, Dr. Stiglitz, was Jack LaLanne–fit and sported a crew cut. People called him arrogant and condescending, and he was, but as another professional in town (there weren't that many of them), Phil had been somewhat friendly with him for years through the Monroe Tennis Club. Madeline played with his kids and she'd gone to him for checkups since she was a baby. Stiglitz quickly diagnosed her with rheumatic fever and prescribed penicillin. He assured Phil her symptoms would subside in a few days.

At home, when he gave Madeline her medicine, Phil explained that it would make her feel better, but she'd have to take it easy for a while, even after she seemed well, because her heart could potentially be harmed if she was active too soon.

She could barely lift her head from the pillow. "Am I going to die, Daddy?"

That stunned him. "No. Baby, you're going to get well." He put her stuffed bear beside her, kissed her cheek, and left the room. As he was walking downstairs to his office, he heard her talking.

"Don't be sad."

He guessed she was speaking to the teddy bear.

"It's okay if I leave here, because I'll go to a place where everyone's happy and no one is mean."

Did she *want* to die? He had to sit down on the stairs. Was his little girl so miserable she thought death would be a relief? This felt like the nadir of fatherhood. Phil wished he had his own father to tell him what to do. He drank himself to sleep that night.

Over the next few days Madeline's symptoms grew exponentially worse. She couldn't keep *anything* down, not the medication, not even water. Her fever soared to 106. Velma was done with Stiglitz. She found another pediatrician, called his emergency after-hours number, and thankfully he agreed to see them. They carried Madeline into his office in a blanket. After examining her for just a few minutes, Dr. Suvari sounded calm, though Phil knew he was alarmed, because he told them to get her to Arden Hill Hospital in Goshen *immediately*. He'd meet them there.

She was quickly admitted and given an IV.

Suvari's skin was browner than Phil's, an anomaly in the area. Phil sensed a mutual affinity. The pediatrician addressed him without the air of condescension he'd grown inured to in interactions with locals who didn't know him. Suvari was sure Madeline did *not* have rheumatic fever, but he wasn't sure what she did have. They would run tests.

By the next afternoon the dehydration had abated, and her temperature was down to 102. But when Dr. Suvari came to her room, his face was grim. He took Phil into the hallway.

"We think it's viral, not bacterial, but there's still no diagnosis. We need your consent for a lumbar puncture to test for meningitis."

"She's better, though. Right?"

He eyed Phil directly. "She's hydrated. Not better."

Phil leaned into the wall. He needed it to hold him up as he realized this was serious.

The next day he arrived at seven in the morning. Visiting hours didn't start until ten. Perhaps because Madeline was a child, the nurses pretended not to notice him pacing her room while she slept.

Phil didn't believe in prayer. Instead, he did something reminiscent of it. He sat down, closed his eyes, and thought of his father. It'd been thirty years, and yet Phil remembered his deep voice, soothing and smooth as a calm sea. For a while he heard it in dreams. He longed for it now. His father would tell him to be brave, he imagined. *Don't lose hope. Think of the best that could happen, son, not the worst.* He'd put his large, brown hand on Phil's shoulder, look him in the eye, and Phil would feel less alone.

Crying wasn't something he was willing to do in his daughter's room. Nurses were in and out. He needed a smoke but wanted to be with her if she woke up, in case she felt afraid. Velma wouldn't be there for hours.

Madeline stretched her curled legs straight and opened her eyes. She yawned.

"Hi, kiddo," he said. "How're you feeling?"

"Grandpa says to tell you he'll watch me, Daddy," she whispered. "You can go have your cigarette."

Phil blinked. "*What?*"

She closed her eyes again.

"What did you say, Madeline?" She didn't answer. He sat still as a corpse. His heart thudded. Phil couldn't see his father or sense his presence, and yet a tingle brushed up his neck and across the backs of his ears. *Thank you, Daddy*, he said silently as he stood and left the room. Was he imagining things?

The pistachio-green visitor's lounge was empty, though not private. Nurses and orderlies passed through. Phil smoked for a minute, and then it occurred to him, *What if he came to take her to the other side?* He didn't believe in such things, and nonetheless, he dropped his cigarette into an ashtray and ran back. His shoes clomped down the hallway. A nurse chided him for running. He kept going.

Madeline's chest rose and fell rhythmically as he stood above her. She was tiny and thin from the illness, her eyes sunken, her mouth open like a nestling, lips dry. Why couldn't he make her recover? A father should be able to fix things. He wanted to scream and pummel something.

Once Velma arrived, he called Abby from the payphone in the lounge.

When he pulled up to her studio, the venetian blinds were closed. The door swung open. She stood resplendent in a black lace bra and panties. She wore platform sandals, toenails painted blood red. Her taut body was a work of art.

And yet his second brain seemed impaired.

As he carried her to the sofa, her hips, skin, hands, lips, and tongue were all over him.

Still nothing.

Abby kept trying until Phil finally nudged her away. Zipped his pants. He pushed her back on the couch and was about to do what he could, when something cracked inside him and a torrent of grief gushed out. He could only turn away.

Abby hugged him from behind, draping her arms and torso around him like an afghan. "It's okay," she said.

It took Phil several minutes to compose himself. "It's not." He wiped his face with his hands. "Something happened to her. She won't talk about it and hasn't been right since. I think she wants to die."

Abby didn't say anything. She let him sit there. When he had to leave to see patients, she surprised him with a gift for Madeline. A whimsical sculpture of a bird she'd made out of three stacked rocks glued together, the size of two fists, one atop the other. The grey rocks had a clear varnish coating that shined them up like pewter. A purple feather was stuck to the uppermost, smallest rock that formed the head. Eyes and a beak were painted on in lustrous black. Wings on the middle were painted fuchsia and orange. The bottom rock was flat, a little thicker than a pancake. It was for the feet, which were royal blue outlined in black.

He took it and hugged her. "Thank you for being just what I needed today."

After work he went back to see Madeline and found her alone, sleeping. He sat in the bedside chair and set the bird sculpture on the table beside the bed, next to a vase of yellow daffodils from Velma's parents.

"Her temperature's still at 102," a young nurse said as she entered. A bun of auburn hair protruded from the white hat on her head.

"She had a spinal tap today, and what a brave girl. She did it all alone, without Mommy or Daddy."

"My wife wasn't here?" he asked.

The nurse shook her head. "No one was. She's a trouper. It's an uncomfortable procedure. She didn't even cry. Most kids do."

"When will they have the results?"

"Not for a couple of days ... Hope you don't mind, I asked Maddie what she was, and she said, 'I'm *Afro-American*.'" The nurse smiled as though amused. "Very formal. But you're not really Black, are you?"

Poor Madeline, Phil thought. A spinal tap and she had to deal with this nonsense, too? "Why do you want to know?" he asked without smiling.

The nurse's eyebrows crept up her forehead. She flushed. "Oh. Um, sorry if, uh ... Never mind." She walked out as Velma strode in wearing a sleeveless blue dress, heels, and a matching bag.

"What're you all dressed up for?" Phil asked.

Her eyes went straight to the bird on the table. "Where'd that come from?"

"Why?"

"What do you mean why? If it's for Maddie, I want to know who gave it to her."

"A friend of mine," Phil said.

"What friend?" She crossed her arms.

"What does it matter?" He picked the bird up and held it.

"Listen," she hissed, "your mother's in the restroom. I drove into the city and picked her up." She pointed at Phil across the bed. "I don't wanna get into it with you right now, but that is *my* fucking child." She jabbed her finger in his direction again. "And unless you want to unleash a lunatic like you've never seen, you will *not* involve my kid in your *openness*."

"His openness?" Phil's mother said, clunking into the room in her orthopedic shoes.

"Have a seat, Emily." Velma dragged a straight-backed chair to her. It was the only one in the room besides Phil's.

Emily plopped down opposite him and looked at Madeline. "Asleep, huh?" Her tone implied laziness.

"Have you come to rub in how I couldn't keep my child healthy, Mother?"

"Give your wife that chair."

He looked at Velma across the bed standing beside Emily.

"I don't want it," Velma said. "I'm sick of sitting on these hard, uncomfortable seats every damn day." She held out her hand. "Give me that thing."

"No." He held tight to the bird.

"Give it to me, Philip."

"It's for Madeline," he said. "You want to carry on like a crazy person, go right ahead. Let them throw you out of here."

"What is that?" his mother asked.

He held it up. "It's a gift from a friend. To lift Madeline's spirits."

Emily's gray eyebrows came together as she squinted and leaned closer. "What?" She adjusted the crocheted white shawl on her shoulders. "What would possess someone to give a sick child a bird with wings made of *rocks*? How is that uplifting?" Her chin-length gray curls swayed as she shook her head. "That thing is an insult," she said. "And it's ugly, too."

Velma's laugh exploded from her like flatulence.

"I'm sick of both of you and your hostility," he said, taking care not to raise his voice. "Why don't you get the hell out of here? You're not doing Madeline any good." He set the bird between his knees.

"Oh, *I'm* not staying," Velma said. "I just came to bring you your mother and to say goodnight to my daughter." She leaned down and kissed Madeline's forehead. "Emily, please see that that thing goes in the trash." She looked at Phil. "If I see it in my house, I'm going to break it." She spun on her high heels and left.

"Where's she going?" he asked.

"She's *your* wife, Philip. I don't know."

Now he was stuck with her. "Hope you have an overnight bag at the house. I'm not driving into the Bronx tonight."

"That's how you talk to your mother?"

"I don't know why you bothered to come."

Her wrinkled hands lay in the lap of her gray-and-white ging-ham dress. She stared at them. "I know you don't think much of me."

He didn't rebut that.

"You think I didn't love you, eh?"

"What would have given me that idea, Mother?"

Her lips pressed together tightly.

"Lawrence was your son, and I was some kid you got stuck taking care of."

She closed her eyes. "I thought you'd have it easier."

"Easier?"

"You were lighter."

He could've slapped her. "Be quiet. Don't say another thing."

"I needed to build him up."

"What did I just say?" He picked up the bird and drew it behind his shoulder like a baseball he was ready to pitch at her.

She shielded her face with her arms.

"Oh my," the auburn-haired nurse said as she entered. She brought a hand to her mouth.

Phil lowered the bird. "I wasn't really going to . . ."

The nurse showed her palm and turned her head as if to say, *I don't want to know*. She felt Madeline's forehead. "Sweating," she said. "Could be a good sign." She rolled Maddie onto her side and inserted a thermometer. Without looking at Phil or his mother she said, "I'll be back," and walked out.

"Easier, huh?" Phil snorted in disgust. "You ever consider how long I spent in school, Mother? *Twenty years* including postdoctoral studies. Why do you suppose I needed so many degrees? You think my abilities weren't questioned because of my race? *Easier?* I had to do exceedingly well *and* make a living to support families the entire time. When I came here for work, bigots threw rocks and eggs at me. Even though I was lighter than my brother. Imagine that."

Emily stared at the floor.

"I made my own way on a path that didn't exist. I had to mow it down myself," he spat. "I had to mow *you* down too, Mother. You did just as much to try to stop my progress as any racist." He shook his head. "There are few things more harmful to a person's psyche than knowing his own mother hates him. I was *lighter*? Go to hell."

Emily did not look up from the speckled, beige floor.

Madeline opened her eyes.

"Hi, baby," Phil said. "How're you feeling?"

She stared at him. "What's wrong, Daddy?" she whispered.

He tried to smile. "Don't worry about me. You rest."

"I prayed for you every day, Philip," Emily said. "Of course I cared for you."

"Oh, be quiet," he said without looking at her. He touched Madeline's face. "Daddy loves you, baby."

"You'd do *anything* to make Madeline well right now, wouldn't you? You're not special in that regard. All parents feel that for their children. Even when they can't show it or when they've said something terrible they didn't mean when they were overwhelmed with grief."

"You never had anything good to say to me, Mother."

"Philip, do you think you've always been a perfect parent?"

"I'm thirsty, Daddy."

He leaned close to Maddie, his nose nearly touching hers. "The nurse will be right back. I'll ask if you can have some water."

She closed her eyes.

"You decided I was against you," Emily said, "and nothing good was all you could hear."

"Mother, *no*. I didn't decide that." His backside was sore on the chair. "That was you." He looked up at her and frowned. "You turned against me as I was being born, and you've been against me ever since." He was dying for a smoke.

His mother stared at her lap as she stroked the knuckles on her wrinkled fingers. There were ridges on the nailbeds. She'd married late, forty by the time she had him and he was nearly that age now.

"I know you're not capable of taking responsibility," he said, "but you will not misplace the blame. It wasn't me. And it wasn't my color. It was your choice to treat me like you wished I wasn't there because that's the kind of person you are."

She looked up at him. "Of course I didn't wish that, Philip. You come from me. You're *mine*. I may have hurt you when I tried to make you compete with your brother. Your grandmother did it with me and my siblings."

"Don't make excuses."

"That was how people inspired children to work harder." Her eyes were brimming. It causes hurt feelings. I see that now."

"Mother—"

"No one talked about children's feelings in my day, Philip. We didn't know better." She lifted her glasses to pat her eyes with the edge of her shawl.

"I'm not moved by your tears," he said. "Do you know I drink because of you?"

She stared at him.

He saw a barely perceptible smile on her lips and he had to resist the urge to sling profanities at her.

"Nothing can change that you're a part of me," she said. "And so is Maddie. Even if I *was* a terrible parent, that doesn't change the fact that you're my children. I've seen you *and* Velma be terrible parents."

"Okay, stop." He *really* needed that cigarette.

"People aren't perfect, Philip. It doesn't mean they don't care for you. In your worst moments as a father I've never doubted that you care for your daughters. And no matter how awful you think I've been, you and Madeline are mine, and I love you. I've always loved you."

Her words didn't land. At least not with Phil. He thought Madeline might have taken them in. For him, they floated in the stale room like smoke and came nowhere near his heart. He had no memory of his mother *ever* having said those words to him. What could they possibly mean now? He held tight to the bird of rocks and did not look at Emily. Instead, he kept his eyes on his daughter. She seemed to be sleeping. Would Maddie one day think his failures meant he hadn't loved her? The rocks were heavy in his hands. His chest felt heavy, too.

When he finally did look at Emily she smiled in a way he'd not seen before. Unguarded. Kind. It was perplexing.

She said, "Your father was in my dream last night. He stood in the room at the foot of the bed and touched my big toe to wake me." Her voice was girlish. "He used to do that you know?" She giggled. "Oh, wasn't it good to see that handsome face again. How I've missed him. 'My Emmy,' he said, 'tell Philip not to worry.'" Tears glimmered in her eyes though she was smiling. "He's still there, Philip. Caring for you. As you will for yours even after you go. It never dies."

A tingle brushed up Phil's neck as it had earlier.

"She's going to be okay," Emily said. "Will *you* be okay?" She extended her hand across Madeline toward him.

He only stared at it. "I don't know, Mother. I hope so."

The nurse returned.

Emily placed her withered hand back into her lap.

The young woman wiped Madeline's face with a washcloth. She removed the thermometer, looked at it, and smiled. "Fever's broken."

Phil felt a wave of relief wash through his body.

Emily clapped.

The expression of happiness startled him. It was out of character.

The nurse stood near the foot of the bed now, disinfecting the thermometer.

"Can she have some water?" Phil asked.

"The doctor has to okay that because she's still on the iv. I'll go call him." She trotted out again.

Thin streams slid down Emily's cheeks. Her eyes twinkled like a sweet old lady Phil had never met.

"Thank you, Daddy," Madeline whispered. She rolled onto her back. "Hi, Grandma."

"Hello, Maddie. How's my little darling?"

"Better," Maddie said.

"Oh, I was hoping you'd say that." Emily beamed at her.

Maddie's cheeks flushed. Her eyes shined. The adoring way she smiled said this bit of affection from her grandmother had moved her.

As Phil watched his daughter embrace his mother's warmth he sensed something begin to disarm inside his chest. He wanted to resist this release and yet, he couldn't. There was a prickle in his nose that came before tears.

Maddie closed her eyes and stretched her arms out, reaching for him on one side and for Emily on the other. Phil set the bird of rocks on the bedside table and took her fingers in his. Emily did the same on her side.

As the three held hands, he imagined his father observing from another dimension. The feeling in Phil's chest began to expand. Maddie would be okay. The past with his mother would not change, but the joy on his little girl's face lifted his spirits and filled him with the lightness of life.

better

Orange County, New York, 1975

The back seat window of the Chevy Monte Carlo frames a view of trees. Nothing but trees—maple, oak, birch, and pine—all blending together. Lulling. For miles.

Twelve-year-old Maddie can barely keep her eyes open.

"You know how fortunate you are to be coming up surrounded by all this green?" Velma says from up front. "Just gorgeous."

"Just *boring*," Maddie says. "I'd rather see buildings. And people who look like us."

Velma turns to Phil, who's driving. "You believe this?"

"And the marquees on Broadway, the lights in Times Square."

"Who're you supposed to be? Eva Gabor in *Green Acres*? Times Square is a cesspool, Madeline."

"Not to me. Can't we *please* move to the city?"

Phil turns the radio on and lights a cigarette.

"Da-ad."

"Roll your window down, kiddo," he says.

She does. Maddie tilts her head out of the car and extends an arm. Despite the August heat, the breeze is cool diving through her fingers. Her thighs, in cutoffs, stick to the warm leather, even with the air-conditioning on.

Velma begins humming to the radio—Captain and Tennille. Maddie draws her hand inside and covers both ears.

"Mo-om."

"Maddie, stop complaining," Phil says.

Her mother's head tips left and right. "*Mm . . . mm mm mm mm mm mm mm . . .*" She's off rhythm, like a maladjusted metronome.

Maddie groans and bumps her head back into the seat repeatedly. Her side ponytail flops against one arm until some split ends catch her eye. She picks up the hair and peers at it through smudged octagon-shaped glasses.

"Hope it's worth this."

"Worth what, Velma?"

"I left my shop. *On a Saturday*, Phil. I'm missing sales."

"It's not like those sales pay for anything," he says.

Maddie looks up at them and the cigarette haze rising around her father's Afro. The way it halos his head reminds her of the album cover from the musical *Hair*.

"What are you talking about?" Velma says. "Who do you think buys her clothes? And pays for her school supplies? And takes her to the movies, and out to eat on Fridays when you stay in the city?"

His head swivels through the smoke toward Velma, mouth angled down in the shape of a horseshoe as if he's impressed. "They asked to meet the whole family. Saturday's the day nonmembers are invited," he says. "Sorry."

"It's all right. I just hope it's worth it, that's all. I'm losing business." She pats at the hair-sprayed curls on her coiffed head.

"Isn't Peggy there?" Phil asks.

"Peggy's a very nice lady, but she couldn't sell drinks to a drunk."

"Then why'd you hire her?"

"Because I *like* her. She's good company. And she puts White people at ease. When they come in and see me first, that kinda throws them. Then they see *her* at the other end of the showcase. And they smile. Then they say hello. Sometimes they'll tell her: *nice shop*. But if they have a merchandise question, she's gotta point 'em back to *me*, because Peggy doesn't know tick from tock about antiques."

"Dad?" Maddie leans forward toward the front seat. "We gonna be the only Black people at this place?"

He exhales and his breath carries a hint of scotch. It mixes with his woodsy aftershave and cigarette smoke and all three creep up her nose.

She sniffles. "Well . . . are we?" she asks, staring at his diamond stud earring.

"We'll see when we get there, honey. I don't know."

Velma tosses a glance over her shoulder. "Of course we are." She turns back to Phil. "In fact, y'sure they're even gonna let us in this place?"

"Dad, you should take your earring out before we get there."

"Oh, you two, just be quiet, will you please?" He turns up the radio.

They emerge from a flight of stairs onto a patio level, where Maddie sees a huge, kidney-shaped pool to the left. It's filled with squealing little White kids, too many to count, splashing around in the shallow end. There are a few teenagers treading water and talking near the deep-end ladder, and about two dozen grown-ups, a few in the pool, more scattered on the sides in their swimsuits. They're standing, chatting, some smoking cigarettes, others reclining on green chaise lounges. To the right, across from the pool, there's a white Cape Cod–style building with green shutters and an outdoor bar and restaurant. Round white tables with green umbrellas that match the shutters fill the space between the pool and the building. The air smells like burgers grilling. Maddie's mouth waters.

She watches her father adjust his Ray-Bans and scratch at the back of his kinky curls as he scans the bodies by the pool. He's dressed for tennis in a white Lacoste shirt and shorts. Her mother's navy linen dress seems too fancy for this setting, but she looks nice. Except for her feet: pantyhose with sandals. And unpainted toenails. Beautiful from head to ankle, Maddie thinks.

She looks around and sees a few people eyeballing them: an overweight kid with white stuff smeared on his nose, a bald guy with a hairy chest, whose legs straddle the chaise lounge as he eats from a basket of fries between his thighs, and a gray-haired couple perched on the tiled edge of the pool with their age-spotted legs dangling in the water. None of these people seem shocked to see them like Maddie worried they might. They're just looking. Her father's not the swiftest when it comes to this kind of thing, though.

At the tennis club down the street from their house, she's heard plenty of comments—mean things—said about her, and her father.

He acts like he doesn't hear them. One lanky old jerk, with a white mustache thick as shag carpet, always shakes his finger at her and says, "Now, don't steal my hubcaps, kid." Then he laughs. She once told him he could shove his stupid hubcaps, but it made no difference. He said it again the next time he saw her. Some people in Monroe irk the hell out of Maddie. They're a couple of towns away today. Maybe this club's members are a different breed? She hopes they're more like city people who don't make a big commotion about people like her.

"What do you think?" Phil asks, without looking at her or her mother. He's watching the ladies in swimsuits, sunning themselves.

"Is the pool heated?" Maddie asks.

"You're not swimming," her mother says.

"Aw, man." Maddie sucks her teeth.

"Phil! Phil!" A thin White lady with long, wet hair framing a narrow face waves at her father. She's tanned, in a yellow bikini, and she glides toward them on her lean legs. Her thighs are as narrow as her calves. Water trickles down from her hair and runs along her arms like veins. The lady keeps looking at her father and smiling. He waves and keeps looking at her, too. As she gets closer, Maddie can see that her teeth are thin like her legs. Yellow, too. A smoker, probably. Her toenails and fingernails are hot pepper red.

Maddie's father steps forward to meet the lady. They kiss each other on the cheek and stand together by the side of the pool.

"Who's that?" Maddie asks.

The strap of her mother's Coach bag slips off as her shoulders notch up and down. She slides it back up. Maddie stares at her father and the wet White lady. Her mother stares, too.

He waves them over, lifts his Ray-Bans, and rests them on top of his Afro.

"Velma, Maddie, this is Abby Goldberg," he says. He places a hand on her bare back. With his other hand Phil gestures, "This is Velma, and my daughter, Maddie."

"*Our* daughter," Velma says, staring at the woman.

Abby Goldberg's mouth twitches as if she's uncomfortable. "I, I used to be a patient," she explains. "Years ago."

"Hello," Velma says flatly.

"Don't you have a girl about the same age?" Phil asks.

"I do," Abby Goldberg says, smiling with her skinny teeth.

Maddie says nothing. Abby Goldberg smells like chlorine and Coppertone. It reminds her of a real vacation.

Her mother stares at her father. His hand is still touching Abby Goldberg's back. "Nice to meet you," she says, in a tone that's not friendly at all.

"Oh, you, too, Velma," Abby says. "Your home is so elegant."

"My home?"

"When I used to come for sessions, I saw—you have excellent taste. Haven't seen you all here before. When did you join?" She steps forward, away from Phil's hand.

"We—"

"We haven't yet." He cuts Velma off. "We're thinking about it."

Maddie watches her mother squint at her father.

"Well, good luck," Abby says. "Hope you brought your suits. The water's divine."

"We're not here to swim," Velma says. "I'm going back to work. I have an antiques shop in Tuxedo."

"Oh, yes. I've passed it. I live in Sterling Forest. Looks darling."

"You should stop in sometime."

"Abby," Phil says, "where are the tennis courts?"

"Behind there." She points to a tall white fence in the back.

He turns toward it. Maddie looks, too. She can faintly hear balls bouncing and being smacked.

"One of these days," Abby says to Velma. "But, really, I prefer *new* things."

Phil walks toward the *clokt—ting* tennis sounds.

Velma crosses her arms. "I also sell jewelry and paintings."

"Paintings?" Abby sweeps her dark hair to one side. Water dribbles down to the tan line where skin white as clouds peeks out of her banana-colored bikini top. "Oh. That, I didn't know. I paint, actually. I'm an artist."

"*Mmm*," Velma says. She smiles with her lips closed.

"Do you sell on consignment?"

Velma nods. "Established artists. No one *new*."

Abby smiles with her lips closed, too.

"Let's go look at the courts," Phil says, returning. "Want to join us, Abby?"

"Can't," she says. "Flora's in the pool." Her eyes dart over there and then back to Maddie. "They have towels if you want to swim." She points to a kiosk over by the fence.

"I do have my suit on under my clothes." Maddie turns to her mother, hands in prayer position. *Please.*

"She's not swimming today."

"Too bad. Why?" Abby asks.

Velma cocks her head as if Abby Goldberg has some nerve asking. "We're going to a play in the city tomorrow. I washed and set her hair."

Her father walks toward the fence again.

"And Madeline sees about as well as a worm without her glasses. She'd be a hazard in the pool."

"Oh, my Flora's a little four-eyes, too, and she does fine. We keep her glasses on the chaise with her towel." She looks at Maddie. "I could put yours with hers if you like." She points to one of the lounges.

"Sure," Maddie says.

"I said *no*. You know how long it took me to do this." She taps Maddie's head.

Maddie looks at Abby. "I'm twelve and I'm still not allowed to wash or dry my own hair. She only washes it for special occasions."

"Maddie."

"First day of school. Thanksgiving. Easter. School photos. And once in the summer. Yesterday was it."

Abby laughs.

"See?" Maddie turns to her mother. "She thinks I'm joking. *That's* how weird it is."

Velma's cheeks lift as if she's smiling. She's not. She places a hand on the back of Maddie's neck and pinches the shit out of it. Maddie winces.

"She has the kind of hair texture that dries out and breaks off easily. It's not meant to be washed often."

Abby's eyebrows inch up her forehead.

Phil returns. "C'mon, you two," he says snippily. "I came here to see the tennis courts."

"Fine. Go ahead. We'll follow you." Velma turns to Abby. "Excuse us."

Maddie waves and moves off behind her parents as a tall man with salt-and-pepper hair and a scraggly goatee exits the restaurant and walks toward them. He raises a hand and wiggles his fingers. His other hand holds a clipboard and he wears a white shirt with "Greenwood Hills" embroidered on it. "Your name?" Sounds like he needs to clear his throat.

"Philip Arrington. We have an appointment."

"Arr-ing-ton?" He looks at the clipboard. Coughs. "Oh. Right. *Dr.* Arrington?"

"Yes."

"Oookey dokey." His eyes move back and forth across them. "Indeed you do. Welcome." He offers his hand. "I'm Adam David."

"Phil," he says, shaking hands. "It's a pleasure."

Adam David backs toward the restaurant again. "Bear with me, please. I've got something to tend to in the office. I'll be out shortly to show you around."

Maddie watches her parents look at each other.

Abby moves toward them. "Shame you can't enjoy the water, Maddie." She turns to the pool and shouts, "Flora!" She hurls her skinny arms overhead and crosses them in the air like she's signaling a search plane. "Flora, darling! Come here, please."

A potbellied girl climbs out of the deep end. With dark wet hair stuck to round cheeks, she trundles toward them in a pink one-piece. Thick marshmallow thighs (nothing like her mother's) are reddish from the sun and they mush together as she moves. Abby introduces Flora to Maddie and her parents.

Flora wipes hair from her face, squinting her deep-set, light brown eyes. "Nice to meet you!" She turns to Maddie. "Water's warm. Coming in?" She sounds friendly.

"Not allowed."

"Why?"

"You can swim, Maddie," her father says. "Go ahead."

"Phil."

"Oh, Velma, let her enjoy herself."

"Don't complain about how she looks tomorrow. I'm not spending another two hours on her hair."

Maddie kicks off her sandals. "Thanks, Daddy!" She hands Abby her glasses, sheds her cut-offs and T-shirt, and shows off a purple two-piece.

Flora grins. Her teeth are narrow like her mother's. She turns and Maddie follows.

In the pool Flora does a handstand. And she holds her breath underwater *really* long. Way longer than Maddie can. Then she wants to race from the shallow end to the deep end, even though there're tons of bodies in the water. Maddie bumps into a red-nosed man who scowls at her. Flora wins.

"Don't feel bad." She rests a chubby hand on Maddie's shoulder as they grip the chrome ladder. "I've been practicing. Hey, you know how to dive?"

Maddie hesitates before shaking her head.

"Oh! I'll show you. Let me show you!"

Flora climbs up the ladder and leads Maddie by the hand to the edge. She squats and falls in headfirst, butt last. She comes up and says to practice that a few times. Maddie does. Then Flora demonstrates how to crouch, lean forward, and glide into the water. Maddie does it and comes back up.

"Very good," Flora says, treading water near the ladder. "Now practice that about ten times and you'll be ready for the real thing."

"Ten times?"

"You wanna get better at something you have to practice."

Once Maddie masters that, Flora climbs out and takes her to the edge again. She stands so close her thigh rubs skin to skin against Maddie's. She lifts her arms overhead, hands flat, one on top of the other.

As Maddie mimics Flora's moves, she hears laughter. She throws a glance across the pool and vaguely makes out a couple of boys, teenagers, pointing at them, cracking up.

She takes a step away from Flora. "Maybe that's enough for today."

Flora reaches out, grabs Maddie's arm, and tugs her close again. "Don't worry about those schmucks. We're not here to impress them."

Maddie stares at her toes and thinks for a moment. Flora's right. She takes a breath. Nods. Flora dives first. Maddie follows, copying as best she can. While she's under, worrying about how it looked, she accidentally breathes in some water, and then comes up coughing. The boys laugh. They're practically howling. At her form? The coughing? Both? Chlorine stings her eyes and she can't see their faces. Being nearsighted sucks almost as bad as being made fun of. She's used to it, though. Kids pick on people who're different. She's always the one who's different.

"Remember to blow *out* of your nose," Flora yells.

Maddie swims toward her at the ladder. When she's closer she sees that Flora's smiling at her. *Staring* and smiling in a weird way. Not sure what to make of it, Maddie climbs past her and out. Though she still can't see the boys clearly, she hears them snickering as she walks, dripping and barefooted, through the sunbathers and the socializers. When she makes it to Flora's lounge chair and her glasses, and she can finally see, she spots her mother sitting alone at one of the restaurant tables looking pissed. She wraps the borrowed towel around her and walks over there. Flora gets her glasses and follows.

"Where's Daddy?" Maddie asks.

"No idea," her mother says. "But I wish he'd hurry up. I'm ready to get the hell out of here. Look at your hair." She shakes her head.

Maddie's ponytail is wet and curly now. As it dries it'll kink up.

"Are those my mom's cigarettes?" Flora asks, pointing at a pack of Marlboro Lights on the table.

Velma shrugs. "I guess so."

"Where is she?"

"I don't know. She walked off somewhere."

"I see her." Flora skips toward the restaurant entrance, dripping and jiggling as she goes.

Maddie's father and Abby Goldberg, with her towel draped around her hips like a sarong, stroll out of the building and head toward them. Flora barnacles herself to her mother's waist.

Phil smiles at Maddie. "Enjoy your swim, kiddo?"

She shrugs. "Where were you?"

"Taking with someone about joining."

"We met with one of the owners," Abby says.

Maddie's mother stands. "What?" She smoothes her dress.

"I'll tell you about it in the car," he says. "Listen, Maddie, Flora's taking a musical theater class for kids at Orange County Community College. Starts next month. Doesn't that sound fun?"

Maddie gives her father a deadpan stare.

"Oh!" Flora bounces on her toes. "That'd be fan*ta*stic. I've been wanting to find someone to take it with me."

"Excellent. We'll carpool," Abby says.

Eyes still stuck on her father, Maddie crosses her arms.

"You think about it," he tells her. "Dry off. We're leaving."

"Can't believe I missed work for this bullshit," Velma shoves her seatbelt buckle together. "Think I came all this way so I could sit there by *myself*?"

"Look, Abby was showing me the courts, and we ran into one of the owners. He gave me a tour of the locker room, the main restaurant, and the offices."

"Why didn't you bring us with you?"

"Because it happened spontaneously."

Velma exhales and turns to look out at the trees.

Maddie hears the cigarette lighter snap into place.

"He asked what I do for work. Went over the cost of dues. Asked for references. Abby vouched for us."

"So that's how you want to spend your weekends?" Velma doesn't turn from the window. "Hanging around those White women at the pool?"

"I'll be joining for the *tennis*." Phil lights a cigarette. "Summer's almost over."

Maddie rolls her window down.

"What's wrong with the courts right down the street?" Velma asks.

"If it's all right with you, I'd like to play with some other people."

"Yeah, I bet you would."

Phil turns the radio on. "Jive Talkin'" by the Bee Gees plays. "Did you like the place, Maddie?" He finds her eyes in the rearview mirror. "You want to go back?"

"Neither of you care what I want."

"I asked you, didn't I?"

"I can hardly do *anything* I want," she shouts. "Can't do my own hair or live in the city or go anyplace where I'm not the only Black kid. Now you wanna pick my friends for me, too?"

"But you're always saying you want to sing. The class sounds great."

"Don't expect me to drive her up there," Velma says.

"I'll drive her," he says.

Velma's head whips toward Maddie. "And what is wrong with you telling that woman I only wash your hair for special occasions?"

"It's true! I get made fun of because my head is greasy and smelly."

"Y'know what? You wanna take care of it yourself so badly, go right ahead."

"Really?"

"Wash it all you want. And when it breaks off or falls out don't come crying to me." She turns back around.

Maddie throws both fists in the air, hitting the car ceiling. "Finally!"

The first time they carpool Phil drives.

"Ooo, your hair looks *good* like that," Flora says as she climbs in wearing a skirt over a leotard and tights.

Maddie smiles. "Thanks. I set it and sat under the dryer. Trimmed it, too."

Flora strokes Maddie's hair. "Soft," she says, sounding surprised. "And long. Much better than when it was all curly. You look pretty. Almost like you're White."

Maddie leans away from Flora and turns toward the window. Green leaves blur by. She knows that was *supposed* to be a compliment, but if someone calls you pretty only because you look almost White, it means that when you look like yourself, you aren't pretty, and that's not a compliment at all. Even if White-girl hair *is* kind of what she was going for.

"So, you like musicals?" Flora says. "Which ones?"

Maddie stares out the window. She heard her. That doesn't mean she feels like answering.

"Which ones do *you* like, Flora?" Phil asks.

"Well, we have the original cast recordings of *Man of La Mancha*, *Godspell*, and *Hair*. I like those a lot."

"Maddie likes those, too. Right, Maddie?"

She exhales, annoyed that he's ignored what Flora said about her hair, but he won't shut up about musicals.

"Have you heard of *Raisin*, Flora?" he asks.

"Yeah! We went in June. It's based on *A Raisin in the Sun*. And Michael from *Good Times* is in it. He sings 'Sidewalk Tree'. That was my favorite song."

"Hear that, Maddie?"

Maddie turns to Flora. "*You* saw *Raisin?*"

Flora nods.

"We saw it," Phil says. "Maddie thinks Michael from *Good Times* is a fox. Right, Maddie?"

"God, Dad, stop."

"None of her friends wanted to go see him with us."

"Really?" Flora says. "I think he's great."

Maddie looks at her. She's never met a White girl who's been to the city to see a Black show. Maybe she's not that bad.

In class they're given sheet music. Maddie gets "How I Feel" from *The Me Nobody Knows*. And after the teacher, Mr. Jansen, sings it to her and she sings it back to him, he smiles with his sparkling teeth, and he nods, shaking his dark David Cassidy shag, and he says she has a great voice. Maddie smiles so hard her cheekbones ache. She tells him she has a piano and she'll practice at home.

When Flora sings, Mr. Jansen sighs and runs both hands through his black hair. He tells her where to take her breaths and makes her do parts over. And she does, without complaining. Maddie admires how she keeps trying.

Flora's mother picks them up in her cranberry-colored Oldsmobile. When she asks how it went, Flora says, "Okay."

Maddie says the same, though to her it was *waaay* better than okay.

Abby drives Maddie back to their house, because her mother's shop is nearby and Velma will pick her up on the way home.

The Goldbergs' walls are filled with Flora's mother's abstract paintings. They remind Maddie of cells under a microscope. She pretends to like it, walking around the living room as if she's in the Museum of Modern Art. She stops to stare at one. Its fuzzy outline shape seems to be two bodies, one over the other. And they're filled with amoebas.

"My father has one like this in his Manhattan office," she says.

"Yeah," Flora says smiling up at it. "People buy them because she's talented. Runs in our family."

Maddie blinks. "It's nice," she says, lying. The painting makes her queasy. And anxious. The large body on top of a smaller one reminds her of being alone with that man in Africa. She exhales long and slow, like an unplugged beach ball. "Where's your room?" she asks.

Flora's walls are lavender, same as Maddie's, except Flora's mother has painted little white flowers on them, too. And there's a portrait of Flora when she was younger, and two posters of Karen Carpenter. "I know another girl who's a fan of hers," Maddie says. "She has all the Carpenters' albums."

"Yeah? Did you like them?"

"Didn't get to hear them. I'm not allowed over her house and she can't come to mine."

"Why?"

Maddie sighs. "Take a guess, Flora. Why do you think?"

"Oh." Flora nods. "They're prejudiced. Sorry. I know what that's like. Jews aren't everybody's favorite, either. But you don't need to listen to hers. I have their albums."

Flora laces her arm through Maddie's. She leads her out of the room and into the doorframe of another across the hall. Its walls and ceiling are baby blue with cotton puff clouds. Her little sister lies prone on top of her bed, backward. Her toes touch the headboard and her head is at the bottom. "This is Amy," Flora says. "She's six. She didn't come out to meet you because she's shy."

Amy has light brown bangs and eyes as dark as Maddie's. She rocks on top of a pillow that's under her body and between her legs and she peers up at them from the pages of a Maurice Sendak book.

"What's she doing with that pillow?" Maddie whispers.

"My mom calls it self-soothing. Amy has anxiety."

"What's she soothing? Her private parts?"

Flora doesn't answer. She leads Maddie back to the living room and plays the Carpenters' "Close to You." They sit on the floor. As Maddie flips through the other albums, Flora begins singing along with the record, performing *right to her*, emoting, as if she's a boy Flora wants to be close to. Maddie thinks it would be unkind to look away, but God, how she wants to crawl behind the couch. The performance feels endless. *What is wrong with this girl?*

Thankfully, Flora is interrupted when Maddie gets invited to join her and her family at their dining table for vegetarian chili over brown rice. Different. Interesting. She actually doesn't miss the meat. Flora's father has longish dark hair and a beard. He looks like the guy she's seen in the illustrations from *The Joy of Sex*, except without the muscles. When Maddie refers to them as Mr. Goldberg and Mrs. Goldberg, Mr. Goldberg insists, "Call us Harry and Abby. We're not formal here."

"Okay," Maddie says, though it makes her uncomfortable. She's not allowed to call grown-ups by their first names. Not even Miss Dowd, their housekeeper, whom she's known since third grade. She said Maddie could call her Gertie, but her mother won't allow it.

When she climbs into her mother's station wagon later, she's surprised to see Brutus and their shaggy mutt Max in the back seat.

"What are the boys doing here, Mom?"

"Oh, your father said he was having work done at the house

today." Velma screws up her face. "Jesus, Maddie. You couldn't break wind *outside* the car?"

Maddie smiles. She eyes the dogs. "How do you know it's not them?"

"Please. I've been with them all day. My God. What the hell've you been eating?"

"Sorry," she says, and squeezes her butt cheeks together.

When they get home, Phil calls Maddie and her mother downstairs into his office and shows them that one of Abby Goldberg's paintings is now hanging above his desk. It's huge and multiple shades of green and painted on a piece of canvas-wrapped wood, carved into a shape that vaguely looks like bodies entwined. Her mother makes the same face she made when she smelled that fart.

In voice class, Mr. Jansen stops Flora every few seconds as she tries to sing "Far from the Home I Love." Her pitch is off, he says. Her breathing isn't from her diaphragm, her posture's bad, and she's not connected to the emotion. Flora doesn't get defensive or let on that her feelings are hurt. She gives it her all until he tells her to stop.

Man, Maddie thinks. She admires the girl's grit.

During a snack break, the two of them stand at the soda machine in the hallway outside the auditorium with some classmates. There are a couple of well-dressed girls, sisters, pretty, with blond hair, and a boy named Shaun, who's also pretty and blond and wears jazz shoes from Capezio. As Maddie sticks her coins into the machine, Flora stands behind her munching potato chips from a bag.

"My mother said you have a big ass, Maddie," Flora says, loud enough for everyone in the hallway to hear.

There's a laugh. Maddie can't tell whose. She doesn't turn around. She feels a prick of pain inside her chest as if she's been poked there with a large pin. Her cheeks feel hot. She's the only Black kid in this class and her ass *is* big, compared to the other girls'. The Danskin pants her mother makes her wear don't help. It's times like these that she *really* wishes she didn't have to live here. If she were in the city or in Queens or on Long Island where her cousins live, her big ass would be no big deal, because Black folks have big butts and that's just how it is. She slaps the button on the soda machine and her Mountain Dew clunks down to the bottom. She yanks it out and spins around to face Flora.

"Your mother was my father's patient. Did you know that? And did you know my father's a shrink? That means your mother's a crazy nut. I don't give a crap what she says."

Flora stops munching. Her deep-set eyes get ginormous. The pretty blonds behind her crack up. Shaun in the jazz shoes says, "At least she's not fat like you, Flora. And *she* can sing."

Flora flushes, looking like she's been smacked in the face. She marches away.

Maddie finds Shaun's eyes shining, sending kindness toward her. She's more grateful than she can say. The whole class knows he likes boys, and no one makes fun of him, maybe because he's never tried to hide it. He's not ashamed. Maddie wishes she had his confidence. She would hug him, but her eyes are pooling up, so she only nods her thanks and heads back into the auditorium.

She has to ride home with Flora and her fucking mother. She slouches in the back of the Oldsmobile and watches the red, gold, and orange leaves on the trees outside. She wouldn't admit this to her parents, only to herself: they're spectacular.

Abby Goldberg plays some singer Maddie's never heard of.

"His name's Boyd Paley," she says. "I went to high school with him in Chicago. Isn't he great? He's influenced by Burl Ives."

Maddie's never heard of Burl Ives either. And no, he's *not* great, in her opinion. He's not even on the radio. They're listening to a rinky-dink cassette on a Panasonic tape player.

In the front seat, Flora sings along with her mother: "It's my world, and I do what I want. / I got a girl, don't mind me if I flaunt. / I know I'm the greatest and my life's a special one. / Don't be mad 'cause it's better than yours, hon."

Boyd Paley's voice is barely more bearable than Flora's, and her mother's is no better. Maddie never did like Abby Goldberg or her ugly artwork.

She won't tell her parents what Abby Goldberg said about her ass because she knows her mother. Velma's sharp tongue is apt to shred Flora's mother to pieces and then the whole carpool thing would be off and she might have to drop the class. She can deal with Flora and Abby's insults. She's been dealing with insults all her life. Maddie's good at singing, way better than Flora, and she's not gonna be run out of the class by either of those bitches.

When she gets home that Saturday she stands in the doorway of her father's smoky office, where that butt-ugly painting hangs on the wall above him and the dogs lounge at his feet while he's hunched over his desk. Ice melts in a glass of scotch beside the yellow pad he's writing on.

"I'll keep doing the carpool," Maddie says, "but I am not going to Flora's house *ever* again, and I don't want her coming here."

Phil lifts his head. "You need to learn to get along with all kinds of people in this world, Maddie."

Her eyes narrow thin as the side of his legal pad. "You pick your friends, Phil, and I'll pick mine."

"Phil?"

She stomps away.

A couple of weeks later Brutus eats a whole stick of butter off the dining table just as Maddie sits down to eat with her parents.

"Goddammit. Get your ass away from here," her mother screams at the dog.

"Calm down, Velma," Phil says.

That sets her off even more. As they argue, Maddie gets up from the table and goes to the piano across the room. She plays and sings the new song she's doing in class: "Easy to Be Hard," from *Hair*. Her favorite is the part about evil and social injustice. She loves that the song does more than entertain. It says something that matters.

Phil and Velma stop their bickering. It was good, they tell her. Maddie likes the compliments. And the change in conversation. She sits back at the table across from Phil. There's a window behind him that faces the backyard. Leaves drift by, falling like snow.

"And what's Flora singing in class?" he asks.

Maddie scoffs. "Why?"

"Just curious."

"Already told you she can't sing."

"That's not nice, Maddie."

"Flora's not nice."

Phil cuts his fried chicken from the bone. Her mother picks hers up with her fingers. Maddie does, too.

"It's good, Mom. Crunchy."

"Better than that vegetarian chili, huh?" Velma winks.

This has become a joke between them. *Anything* is better than that flatulence-inducing chili.

Apropos of nothing Phil begins to hum and then softly sing to himself: "It's my world, and I do what I want. / I got a girl, don't mind me if I flaunt. / I know I'm the greatest and my life's a special one. / Don't be mad 'cause it's better than yours, hon."

Maddie sets her chicken breast down.

Phil continues to hum the melody as he heaps cucumber salad onto his plate. He feels her eyes on him and looks up. "What?"

"How do you know that song?"

"Must've heard it on the radio," he says. "Found its way into my head and now it won't leave."

Maddie stares at her plate. Her heart hammers.

Across the room, little Max climbs onto Brutus's hip and begins to hump it.

Her mother pitches a napkin holder at him. "Cut that out!" she yells. He stumbles off.

Maddie looks Phil dead in the face. "Whatever happened with the tennis and swim club?"

"Why?"

"Why'd you even bring me there? Are we joining?"

"No."

"*Good*," Maddie says.

"Good?" he says.

"There're no Black people there."

"Tell her *why* we're not joining, Philip," Velma says.

He dabs salad dressing from his mouth with a napkin. "It was more than I wanted to spend."

Velma sucks her teeth. "Oh please, tell her the truth. It's not like she doesn't understand prejudice."

"Velma."

Max mounts Brutus again.

"May I be excused?"

"No," her mother snaps. "Finish your—"

"If she wants to go, let her go! Why're you always telling her no?"

"Who the fuck do you think you're raising your voice at?"

Maddie gets up and runs upstairs. She hears Max panting and whining (still humping) even after she closes her bedroom door.

He could've heard the song when he went to buy the painting, she figures. But would Abby Goldberg have played it for him then? He knew most of the words. How long was he there?

As she sits on her purple bed, Maddie has an uneasy feeling. One she doesn't want. She shoves it way in a corner in the back of her head where she stuffs all the other shit she'd rather not feel.

Another Saturday, after musical theater class, Phil picks Maddie and Flora up. He tells the girls Abby said to take Flora home with them. She'll pick her up later. Maddie tries to evil eye him in the rearview mirror. It doesn't work. He drops them off and then leaves without saying where he's going. Shit, she thinks.

After introducing Flora to the dogs in the kitchen and then having a snack, Maddie takes her into the living room, where Flora flops down in her sweatpants beside the stereo and rifles through the record albums.

"Ooo, Petula Clark," she squeals, "She's beautiful."

Maddie sits cross-legged on the rug near her.

"Don't you think?" Flora asks.

"She's all right." Maddie picks some dog hair off her stretchy Danskins.

"She's *excellent*," Flora says. "Can you play this?"

Maddie exhales. "That's my father's. I don't feel like listening to her."

"She was on TV with Harry Belafonte."

"So?"

"So, my mom said it was *major*, because Petula linked arms with him, and a White lady had never touched a Black man on TV before that. You should like her."

Maddie rolls her eyes so hard they almost fling out of her head. "As handsome as Harry Belafonte is, that lady's lucky he *let* her touch him." She flips to a Billie Holiday album. "*This* is the voice I'm in the mood for."

Flora huffs. She hoists herself off the floor and plods over to the upright piano. Clinks a few keys. "Let's practice our songs."

"You know how to play?"

She sighs. "Can't you play for me?"

"I'd rather listen to Billie Holiday."

Flora plunks down onto the bench. Maddie walks on her knees to the turntable. She sets the record down and places the needle onto: "You Go to My Head." She sits on her feet and closes her eyes to listen as Billie sings of a lover who gets in her brain like a glass of champagne.

"She sounds drunk," Flora says, as if that's some kind of disgrace.

"She sounds *different*," Maddie says. "And she sounds like she *loves* sounding different. That's why she's amazing."

"Petula's a better singer."

Maddie snorts. Flora's so wrong it's not worth arguing. How is she going to get through this miserable visit? After a moment she says, "Hey," as an idea occurs to her. "*We* could get drunk."

Flora raises her eyebrows.

Phil's liquor cabinet is downstairs in the den that doubles as his waiting room when he sees patients. They each slug a bit of every open bottle: scotch, gin, vodka, vermouth, rum, Campari (*elch*!), Kahlúa, and crème de menthe. Soon they're sliding around in their socks, laughing, as they stumble through some Fosse-inspired choreography they learned in class. Flora giggles and falls in a thudding heap onto the black-and-white checkered floor. The walls shake. Maddie crashes down beside her.

"Everything's spinning," Flora says.

The hefty bang must have roused the dogs, because they push through the swinging door and barrel down the stairs into the den. The girls play dead, trying not to laugh, as Max and Brutus check them out with sniffs and licks. Brutus drools. After a while, he sighs and lies down. Max promptly climbs his shaggy self onto him. As he begins to whine and thrust his privates into Brutus's hip, the girls sit up and watch.

"Wow," Flora says. "Never seen *that*."

"Really? Dogs are always humping."

"Never around 'em. My mom's afraid." Flora sucks in a gasp. "O-my-God." Her voice rises to its upper register. "*Ew!*" His red thingy scootches out like lipstick!" She watches and then turns to Maddie. "Ever see a boy's thing?"

Maddie stares at the floor. She nods.

"Yuck." Flora laughs. "Was it disgusting?"

Maddie nods again. She feels sweat beading on her scalp. And she's dizzy.

"Whose was it?"

Maddie draws her thighs to her chest and shakes her head. She won't say.

"Ever been tongue-kissed?" Flora asks.

"What do you think?" Maddie exhales a burst of irritation. "Boys don't kiss girls like me around here."

Flora cracks a wide thin-toothed smile. "I could show you. We could practice."

Maddie slides her a look. "You mean . . . on each other?"

Flora's shoulders rise and fall. "Why not?"

Brutus shifts, shaking Max off.

Woozy, and balancing on her backside, Maddie straightens her legs to keep from tipping over. Her thoughts are a bit hazy.

Flora leans toward Maddie. Maddie leans toward Flora. Their eyeglasses clink and their front teeth smash together. They fall back, laughing, hands over their mouths, their bodies flopping on the floor like Max's tail when he sits for a treat. Flora touches Maddie's arm and rolls toward her. They move together, slowly this time. Lips touch. Tongues meet. Maddie's pulse quickens. Flora sighs softly and rests against her and Maddie remembers, *This is a girl*. Girls aren't supposed to do this with each other.

"Wanna take off our clothes?" Flora says.

We shouldn't, Maddie thinks. This is bad. Forbidden. But there's a throbbing tingle between her legs and she says, "Okay. In my room."

She leads Flora up both staircases and down the hallway. They set their eyeglasses on her night table. Flora slips under the grape-colored bedspread. She pulls off her sweats, top and bottom, her bra and panties, too, and she tosses them onto the carpet.

Maddie undresses and gets in beside Flora. Their bare thighs touch. "This is just practice for being with a boy, right?"

"Uh huh," Flora says. "We'll take turns. I'll be the girl first. Suck my boobs."

Maddie can't help but think of that asshole in Ivory Coast. She didn't have any boobs (still doesn't), but he suckled them anyway. Though the memory of him is fuzzy, bits of it are still alive like a dormant virus that flares up sometimes. She rolls onto her side to face Flora's boobs. *She* actually has some. They fill a real bra. They're probably nothing more than extra fat, but they're there. Maddie leans in to put her lips on one. She hesitates, remembering. Her heart beats with anxiety.

"C'mon," Flora says.

Think of someone else. Not him. Forget him. She thinks she should pretend to be a guy, but a different guy. She doesn't want to be sad right now. Maddie realizes she needs to *act*, like when Mr. Jansen says to become the character in a song. She pictures the long-haired hippie from the pictures in *The Joy of Sex* and the way she's seen him suck a breast. It's hard to *be* him, though. He's only a drawing. A piece of art. The other guy had a smell, a touch, and sounds . . . She begins to breathe like he did. Not unlike Max, panting, downstairs. She twirls her tongue around Flora's nipple the way he did around hers, and she feels kind of gross. Still, she sucks on it and nibbles it softly. It's salty and smells a little like salami. She nudges Flora flat onto her back, and moves on top, pressing against her. Despite the uneasiness, a swelling pulsation between her legs drives her to rub into Flora's thigh.

Flora cups Maddie's butt cheeks. She squeezes them hard as she lifts her own pelvis and moans. Her hands slide up Maddie's back to her shoulders. She gently pushes her from her breast and laughs. "You should see your hair," she says. "It's frizzing out like you stuck your finger in a light socket."

Maddie slides back onto her knees.

"Kiss me," Flora says, as if she's running this show.

"No." Maddie's heartbeat thrums in her ears. "My hair's frizzy, my ass is too big. Fuck you *and* your mother, Flora!"

Flora gapes at her. "Why are you so mad?" She seems genuinely astonished.

Maddie stares down at her as the feelings she'd stuffed away come bursting out. "I don't even like this," she says. "I didn't want to suck your flabby boob. I don't *like* girl parts," she yells. "But you sure seemed into grabbing *mine*."

Flora wriggles from under her. She sits up and leans away from Maddie, against the brass headboard. Eyes shiny with tears, she covers her breasts with fleshy arms.

Maddie stares at her. "Why do you always have to say mean things about me?"

"I don't know. I didn't think they were that bad." Flora sniffles. "I'm sorry."

"But why do you do it? Why do you act like you're better than me? You're not. You're big as a boat. Your voice sucks. And you like girls."

Flora's face deflates. Her body follows, caving in on itself like a falling cake. She shakes and sobs.

"Oh." Maddie's eyes widen. "You really *do*, don't you? Is *that* your problem?"

"Shut up!" Flora lurches out of the bed, throws on her glasses, and grabs her clothes from the floor.

Maddie moves into the doorway, holding the frame to keep from swaying, and watches her stagger, barefoot and weeping, down the hall into the bathroom. She hears her puke. Shit, she thinks, as she goes to put her clothes on. It was just a good guess. She should apologize.

When Flora comes out, dressed, she lumbers down the stairs to use the phone in the kitchen. She stays in there for a long time, too long, Maddie thinks. She goes down to see what she's doing.

Flora's gone. So are her coat and shoes. Maddie turns and heads for the den, where the dogs are, to look out the front window. She sees Flora outside, standing near the top of the driveway, under the leafless maple trees, waiting in the cold. Even from behind, Maddie can tell she's crying from the way her shoulders shake.

She could go out there, say she's sorry, and try to comfort Flora. But what would be the point? There's only one more musical theater class. She doesn't want to see the girl again, and she's pretty sure Flora won't want to see her either, after today. Maddie'll say she's sick and miss the holiday performance for the parents. That's fine. Parents are overrated. She doesn't move. She watches Flora through the window standing there, sniffling, with nothing but the spindly trees to keep her company. She's wounded, but she'll be okay. Eventually. People get better. They do. Maddie knows, because she did. That's how it works, she figures. You die inside and then after a while you come back. Just like the trees. They're barren in one season, but slowly over time, they transform. She watches out the window and waits.

light skin gone to waste

Monroe, New York, 1976

Maddie pestered Velma to drive her to Julia Romano's house, because she really wanted to tell her. Julia was the best new friend she'd made in seventh grade. They were both turning thirteen that summer and Julia was the one person she wanted to tell after her cousin Suzy, who already knew, because Suzy was there.

When Julia came to her door, she looked *so* perfect in cutoff shorts and a white bikini top.

"Man," Maddie said. "Wish *I* could look that cool."

Julia's cheeks turned all rosy. She smiled and cast her hazel eyes down. "Oh stop," she said. They hugged, and Julia's back was sweaty against Maddie's palms, but she smelled sweet and powdery, like Love's Baby Soft.

She turned and waved to Maddie's mom, who was behind the wheel in her big boat of a Chevy station wagon filled with musty antiques.

"Hi Mrs. Arrington!"

Velma's windows were up, with the air-conditioning on and the radio playing "Love Rollercoaster." All you could see was her short dark hair because she was looking down at her datebook for directions. She was on her way to deliver a pair of Biedermeier chairs.

Maddie cupped her hands around her mouth and yelled, "Bye, Mom-my!" She was relieved to be away from the grouch for a while. That morning Velma had slapped her for breaking a glass while she was loading the dishwasher. It was wet and it slipped out of her hand, and even though it was an accident, Velma hit her and said it wasn't her glass to break and she needed to be more careful. There was still a red splotch on Maddie's upper arm.

Velma finally looked up with a pen in her teeth. She waved.

"Gosh, Maddie. Your mom is bee-uuu-tee-ful," Julia said.

Maddie didn't know why Julia pronounced it that way. She had the urge to correct her, but according to her mother people hated being corrected, so she didn't.

"Her skin is like gold," Julia said. "She glows."

Maddie grunted. Sweet Julia. She was exaggerating. Her mother had been a model in a couple of ads in *Ebony* magazine when she was a teenager. She was pretty but she damn sure didn't glow. Maddie's cousin Suzy said people in Monroe expected Black women to look like Aunt Jemima and that's why they were so amazed Velma was attractive.

Velma tooted the horn and backed out of Julia's driveway. When they'd pulled in Maddie mentioned that it was spotless. She asked why *their* driveway was always dusty and full of oil stains. Velma gripped the steering wheel and grit her teeth. "Our house is in a more affluent area," she snarled. "And it's architecturally superior to this cookie-cutter crap. Can't you see how this box looks like all the other boxes in this development?"

God, Maddie thought. Shouldn't have asked. Her parents used to rent in this neighborhood when they first moved to Monroe. Livia told her people called them names and threw stuff at their car. That's why her mother always scowled whenever they drove through here.

Maddie was about to tell Julia her news, when she saw her mother pull over to talk to Mrs. Sibella, who was on the sidewalk with her little white poodle. She had balloon-sized breasts, and permed hair, and she was one of her mother's regular customers.

"Roberto told me his grandma says your mom really knows her antiques."

"Yeah, she does. She reads a lot of books, and she takes night classes in the city."

"He said his grandma loves her shop. Guess she goes there a lot?"

"Yeah. She brought him in with her the other day. I was there."

"He *told* me," Julia said, smiling. There was something mischievous gleaming in her eyes.

"What? What's that look, Jules?"

"Nothing." Her cheeks flushed again.

Maddie wished she could blush that same pretty color. When her own face turned red it was blotchy and she looked more like a pepperoni pizza than flower-petal cute like Julia.

"If Mrs. Sibella's impressed, it must be top-notch. She's from the old country."

Inside, Maddie groaned. Julia was nice, which is why she didn't tell her that, yeah, Mrs. Sibella was from Italy. *Like a hundred years ago.* So what? Julia thought anyone European automatically had class. Maddie had actually been there; she knew it wasn't true.

Julia reached inside her front door, pulled out two black bags stuffed with trash, and handed one to Maddie. The damn thing was heavy. It smelled sour, too, like spoiled ricotta. Julia stepped off the front porch with the other bag and headed down the walkway. Maddie followed. The plastic made her arms sweat, and her bare thighs bumped into empty cans inside the bag. Her wooden sandals clunked down the concrete. She thanked God her mother was driving away. She worried Velma might act insane if she saw Maddie taking out the Romanos' trash like she worked there.

"Roberto said he liked your mom's shop, too."

"That's cool," Maddie said, breathing through her mouth and thinking something must've died in this bag. Roberto was cute. He was *really* Italian. Fresh from Firenze and he barely spoke English. When he did, his accent was *so* sexy.

"He said she was yelling when they came in, though. What was she yelling about?"

"Who knows?" Maddie said. "She's always yelling about something."

Her mother was happier in her shop than she was anywhere, but she really did yell a lot. At home she was almost always in a bad mood and took it out on Maddie. Today, however, Maddie appreciated her, because the day before, Velma had stood up to Phil, so Maddie could go to the Fourth of July party at her cousin Suzy's house in Long

Island. He was insisting they go to some White lady's apartment in Manhattan to see the tall-mast sailboats in New York Harbor for the Bicentennial. Boats? Please. Maddie wanted to see *boys*.

She was in the kitchen when Velma asked Phil if he'd really prefer to look at some old ships rather than spend time with family. He sighed all loud and said, "That would be my preference, yes."

Her mother was in her bathrobe and her pink rollers, loading the dishwasher, and her father with his 'fro wet from a shower sat at the oak table smoking a cigarette in his tennis shorts.

"*That* is some White folks' foolishness," Velma said. "We live among White folks all year round, Philip. You run around here doing what *you* want to do almost all the time. I'm entitled to a Fourth of July holiday with my family, and so is Maddie."

Maddie moved from the fridge to stand in the kitchen doorway with a handful of grapes and she watched as her dad blew smoke through his nose.

"Velma," he told her, "I didn't spend years of my life getting multiple degrees and a PhD to spend my time listening to your family's mind-numbing nonsense."

"Oh, really?" her mother's neck slid from one shoulder to the other. "And who *worked* and helped you *pay* for that doctorate *and* put half the down payment on this house you're sitting up in while insulting my folks? You've gotta be the biggest idiot with a PhD there ever was."

Maddie wished she could laugh with Julia about this, but neither of her parents went to college, and Julia might think she was being stuck-up.

They reached the side of the house, dumped the trash into a shiny metal bin, and then thunked back up the walkway. They kicked their Dr. Scholl's off right inside the door. Ah—relief. It was cool in there, and it smelled like lavender-scented potpourri.

"I have something really good to tell you," Maddie said.

"Yeah?" Julia said. "Cool. Let's save it for when we get downstairs, 'kay?"

Maddie nodded. The basement was where they usually told their good stuff when she came over. She heard the vacuum cleaner running upstairs. Every time she was there, Julia's mom was running that vacuum cleaner. Maddie thought it was because Julia was allergic to everything. She'd only been to Maddie's house once. Miss Dowd cleaned twice a week, but her father smoked, their dogs shed, and her mother's musty antiques were every-damn-where. Their house would probably kill Julia.

Maddie walked behind her down the plastic runner over the carpet in the hallway. Julia's honey-brown hair was in perfect Farrah Fawcett wings. Man, Maddie thought. All the cool girls in junior high had them. She *tried* to have them, but of course hers always poofed out and went wild. "Your hair's *so* smooth," she told Julia. "Even in all this humidity. Mine would be a gigantic frizz ball if it were still long."

Julia glanced back at her. "You look good with it short. You got a pretty face. I'd be a dog with short hair. Woof."

Maddie laughed. "You would not," she said. And she meant it.

They got to the kitchen. It looked like you could lick the linoleum floor. Julia washed her hands with Palmolive, and Maddie did, too.

"I got droopy eyes and fat cheeks," Julia said. "When you got a face like mine, you *need* hair."

"Yeah, right," Maddie said. "That's so not true."

They dried their hands. Julia took two bottles of Tab from the refrigerator and Maddie saw her inhalers lined up on the shelf inside the door. During school there was always one in her book bag.

She handed Maddie the bottles of diet soda, then opened a tall cabinet next to the stove. She grabbed a can of Pringles and set it on the counter. When she moved to another cabinet, Maddie peeked at her little butt and thin thighs and felt a pinch of envy. She starved herself all through seventh grade and she still didn't look that skinny.

Julia's eyes *were* kind of droopy, but no one noticed, because they were an amazing mix of green, light brown, and yellow. Maddie didn't think Julia even realized how fascinated boys were by the way they turned different colors sometimes, and the way they sparkled and brightened her face. Maddie's eyes were just brown. Like mud.

"Even if you had *no* hair," she said, "there'd still be more boys that like you than like me. Do you know how hard I tried to get my hair to feather like yours?"

Julia found the bowl she'd been digging in the cabinet for. She whipped around. "Is *that* what it was?" She eyed Maddie's head. "I wondered. I did notice you trying to flip the front back. Looked like you used a curling iron?" She lifted her cheeks and lowered her brows as skin squeezed up around her eyes like something hurt. Or like she was taking a poop. It was a painful strain to remember her hair. God, Maddie thought.

"You gotta cut it in *layers* to make it feather," Julia said. She tilted her head and gave a sad smile before turning back around. She meant to be nice, but that look was all pity.

Maddie brushed a forearm over her head. Tiny curls. Almost nothing there.

Julia pried open the Pringles can and emptied the chips into the bowl. Maddie leaned into the potato-y smell with her eyes closed until Julia took it away.

She carried the soda and followed Julia back down the hall. Her feet stuck on and peeled off the plastic runner with each step.

"I'm glad I don't have long hair anymore," Maddie said. "I blew-dry the crap out of it trying to get those wings. Burned my scalp and my forehead, too, with that evil curling iron."

Julia looked back, scrunching her face. "But . . . you're pretty."

Maddie didn't know what *that* had to do with it. She didn't ask. They tromped down a flight of stairs to the basement. Her eyes were rapt by Julia's hair, the way it flowed over her bare shoulders and glided across her back. Man.

When school ended a couple of weeks earlier, Maddie decided to have all her so-called "good hair" cut off. Good? Her mother called it "good," and so did her cousin Suzy, but Maddie's hair wasn't flowing all down her back, shiny and smooth like Julia's.

Suzy had nappy hair. She had to have those naps pressed every two weeks since she was a toddler. "Don't cut it," she warned Maddie. "No guys are gonna like you. Just keep your hair in a long ponytail."

What did it matter? No guys in Monroe liked her anyway. Not even Zeke Odom, the cute new Black guy in town whose attention Maddie had tried and failed to get. She was sick of trying to make her hair look like the girls' in Monroe. And her mother was sick of hearing her complain that it didn't. Velma drove Maddie fifty miles, all the way down to her childhood hairdresser in Harlem, fussing the whole time about how she didn't wanna hear it if Maddie didn't like it. "It's your decision and I'm not gonna be responsible," Velma said.

Maddie got it cut into a curly Afro. She thought it looked good. They came home and her father hated it. He took her back into the city, not to his old neighborhood in the Bronx, though. *Nooo.* They went to Manhattan, to the salon at Henri Bendel's, where a snooty stylist shook his head at her ghetto cut, recut it, and charged three times what her mom's hairdresser had. Maddie's hair was so short now you could barely tell if it was curly or nappy. Among Black people this was not considered a good thing.

Yesterday, when Aunt Syl, Suzy's mom, saw Maddie, she stared at her head and went, "*Tsssk,*" sucking her teeth in that Jamaican way of hers. "Gyal," she said, "you've barely a touch of de tar brush, but now your light skin's gone to waste."

Maddie wished she could share that with Julia, but she knew she wouldn't get it.

Soon as they were down the steps, Julia set the bowl of chips between two cream-colored beanbag chairs. "Okay. Tell me."

Maddie plopped onto one of the beanbags as she held the soda bottles in the air and yelled, "A boy finally tongue-kissed me!"

"No. Way." Julia's eyes opened as wide as Walton Lake and stayed that way for a few seconds. She flopped down and leaned closer to Maddie. "Who? When? Was he Black or something?"

Maddie set the bottles on the floor and watched Julia pull her chin.

Of course he would have to be Black, "*or something.*" Maddie guessed she meant Puerto Rican. Boys in Monroe acted like she had cooties. Just before school let out for the summer, their English class played spin the bottle when Mr. DiPrima left sick and the substitute wasn't there yet. The assistant principal came and told them to read the next chapter in their textbook until a sub arrived. Instead, everyone got on the floor, in a circle, sitting boy-girl-boy-girl except Ralph, a husky guy, who went and stood watch by the door.

When Maddie sat down, her neighbor Tobias stood back up and said, "*Maddie* can't play."

At first everyone was still talking and didn't pay stupid Tobias much attention. Maddie couldn't stand his dumb ass with his American-cheese-colored teeth and his choppy bowl hairstyle that looked like he cut it himself with a knife.

He said it again, louder. "*Maddie can't play.*"

Some kids snickered. A couple seemed confused. Julia was there. She gave Maddie a look like she felt bad. No one spoke directly to Maddie, not even Tobias. They talked *about* her, around her. The back of her neck began to sweat. She'd worked really hard blow-drying her hair that morning and she could feel it frizzing up.

Bob Jones, a cute blond boy that Julia had a serious crush on asked, "Why can't she play?" Sounded like he was defending her, which Maddie thought was super cool.

Tobias said, "*She knows why.*"

Then it got quiet. Everyone stared at her: the girl banned from spin the bottle. God.

She looked up at Tobias and climbed off the floor. Then she cleared her throat. Her father told her that if you're about to cry, and you don't want to, you can clear your throat, and that'll stop it. Maddie looked Tobias right in his bigoted brown eyes. A few people laughed but she stared at him until he looked away first and plopped back down. Jackass. The two of them used to play from morning till night. Now he thought he had to protect other kids from her? Like she was contagious?

Maddie hated the fuck out of Monroe. She wished she could live where Suzy lived.

She went and stood near husky Ralph at the door and pretended to look through the tiny window into the hallway. Julia came and stood by her, even though Bob Jones was playing and she'd *love* to kiss him. She was a good friend.

"Well? Who was it?" Julia asked now. "Tell me, already!" She burrowed her butt into the beanbag and it made crunchy sounds as she looked at Maddie.

"No one around here," she told her. "Yesterday, we went to my cousin Suzy's house."

"In the city?"

Julia thought *all* Black people, except Maddie's family, lived in the city. Maddie explained more than once that it wasn't true, but Julia only knew her, and the Black people she saw on the news.

"No," Maddie said. "On Long Island. And my cousin Treavor, Suzy's brother, had a house party last night in the basement."

"*A house party*," Julia repeated, as if she were learning a new language.

"I wore my white embroidered Indian shirt and the puka shells you gave me, and my new black pants. My butt looks good in those. Guys around here never think I'm pretty, but where Suzy lives, they do. They actually *like* big butts."

"Yours isn't *that* big, Maddie. But why do they like big butts?" she asked, scratching her cheek. "That's weird."

Maddie shrugged, like she didn't know. She *did* know. Suzy said big round behinds were sexy. Nobody thought so in Monroe, though. They liked scrawny, little anorexic butts. If Zeke Odom liked big butts, he certainly hadn't let on. Maddie went to three of Zeke's Pop Warner games just to try to meet him and he ignored her and chatted up the White girls.

"Okay," Julia said, "but you're wrong about no one around here thinking you're pretty." She grinned, with perfect round dimples gracing her full pink cheeks.

"Please," Maddie said. "I had to go all the way to Long Island just to get kissed."

"We-ell," Julia said, singsongy, "not supposed to tell you, but I know someone who wants to kiss you."

Maddie was quiet for a moment. "Are you teasing me?"

Julia shook her head.

"You do?"

Julia nodded, her pretty dimples still deep. She twirled a shiny lock of hair around a finger, took a long swig of Tab, and stared at Maddie the whole time.

"*Who?*"

Julia's eyes were glittering now. Green and gold, they really were something. She giggled but didn't say a word.

"Tell me!" Maddie shrieked.

"Guess."

Maddie squeezed her eyes shut. *Please God*, she thought. "Zeke Odom?" She opened her eyes.

"*No,*" Julia said, as if that idea was preposterous.

"Then I don't know." Maddie slumped in the beanbag chair. "Is it someone good?"

"Hint," she said. "He lives close, and he's not American."

"Huh!" Maddie gasped. Though it wasn't her first choice, it was better than she could've imagined. "*Roberto?*"

Julia nodded.

Maddie's mouth hung open. She could've died. If she'd been lucky enough to have dimples, they'd've been showing for sure. Man. Roberto was a fox. She sat by him at Julia's barbecue back in June and he had put his hand on her back when he talked to her. And when he came with his grandma to her mom's shop, he smiled at her a whole lot. Even Maddie's mother said he was handsome. Some people thought Roberto was dumb because he couldn't speak English. Those people were stupid idiots who didn't know that people didn't speak English everywhere in the world. Roberto spoke Italian *and* French. He just hadn't learned English yet.

She leaned forward, squishing noisy beans in the chair. "He told you he wanted to kiss me?"

Julia leaned forward, too. "He said, 'I like-a you friend.'" Her imitation was terrible. They looked at each other and cracked up. "He likes that you travel. You're the only one around here that's been to Italy or *anywhere* out of America. He thinks you're different from us hicks."

Maddie's stomach dropped like it was swooshing down a rollercoaster. "I'm *different* all right. Jules. Does Roberto realize *how* different I am?"

Julia bit her bottom lip. "Um . . . I think so. He met your mother."

"Sometimes people think she just has a tan."

"No, you can tell," she said. "You can tell with you, too, especially now that your hair's like that."

"What if he can't?"

"Oh, he doesn't care. He's from Europe. He's coming over." She crossed her legs Indian style and the chair crackled beneath her.

"Really?" Maddie hugged her bare knees. "When?"

"Soon. Now."

She still really wanted to tell her about the night before, but she felt a tingle in her private parts. Roberrrto. Man. She thought Julia was cool to be on her side. And Roberto's. Julia didn't mind being friends with him when other people didn't want to because he couldn't speak much English. And she didn't mind being friends with Maddie, when some kids wouldn't, because they thought all Black people were like the ones they saw on the news.

When Julia had asthma attacks, she wheezed and her hands curled in toward her body. She couldn't speak and it was scary. When it happened at school, they called the paramedics, and Maddie had to go in the ambulance with her a couple of times, because Julia was afraid to go alone. She thought she was defective. She felt fortunate when someone stayed her friend after seeing her like that.

"Let me tell you about yesterday before he gets here," Maddie said.

"'kay," Julia said, leaning over for some Pringles.

Maddie took some, too. "Daytime was dull," she said, munching. "Just barbecuing in the backyard and it was mostly old people, my parents, my aunt and uncle, and their West Indian neighbors. My dad drank too much scotch and fell asleep on the chaise lounge. He even snoozed through the firecrackers going off on the street all day."

"Firecrackers?" Julia asked. "Aren't those *illegal*?"

Maddie shrugged. She figured she shouldn't tell her about her cousin Treavor's pot plants.

"When it got dark, me and Suzy took baths and we changed. She said I should put on makeup. I used her mascara and eyelash curler, and I put this gold sparkly dust on my eyelids. She let me use some nice perfume called Bakir that she said was the joint, because it makes guys horny."

Julia threw her head back and laughed like this was the funniest thing ever.

"What?"

"*Make* guys horny?" She uncrossed her legs and sat forward. "Isn't that just how they are? That's sure how they are around here."

Maddie breathed in and out, took a sip of Tab, and set the bottle back on the floor. "Okay. The point is the perfume makes a guy want to be horny with *you* instead of some other girl. God."

"What's *the joint*?" Julia squeezed her chin with her thumb and forefinger. "Does that just mean *good*?"

"Yeah."

"Why do they call it that?"

"I don't know, Julia. They just do." Maddie huffed out a breath. "All the adults were like drunk and laughing on the back patio, except my dad who was passed out, and they didn't even come down to the basement at all. Before anyone got there, Treavor set up his DJ table."

"His *what*?"

"You know, the table, where he puts the turntables and records and stuff on."

"Oh." Her mouth stretched downward and her eyebrows shot up like she had no idea what Maddie was talking about, even though she'd just explained it.

"He put green bulbs in the ceiling fixture, and a whole part of the room looked greenish."

Julia crinkled her nose like she was smelling whatever that spoiled shit in the trash was earlier. Maddie didn't react.

"There was a huge section of the floor for dancing and then there was a table with sodas and stuff and Treavor snuck some bottles of my uncle's liquor down there—gin, vodka, Jamaican rum—and he hid them under the table. Suzy said I should have some, so I wouldn't be nervous about dancing and talking to boys."

"But you're a good dancer."

Maddie laughed. She wasn't a good dancer. Not really. "At our school dances, yeah, but when I leave here, people tell me I dance like a White girl."

Julia's head lurched backward and her eyebrows met.

"I know. It's not nice, but that *is* what they say."

Julia exhaled. "Go on."

"I did have some rum. Just a little. A lot of people showed up, way more than Suzy and Treavor expected. I got pushed by the crowd up against the drinks table and this guy came up to me and asked if I could do the hustle."

"Now you're getting to the good part. Was he cute?" She folded her legs again and leaned forward, elbows on her thighs, chin in her fists.

"I thought he was. He was light skinned, a little darker than me. And he had light eyes, but I don't know what color, exactly, because I never saw him in the light. He had reddish hair and it was in a giant Afro."

"Red hair?" Julia crossed her arms again and leaned back. "I've never seen a Black person with red hair. Or light eyes."

"Yeah. They never show 'em on the news. It's a conspiracy."

Julia tilted her head and twisted her mouth to one side, looking confused. She didn't get that Maddie was teasing her.

"He had nice lips. Full, without being too big."

"Like yours?"

Huh. Maddie hadn't thought of that, but Julia was right. "His were maybe just a tiny bit bigger. And they had a nice shape. He said his name was Eddie. We got on the dance floor and I really did think I knew how to do the hustle, because I took Miss O'Malley's recreational dance class this past spring and she taught us 'the basic.' She said there were different styles of the hustle, but that if you could get the basic, you could adapt it to pretty much any style. I thought I'd be okay. Well, Eddie started doing these steps I'd never seen, and I couldn't follow. I was lost. And embarrassed. I stopped and said, 'That's different from the one I know. Can you show me *the basic*?' But the music was loud and he couldn't hear me. He put his ear near my mouth and his hand on my back and he smelled *really* good, like some kind of incense. I wanted to lick his ear."

"Incense? On a *person?*"

"*Yes.*" Maddie knew Julia was about to say that was weird and she didn't give her the chance, because it wasn't. "I asked again, 'Can you show me the basic?' He looked at me, cracked a smile, and lowered his chin, 'The *what?*'

"'The basic,' I said. He lifted his shoulders and shook his head. 'Sorry. I don't know about that.' I realized Miss O'Malley didn't know what the hell she was talking about. He told me, 'It's easy. Just follow.' I tried. He went to turn me and I went *the wrong way* and bumped into some girl who called me a dumbass. Jules, I felt like such a spaz. Eddie stopped. He stood still and smiled. His teeth were big and bright. He asked if I wanted to take a walk. Of course I did! I didn't wanna stay on the dance floor looking ridiculous. Some of Suzy's friends leaning against the wall were pointing at me and laughing. I knew I shouldn't say yes, because I was definitely not allowed to leave the party, but I had to get out of there. We went upstairs. Fortunately, my parents were still on the patio and didn't see us slip out the front door. Eddie took my hand and started walking down the street. Our palms were so sweaty they felt like a dog slobbered on them, but Eddie didn't let go, so I didn't either. I asked him where we were going and he said, 'Just for a walk. Too loud down there, don't you think?'

"I think he was just trying to save me from being embarrassed. Or maybe he was saving himself from being embarrassed by me. It was a little scary, because I didn't know him, or where he was taking me." She wasn't being totally honest now. It was scary because Maddie got scared around boys who liked her. Because they might do something she didn't want them to. This fear had been a problem for a while. "'How old are you?' he asked. I figured I'd better lie, or it'd be a really short walk. He looked old. I said, 'Fifteen.' He seemed to believe me. Said he was sixteen. Asked me where I was from. When I told him Monroe, he said, 'Never heard of it. Is that Upstate?' But before I could answer, he stopped and said, 'Do you know how pretty you are, Maddie from Monroe?' First time a boy's ever told me I was pretty. And then he kissed me. Just like that."

Julia stopped crunching her mouthful of Pringles. "Really?"

"Really, what?"

"That's the first time a guy told you you're pretty?"

Maddie nodded. It had been her first real kiss with a boy, too.

"Wow," Julia said. "But I thought you said guys around there like you. You been there before, right?"

Maddie folded her arms. "Jules. Suzy said some guys have told her they thought I was *fine*, but they never said it to me. Okay?"

"Oh. Why's that?"

"I don't know. You think it's because they really *don't* think so? They *do*. Suzy says if I lived around there, I'd definitely have a boyfriend."

"Jeez, Maddie. Calm down. Bet a lotta boys think you're pretty, and just don't say it. Even in Monroe."

"Oh. I doubt that, but thanks. There's more: He held my shoulders and his tongue went *way* into my mouth, and then he spun it in a circle around mine for a really long time. It wasn't what I expected. But it was nice, I guess. He was nice." She was relieved to have finally gone through with it. She'd had an opportunity to kiss Suzy's neighbor once. He barely pressed against her and Maddie almost couldn't breathe. She said she didn't feel well and told Suzy she didn't like the boy. That wasn't true, but he made her nervous when he touched her.

"Wait," Julia said. "Just in a circle? The *whole time*?" She was wincing. "And he was sixteen?"

Maddie sighed, "Yes, Julia. You're killing me with these questions. He kissed me one more time. Then he asked if I was really fifteen. I asked if he was really sixteen. He laughed and said he should get me back to the party. He walked me to the door, pecked me on the cheek, and said, 'I have to go, but it was nice meeting you, Maddie from Monroe. Take care of yourself.' Then I was ready to go home."

Julia didn't say anything for a second. She smiled, but at the same time her eyebrows squinched together in a frown. Finally, she said, "O-kay."

"What?"

Her voice rose higher in pitch. "He didn't ask for your number or anything?"

"What for? I don't want to see him again."

Her hands opened, palms up, and hung in the air. "Thought you said he was cute."

"He was, Julia, but that wasn't the point."

Julia looked at Maddie. "Isn't the point of kissing someone at a party to get their information so you could meet up and do it again?"

"Not always."

"Well, don't worry about it," she said. "That was just practice."

The doorbell rang. It was long and melodic and sang through several tones before it stopped. Ding-dong-dang-dong-ding. Roberrrto. Maddie's heart wanted to leap out a window.

"Think that's him?" she asked.

Julia nodded, grinning hard. They heard footsteps across the ceiling. Her mother was going to the door.

Maddie whispered, "The point was I was tired of being the only thirteen year old who's never been tongue-kissed by a boy. And now I'm not. Anyway, I lied about my age. Wasn't like I could keep in touch with him."

Julia sounded more amused than judgmental when she said, "You used him. Cool."

Maybe she did.

Mrs. Romano yelled that Roberto was there. She was sending him down.

"Perfect," Julia said. "You're free and ready for him."

His feet thumped down the steps.

Maddie's heartbeat was almost as loud. She pulled her Bonne Belle Tootsie Roll Lip Smacker from her pocket and quickly smeared some on her mouth. "How do I look?" she whispered as she slipped the lip gloss back.

Julia made the okay sign with her fingers. Her face was getting all rosy-red again like she was as excited as Maddie was.

Roberto finally appeared on the last step. "Allo," he said softly.

He lingered a moment, as if he was wary of coming into the room. Maddie thought he might be nervous. How could someone *that* good-looking be nervous? She waved. He was *so* fine she couldn't believe her luck.

He had black shiny hair, not too short, or too long. Thick, a bit tousled, and it fell over his ears just right. His brows were dark blocks over eyes that looked like he was thinking of doing something fun and a bit naughty. His skin was suntanned, browner than Maddie's, and his lips were a deep pink. He was tall, with muscular arms, and from what she could tell, a flat stomach. Roberto was only thirteen, like they were, but damn, he looked almost like a man in his light gray cotton T-shirt, faded Levi's, and blue Pro-Keds. He made her mouth water.

He finally moved off the steps and sat by Maddie on the floor next to the beanbag chair. His shoulder touched her bare knee. She was warm and tingling everywhere and smiling way too hard. He smiled, too. They were quiet for so long it felt weird. Julia giggled.

"*Buongiorno*" finally tumbled out of Maddie's mouth.

He chuckled. "Allo. How you are doing?"

She didn't correct him, even though he'd asked her to in the past. "I'm good." Her voice quavered.

"Let's play spin the bottle," Julia said in a perky way. Not subtle at all.

Roberto's thick brows crinkled. "What this means?"

Julia chugged down the rest of her Tab and slid off the beanbag chair onto the linoleum. She set the bottle on the floor in front of her. "Sit down here, Maddie, across from Roberto."

Maddie did as she was told. Julia looked at him. "We spin this," she said, twirling the bottle on its side. "And whoever both ends are pointing at when it stops, has to kiss."

His worried eyes said that was way too many words.

"Do you understand?" Maddie asked.

"Kiss?" he asked. "I know what means, kiss." A grin spread across his face.

Maddie wanted to *scream*. He was *so* cute!

"Okay," Julia said. "Here we go . . ."

She didn't "spin" the bottle. What Julia did was purposefully park it between Roberto and Maddie. She beamed, looked at him, then at Maddie, and then she stood and tugged at the jean shorts riding up her butt.

"Gotta go to the bathroom," she said.

Maddie watched her walk away and thought Julia looked so much better than she did, but when she turned to Roberto, she was all he was looking at.

She hoped she'd never forget the way he was looking at her. Like she was beautiful, and he was happy to be there. No one had ever looked at her quite this way.

He put his hand on her cheek and drew her face to his. He was warm and he smelled like fresh-cleaned laundry and Bazooka bubble gum. Delicious. She didn't want to close her eyes, because she wanted to see him, but you're supposed to close your eyes when you kiss, so she did.

His lips were soft as pillows, and a little moist. Perfect. He let out a sigh that sounded sincere.

Maddie's pulse pounded like it did around boys, though she wasn't afraid in the same way she'd been before.

His hands caressed her short curls and then one moved down over her body and landed on her thigh. Their tongues danced. She felt his heart beating. Maddie could tell that Roberto wanted to know her. He was different from the boy the night before who did not. Yet, part of her felt safer then. That boy didn't hurt her the way she worried he might, and he *couldn't* hurt her the way Roberto could.

She didn't want to, but she began moving out of the moment. She should have been enjoying the way Roberto smelled and tasted and the way he was showing her that he liked her. She should have felt lucky because she liked him, too. Instead, her mind was spinning into the fall and eighth grade when his English would improve and cool girls with Farrah Fawcett wings and tiny backsides would notice him, and boys with bowl haircuts would tell him the rules of the game, and before they even stopped kissing, she knew that she couldn't compete.

the way we fell out of touch

Monroe, New York, 2005

VELMA

Maddie called and told me Phil ran into Gertie up in Goshen at one of those old-folks homes he works with. As bent over and decrepit as he looks, he oughta be living in one of those places himself, honestly. But that's her father and I held my tongue.

Gertie Dowd. Sweet lady. Often wondered what happened to her. Maybe I'll get up there and visit her myself one of these days. We were still living on Stage Road when she started working for us. *Long* time ago. The day we met it was spring, my forsythia bush was blooming in the backyard like a big burst of yellow confetti. The reason I remember it so well is 'cause of the ruckus up the road that morning.

I'd walked Brutus up the road going toward the golf course like I had many times. We're talking back in the seventies before Monroe was so built up. Lots of pine trees, maple, birch, and coming from the city, I thought it was beautiful. Well, ol' Brutus took a dump in what I thought were nothing but some wild plants at the edge of the woods. Looked like weeds to me. So I wasn't expecting it when Sally Gore, in a housecoat with curlers in her frosted blond hair, popped outta the trees, like a horror house monster, screaming at me.

"I catch you lettin' your dog crap in my garden again, I'm gonna slap you!"

I stepped forward and said, "Bitch: you and what brigade? You slap me, Sally, and I promise, that'll be the *last* thing you do this side of the grave."

Brutus growled, and big as he was, that scared her a bit. She back-stepped and pulled her cat-eye glasses off her face. My God, that woman could've made a clock strike thirteen. And what I said must've shocked the sugar cubes out of her, 'cause her eyes went wide and her mouth stretched open big enough to fit a fist in it.

Some of those Monroe White folks, honestly . . . I don't know what they thought half the time. Maybe that I was gonna hang my head, or say "yass'm," or whatever nonsense they saw on television, but she had another thing coming . . . Even though my Great Dane *shouldn't've* been doing his business on her property. I sure as hell wasn't gonna kowtow to silly Sally Gore.

A few years before that her daughter tried to commit suicide in my house. Mm-hmm. She babysat for Maddie, against Sally's wishes, I soon found out. Caitlyn was thirteen or fourteen at the time and nuts about some boy her parents didn't approve of.

Phil used to spend Friday nights at his office in the city—this was back when I was too naive to know what, exactly, he was spending those nights doing—and I'd go up to auction in Middletown. Sometimes when I'd get back, Caitlyn would stick around and chat with me, tell me her lil junior high problems. She needed somebody to listen to her, and I was lonely, so I didn't mind the company.

Well, one night I came home and the damn kid was passed out in my bathroom. She'd taken a bottle of sleeping pills. Had to rush her to the hospital myself, because I didn't trust the volunteer ambulance this little town had. But I couldn't leave Maddie alone; she was four years old. So I pulled her out of bed *and* carried this unconscious teenager to the car and got her down to Tuxedo Hospital. They pumped her stomach, and the head of the ER, Dr. Wagner, came out and told me she was okay. But when Sally Gore and her skinny little runt of a husband showed up and started fussing at me—*what'd I do to their daughter?*—the doctor let 'em have it. Wagner was a mountain of a man, with a voice to match, and it echoed through the halls of the hospital. Caitlyn apparently shared some details about what was going on at home, and he told them they were terrible parents. Said the kid felt unloved and unwanted and shame on them. The guy was known to speak his mind.

I saw Sally eyeing me across the room through her cat-eye glasses. Now, I wasn't one to contribute to anybody's humiliation, so I focused on Maddie. She was whining to go home. Turned out, Sally had forbidden her kid to work for us and she was mortified to have this play out in front of *me*, of all people. Even White trash likes to have somebody they can feel better than.

Caitlyn finished high school and left town, but Sally never got over the incident. She didn't like me before, and she *really* hated me after that. She had every right to be annoyed about the dog, but you have to understand this was a road that bordered the woods, and her house was down a hill from there. Couldn't even see it from the street, there were so many trees. I had no idea it was her property. And I never did walk the dog there again. But threaten to slap me? Please. I didn't back down from that kinda shit when I was a kid in Harlem, and I certainly wasn't gonna take it from some backwoods hillbilly up here.

Sally's tongue tied itself up in a knot after I let her know who she was dealing with. She was so hot in the face even her ears turned red. But with a horse-sized dog beside me, what was she gonna do? She stomped back down her hill and disappeared through the trees.

Soon as I got home, I mean, it couldn't have been more than five minutes later, my neighbor Iris was at my back door telling me Sally called and told her what I said.

Iris had this tickled smirk on her face and she said, "I told her, 'I know Velma, and I don't think she'd say a thing like that.'"

I looked at her and said, "Oh yes, I *did* say it, Iris, and I'd say it again."

She laughed and laughed—got a real kick out of it. Probably because my demeanor was typically feminine as a flower. It was. I couldn't live up here and act like some ghetto wild woman, my husband being a professional and all. Anything we did—including Phil's running around—everybody knew about it. This was a small town back then and we didn't exactly blend in.

Now, Iris was fun. She wasn't prejudiced. Nothing like that stupid Sally. First of all, the woman was movie-star gorgeous, I'm telling you, blond, blue-eyed, shapely figure. Had a handsome husband who loved and provided for her, and kids who didn't give her a whole lot of trouble. Guess she had no reason not to be nice. A lot of women in town had a problem with her, because she really was a beauty, but that didn't bother me, because so was I. Listen, I have never been jealous of another woman's beauty. I might admire someone else's eyes or her figure, or whatever, but not so much that I didn't like my own. Even with all Phil's carrying on ... Well, okay, I *was* jealous about that, but not because I thought they were prettier. Please. I used to model for *Ebony* and win beauty contests at the Harlem Y. And the woman I called my grandmother, bless her crazy heart, was constantly telling me I was the prettiest girl in the world, and I believed her. Shoot, I still look good all these years later in my seventies. And Phil's rickety old ass is with another one of his bow-wows, this one bowwowier than the one before.

My run in with that bumpkin in her bathrobe was the same morning Gertie came. She took the Shortline bus from Middletown to Monroe and got off on the corner where Stage Road and 17M meet and where the waterfall's at the edge of the lake. That waterfall is pretty as a Monet masterpiece. The second I saw it and heard the sound of that water falling into itself, I knew I wanted to live on that street. Gertie walked up the hill from the waterfall, just a little ways, to get to our house. And she did that twice a week for several years.

If she was surprised to find herself working for our kind of people, she covered it quick. First time she showed up, Iris was having coffee with me in the kitchen right after I got through dealing with Sally. When I answered the door and Gertie saw Iris at the table behind me, she *did* look right past me and she waved at *her*. But I introduced myself, and if she flinched, I didn't notice.

Gertie was Irish American and a little older than me, early forties. She was matronly, even then. Slightly pudgy, ruddy skin, deep-set, dark eyes. Her hair was mousy brown and had no sheen. She wasn't ugly. You just got the sense she didn't feel a need to fuss about her looks. No makeup. She wore a light green uniform, faded, and a white cardigan sometimes buttoned unevenly so one side hung below the other. I knew she was fragile, emotionally, because we'd spoken on the phone.

I'd put an ad in the paper looking for a housekeeper. After the sui-cidal-babysitter episode, we tried a couple of live-in Haitian nannies for Maddie that Phil found through an agency in Manhattan. They also cooked and did light cleaning when I started selling antiques on the weekends. None worked out. Phil said it was because they were dark, West Indian maids who reminded me of my birth mother, and this supposedly made me aggressive toward them. But that wasn't it. One lady tried to berate me for spanking Maddie when she misbe-haved. The next one acted like it was beneath her to work for another Black woman. She had the nerve to suck her teeth when I asked her to clean the oven. And the last one refused to dust my nine-teenth-century bureau, because, according to her, it was haunted. So that was that. We'd either take Maddie with us, or if we were going out in Manhattan, leave her with my folks. And I pushed a broom myself for a while. When I decided to keep my shop open full-time, I looked for someone local. Didn't care if they were Black, White, or neon blue, as long as they were willing to work by my rules.

Gertie called and said, "Hello, Mrs. Arrington, my name is Gertrude Dowd. I'm callin' about the ad in the *Times Herald-Record* for a housekeeper."

"Thank you for calling," I said. "Can you tell me what kind of experience you have?"

"Yes, ma'am, my mother's been cleaning some of the big homes in Goshen for a long time now. When I was fifteen she taught me. I been a cleaning lady for twenty-five years. I have references."

"That's fantastic," I said. "But may I ask why you need *this* job? Sounds like you've been busy."

"Yes, ma'am. I, uh, haven't worked in a while, because for the last few months I've been a patient at Middletown State Hospital, and someone took over the jobs I had."

Mind you, Middletown State Hospital was basically an insane asylum, but I was married to Phil and he was a psychologist, so I knew there were different degrees of crazy.

"Middletown State Hospital?" I said. "May I ask, what for?"

Heard her take a breath and let it out. "I had a nervous break-down, ma'am." Her voice was cracking. "But I'm doing better now.

I'm an outpatient and my social worker says I can work twice a week, just like your ad says. Says here you need someone Tues-dees and Fri-dees and I'm available. Y'can speak with her if y'like. I'll do a good job if you'll give me a chance."

I knew I was gonna hire her then, before I even saw her. Because it took a lotta guts to ask for a job and have to admit all that.

GERTIE

Before everything, and after, I was in love with Arthur. I used to clean for Seth, his brother. Seth was a dentist. Arthur worked with their papa (that's what they called him) who owned a drycleaner business. He was a Jewish fella. Shy, like me. Forty years old and still wasn't married. I was thirty-nine and not married myself. It's different now, but back then—y'never married and you were *forty*? People said bad things about you.

Before meetin' Arthur, I didn't think I could get married because I wasn't pretty. Until Arthur. He said I was, so I was.

I lived with my mother, may she rest in peace. She was a devout Catholic, and she didn't want me seeing him because he was a Jew. Mother said such mean things about Arthur. It still makes me sad to think of the names she called him and the way it made me and Arthur feel. I don't think it made her feel too good either, to tell you the truth. She had a cruel side, but she was my mother. I didn't know my father. She never told me who he was. I guessed he was one of the men she cleaned for, but to this day, I don't know. All I had was her. No sisters, brothers, aunts, uncles, or cousins. My mother didn't keep in touch with her own mother, because of me. Because she had me without being married. *I* was a sin. She said that.

I never had a beau before Arthur. Not a real one. There was a boy from church who sat with me sometimes at lunch in junior high. He walked me home once in a while. He called on the phone a few times, too, until Mother told him I couldn't take calls. He was a nice friend. Just a friend. He never held my hand or tried to kiss me.

Another boy did kiss me when I got to high school. It was on the school bus. This boy did not like me. He used to call me a retard. He made fun of my clothes, too. I didn't have good clothes till I started working my junior year. Before that it was mostly hand-me-downs from people Mother worked for. Sometimes they didn't fit, but I had to wear something. For special days she'd buy me a nice dress. Easter, Christmas—once in a while. I was only allowed to wear those things to church, not to school. The boy who kissed me, his name was Jim. He used to make fun of me in class, too, and he'd follow me down the hall and throw things at my head—balled up paper, pens. Once it was a red Jacks ball.

On the school bus one day, his friends watched as he sat next to me. He said I was cute. Then he put his arm around me. His friends laughed and I pushed him off. He kept it up, wrapped his arm around my neck, drew my head to his, and kissed my lips. I tried to pull away. I couldn't. Then he put his hand down the front of my dress and grabbed a handful. I screamed right in his ear. He stopped and cursed me, and his friends kept laughing. Kids.

Arthur *did* like me. He loved me. With him, I wasn't ugly. Or dumb. And I was only shy at first. We could talk and talk . . . boy could we talk. About anything. If I didn't know something, he didn't get impatient like my mother did. He explained it.

He said my eyes danced when he told funny stories. He said I smelled like vanilla. And he said it was sweet the way I chewed my bottom lip with my front teeth when I was thinking. He liked the way my laugh came from deep inside. It was genuine, he said. I'd never laughed as much as I did with Arthur.

He gave me a lovely ring. His brother, Seth, and Seth's wife, Reena—they were fine with it. They were Jewish, but not religious, and though Seth was a dentist and I was just his maid, he said I made his brother happier than he'd ever seen. He was even gonna let us have the wedding at his house.

Mother said it was a sin to wed a Jew. She said God wouldn't bless the marriage and bad things would happen. I know that malarkey was her way to control me, but I had no spine. I gave back the ring. The beautiful ring he picked out and had inscribed for me: "To my dear Gertie, love of my life. —Arthur."

It hurt my heart to see how I disappointed him. He wept. He came to our apartment in a nice suit, to talk to Mother. And he brought a bouquet of yellow mums. She wouldn't let him past the door. She wore a black scarf on her head like a nun's habit and she yelled at him in the hallway for all the neighbors to hear. The names she called my Arthur. Slurs I'd never even heard of. She called him a hooknose hymie, an Easy-Bake shyster, a Christ-killing kike. To hear my mother say those things to my sweet Arthur who did nothing but love me, and to know she'd never let me marry him—I'd have to give him up—it broke me in places I didn't know I had till I felt them crack and give way.

No one wants to be shut up in a mental hospital, but I wanted to die, and I would have if they hadn't put me there. I can't say all of what happened—I don't even know. I just know that whatever makes me Gertie was gone for a while. I slept a lot. Couldn't talk or feel.

Then I got better. After a while. I wasn't *well*. I wasn't happy, but I could function. I got out and my social worker said I had to get a job.

I never had that meanness about people the way Mother had. I never felt better than anybody. How could I? I was a sin. I tell y'this though: I said not one word to my mother about what the Arringtons looked like. In all the years I worked for them. She would've had a few things to say about it and they wouldn't't've been nice.

VELMA

Gertie and I had a great first year. She did what I asked and she was reliable. Gentle. Easy to be around. Occasionally, I'd save her the bus fare and drive her the fifteen or so miles back to Middletown if I was going up there for an auction or to shop. She and her mother lived near the Playtogs. I bought stuff for Maddie there sometimes and she usually fell asleep in the back seat while Gertie and I talked. Got to know a bit about what led her to snap. Her mother said the Jewish drycleaner only wanted to use her. She said things like,

"What would he want with you? You're not pretty. You're not smart. He just wants to get under your skirt, and then he'll move on." She told her God would curse her. Even threatened to have a heart attack if Gertie went through with the wedding. Just your average sweet-little-old religious nut.

When I asked if her mother was always so manipulative, she didn't answer. She looked off for a while, like she was thinking about it for the first time. In ways, Gertie was childlike. Might've been the drugs they gave her, but she almost seemed . . . slow.

"If you love this man, and he loves you," I told her, "you should marry him. Your mother may fuss and carry on. Who cares? She'll get used to it."

Know what Gertie said? "Oh, I couldn't stand to see her so upset. I wouldn't be able to live with myself."

It was okay to have a nervous breakdown but not okay to upset her mother? Made me sad. Especially since her mother didn't seem to give a chipmunk's nut about her.

The next year, she came to work one day and told me Arthur showed up at her mother's door and said he was marrying someone else. But it was really romantic. He said, "If there's a chance you'll marry me, I won't go through with it. I'll wait."

Oh, what I would've given then to have Phil that crazy about me again.

Gertie didn't remember what she said, she was so stunned, but what she *didn't* say was that there was a chance.

When I heard that, I shed a few tears myself. I said, "Gertie! You're the one he loves. Grab your happiness while you can."

She said she wished she could.

My family didn't want me to marry Philip. They thought he was an arrogant SOB. I didn't care. My word, did I love that man. He was handsome, and ambitious, and he was gonna get me the hell out of Harlem. They didn't carry on and threaten me with curses. My brother was a cop. They threatened *Phil*, like normal people.

About a month later, Gertie didn't show up on a Tuesday and she didn't call. When the same thing happened Friday, I knew something was going on, because that wasn't like her. Finally got her mother on the phone. Lady Cruella told me that Arthur had gone ahead with his wedding, and Gertie relapsed. She was back in the hospital. She stayed there for almost two months.

I didn't replace her. Cleaned the house myself those months. Not because she was such a great cleaning lady, she was, but that wasn't why. It was *her*.

GERTIE

After I got sick again, things changed between my mother and me. I was the one who didn't marry Arthur, but I blamed her. When the rage started coming out, I couldn't stop it. My psychiatrist said it was because I'd never been allowed to be angry before. Mother and I couldn't sit down to a meal without me getting mad. I'd snap at her. Then I'd feel ashamed. God forgive me, it got so bad, once I almost threw a plate at her. My social worker said I had to get my own place.

Oh, Mother threw a fit as I packed my bag on the bed. She wailed, "I'll *die* if you leave! And it'll be your fault." She flopped to the floor in the hallway like a bundle of wet rags.

I stepped over her and said, "Well, I'll miss you."

After being sick again I had to fight my way back. It wasn't that I didn't care about my mother. It was a choice between taking care of her or taking care of me, and I'd already seen which choice didn't work. After that, I saw her no more than once a week. She wanted me to visit her at home. My doctor said I had to "set boundaries." I told Mother we could meet for supper on Fri-dee nights at Beefsteak Charlie's in Goshen and that's it. We did that for a few months into the next year until one night in early spring, heaven help me, Arthur came in with his wife. He looked so good. He was in a fancy suit, pinstriped, even though Beefsteak Charlie's was casual. He had on new glasses, wire-rimmed. They flattered his face. He'd been to the barber and his hair was smoother and blacker than I remembered it. Oh, the shine. I wanted to touch it. His wife, she was in a blue, long-sleeved dress. A real looker, that girl. Prettier than me. Chestnut brown hair, blue eyes, rosy cheeks.

She was younger than me, too. She wore a Star of David on her neck and she looked like she had a beach ball beneath her blue dress. It hugged the belly where Arthur's baby was. Mother of God. I think I moaned out loud.

He saw us and said hello to me. He was warm—even kissed my cheek and squeezed my shoulder. I couldn't get one word out. Not even hello. He introduced her. Rachel. She shook my hand and smiled. She had kind eyes, like Arthur's. He ignored Mother, like she wasn't even there, but Rachel introduced herself.

When they walked away, Mother called Arthur a rude hebe.

Something came over me. It was like someone else was in my soul. I raised my hand as if to slap her. The fear in her eyes stopped me and brought me back. I felt awful. My teeth were clenched so hard they hurt. I picked up my purse and coat and walked out of Beefsteak Charlie's.

I didn't want to harm my mother, but I didn't want to love her anymore either.

VELMA

I got a call from Iris while I was at my shop telling me Brutus was loose, and Gertie was running up the street after him. Guess where that damn dog ended up running to?

GERTIE

I tried my best at work, because there wasn't much else, but at times I messed that up, too. I was wiping down the glass on the front door, it was wide open, and the dog ran right past me, all the way up the street. There were a lot of trees along the sidewalk, and the leaves were changing. The fallen ones were wet and had me land on my backside more than once. I finally caught up to Brutus when he stopped to do his business and I was able to grab his collar and catch my breath. He didn't like me having hold of him like that while he was letting out his load. He growled. I talked sweetly to him and he stopped. Brutus liked me. Sometimes I saved a bit of bacon from my breakfast and slipped it to him, so he was always glad to see me. When he finished and we walked away, I heard, "Hey!"

I turned to see this lady charging up the hill through orange, yellow, and red trees. In her black robe and black glasses she looked like a huge ant running from a fire.

"You better clean that up." She shook a finger at me.

"Uh . . ." I said.

"You wait right there. I'll get a sandwich bag. Don't you go anywhere."

I waited like she said, though I was nervous, because I thought I'd left the door open when I ran out. The lady came back with a plastic baggie and gave it to me.

"Stick your hand in there," she fussed. "Then grab it and pull it through. Don't you know dogs aren't allowed to run around and leave their mess on other people's property?"

I put my hand in the bag, leaned down, and picked it up best I could. But Brutus was a big dog. His pile didn't fit in that small bag.

"Why're you the one chasin' after him?" she asked. "This isn't your dog."

"Sorry. He belongs to my boss." I took a step to leave and she stood in my way.

"Your boss?" She winced. "Oh, honey. You kiddin' me?"

She stared at my uniform, then clapped a hand on her mouth.

"I have to go," I said. "Sorry about the dog poop." I tugged Brutus and we moved around her.

She yelled, "You should be ashamed. Working for that family. They're *lower* than dogs."

I didn't look back. I kept going as she shouted things that reminded me of my mother bad-mouthing Arthur. Why do people mouth off about others like they know them when they don't know them at all?

VELMA

When I got home, Gertie was in the kitchen dusting the round oak table with Pledge. Her face was red and blotchy and she was so tense her shoulders were hiked up around her ears. When I asked what happened she told me she was okay, and we didn't need to talk about it. Said she didn't like that neighbor and that's all she'd say.

Iris rang to tell me Sally called and carried on. "Who do they think they are having a maid?" she said. Now, Iris wasn't gonna tell me she said, "*White* maid," but I knew damn well that's what Sally Gore was foaming at the mouth about.

GERTIE

I didn't see that neighbor after that. A couple of years later, though, Maddie was in the sixth grade, and she came home in tears. She ran past me and didn't say, "Hello Miss Dowd," like she usually did. She didn't take her boots off like she was supposed to either and she tracked dirty snow across the floors I'd cleaned, all the way up to her room. She was eleven, and by this time, she mostly stayed out of my way and let me do my work. We didn't talk the way we did when she was little and she used to follow me around and ask me a bunch of questions. But when a kid's crying her lungs out, you go up to see what's wrong.

That room. Sweet Jesus. Everything in it, but the curly-maple bedroom set, was some shade of purple—the rug, the walls, the bed, the curtains. It made my eyes ache. Even her coat was purple. It matched the bed.

I asked why the tears. She sat up and sniffled. "Mrs. Gore met the school bus to pick up her son and she called me a nasty name."

I sat down and told her that my friend Arthur used to get called mean names and he stayed calm because he knew that only unhappy people call others names. "Y'know what he did?" I said. "Instead of getting mad or upset, he sent them good wishes."

Maddie still had the same sweet eyes she had at eight years old when she handed me a chocolate cake made in her Easy-Bake Oven on my first day. Only now she looked at me like I belonged back in Middletown State Hospital. "Miss Dowd," she said, "I hate that lady. No way I'm gonna send her *any*thing good. Ever. Not even a wish. I hope she dies, goes to hell, and burns to a crisp."

It was hard not to smile. "Don't talk that way, dear," I said. "Don't let anyone make you feel that kind of hate. It doesn't hurt her, it only hurts *you*."

She didn't understand. Too young. But it was a good reminder for me. I had to keep prayin' for my mother. She said I'd forget about Arthur. I did not. I thought of him every day, even as the years went by. I always saw him coming back to me. I knew that was unfair to his family. And yet, I couldn't help my thoughts.

I would've done *anything* to change the past and be married to my love. It got to be tough working for the Arringtons. Because . . . Dr. Arrington. That man. He chose Velma, and he married her, and he didn't appreciate what he had. I knew. When y'clean house for someone, y'get to know things.

He saw patients in his office downstairs. Not usually on Tues-dees, though. Tues-dees, he usually went to the city. One Tues-dee, I was putting things up in the pantry after Velma had gone to work. The pantry was just a converted stairway to the bottom floor, closed off with a wall. They put shelves on that wall from bottom to top. His office was right on the other side. When I heard those sounds . . . I could've minded my business and left the pantry. Instead, I crept down near the bottom shelf. I leaned close to the wall and heard Dr. Arrington saying things. Private things. *Dirty* things. And then a woman's voice saying the same kinds of things back. And moaning.

Velma had an IUD, one of those whodingys that's lodged up there for months. I heard her talk about it on the phone once when she had to get it checked. So why did Dr. Arrington have a stash of pro-phylactics stuck in some socks in his drawer? I did not snoop. I was puttin' laundry away. I moved that pair of socks and there they were. I couldn't tell Velma, of course. It got harder to look her in the eye.

VELMA

Phil started collecting this ugly art. And I mean *ugly*. So ugly even Gertie commented, and she was the sweetest woman in the world. I felt guilty having her dust it. Looked like amoebas painted on shapes that looked like people screwing. All by a former patient of Phil's.

I knew who she was. We ran into her once near Middletown at a tennis and swim club Phil was talking about joining. Supposedly, it was a coincidence. Maddie was with us. She made friends with her daughter. The woman wasn't a patient anymore and Phil said she was giving the art to pay a balance she owed.

He told me this bullshit with a straight face. Never ceased to amaze me how stupid he thought I was. Now, why would you accept this hideous art as *payment*? She wasn't famous or even up and coming and she damn sure wasn't talented. She was a dilettante, and I knew the work had no resale value.

Finally, I said, "Are you fucking this bitch?" He denied it, but yes, she *did* turn out to be one of his bowwows. Pink-faced bowwow number one. Or at least the first one I knew of.

We were fighting a lot and one of the fights we kept having was about Maddie. She was getting called the N-word in Monroe, and when she was around my family her cousins were telling her she didn't seem Black, or Black *enough*. Phil thought it would help her to know her real ancestry—what *I* really was.

I said, "It has nothing to do with her." He said, "What are you talking about? It *is* her. It's her DNA." I said, "It's *my* history and I don't feel like telling her about it."

I'd hardly told anybody about it. Friends I grew up with didn't know. Being adopted wasn't something you talked about. The fact that your birth mother worked for your real father as a live-in maid was nothing to be proud of. And the fact that he was a Russian Jew, that you have no memory of him, and that he didn't want you and wouldn't let your mother keep you at his house, which is why you ended up in foster care, was nothing you wanted to tell *anybody*. You didn't want to admit how your mother would visit you sometimes at your foster grandmother's house. And how your grandmother and her son, who became your father, wouldn't let your mother in, or let you out. And she could only stand at the door looking at you while you looked back at her, and she'd say, "I just wanted to see you." . . . When they asked her to stop coming, she did. And you lost touch . . . Phil thought it was Maddie's right to know all that. I said, "What about my right to keep it to myself? Maddie's fine. She's being raised like a princess in a palace. Forgive me if I don't want to tell her about my shitty childhood, and so help me, Philip, if *you* tell her, if you do, I'll tell her how you're screwing White women. You think she's ready to know my secrets, then she's gonna know yours, too.

GERTIE

A few years passed. Years I don't recall much of, because I was numb, when one day, Mother insisted I come home. It was two weeks before Easter. She wouldn't say why. I walked over there in the rain, slowly, though I could've caught the bus. I took a long time, because I didn't want to go. We rarely met at all by this time. No more Beefsteak Charlie's dinners. We'd speak on the phone once in a while. I saw her on holidays at a restaurant, or at mass. She insisted I come.

VELMA

I couldn't do anything about Phil's philandering. I tried. Tried being closer. Tried looking my best, cooking his favorites, making the house as nice as I could. Nothing.

I've always been the type of person to appreciate good quality things. I took care of them, even nurtured them, and watched them increase in value. Everybody's not like that. Some people toss out quality in favor of junk. Only taste they have is in their mouth.

We had everything you could want: a family, enough money, we traveled, lived in a pretty house. I would have kept on loving Phil. He was the one who decided he liked gutter trash better than his wife.

I considered leaving. But I'd gone from my parents' house to living with him and I'll admit, I was afraid. Afraid of being alone. And of having to support myself. I did start putting money aside, though. I was no idiot. I hoped he'd stop. Hoped he'd come back to the marriage. *And* I prepared myself, in case he didn't. 'Cause if he was gonna try to screw me over, I'd be ready to bash his nuts to bits like a street fighter with brass knuckles.

When I got there, she offered me a drink. I'd never known my mother to drink, much less keep liquor in the house, but that day she handed me a vodka and orange juice. She said I'd need it.

In her tidy kitchen, my high school photo still hung on the wall. Mother's frown lines were deeper than when I'd last seen her. Her hands were wrinkled; fingertips shriveled, like mine, dried out from cleaning. She slid an envelope toward me. I recognized Arthur's handwriting. He didn't know my address so he sent it there. The seal was broken.

"You read it?" I asked.

"Your Jew wasn't man enough to ask me where you live."

My hand gripped the glass and time stopped. I was gonna throw it at her. I could have. I wanted to. Her face looked so . . . hard. So cruel. I wanted to smash it. I smacked the glass over instead. The orange juice rained down her white tablecloth and splattered the spick-and-span floor.

She sprang from her seat. "Gertrude! What in God's name—?"

I snatched the letter and ran to the door.

She screamed, "I didn't even have to tell you about it. You owe me a thank you!"

I said, "When you're under a headstone at St. Mary's, maybe I'll thank you."

I rode the bus back to my room. The letter throbbed in my hands like a heart. I didn't open it. My roommate was watching TV. I closed my door, kicked off my shoes, and knelt by the bed. I hadn't prayed in ages, but I said, "God, please. *Please* don't let this hurt too bad."

His wife was gone. Pancreatic cancer.

He wrote, "I must focus on my boys now. Their little hearts are broken, and they need their papa's full attention while they grieve. A year from now, my darling, I'll ask you to marry me again."

I could hardly make sense of all that was in my head and heart—a stew of happy, sad, guilty, and relieved. I jumped up and down on my bed like I hadn't done since I played with dolls. I jumped so much I lost my breath and had to sit myself down. Then I curled up and made my pillowcase soggy. I cried for Arthur and for his kids. God forgive me, *every* day I'd willed him back to me. And the truth is, his wife dying had crossed my mind. I didn't wish for that, though. I never wanted anything bad to happen to her or their children. It was my own fault for losing Arthur, not theirs. And if I was the cause of bad things, bad things would come to me, too.

VELMA

There was a point where Gertie stopped confiding in me the way she had. Even when I'd drive her home, she was quiet, like she'd gone inside herself.

I asked her how she was doing. Was she seeing anyone new? She wouldn't say. I had my own challenges, but I tried to tell her it's possible to fall in love again. The heart heals, and if you had love to give to one man, you can give it to another. She let out a sigh and didn't explain what she was sighing about and then went silent again. I left it alone after that.

I was too ashamed to tell anybody about Phil's carrying on. Couldn't even tell my own mother, because my father had a mistress, and if I complained about Phil, she'd get upset and start crying about Dad. Most of my friends never liked Phil, so I didn't wanna tell *them*. It was a lot to carry alone.

Gertie caught me one day at the kitchen table crying into my coffee. It was awful, oh my God. So embarrassing. Out of the corner of my eye, saw her look at me for a few seconds. I think she was deciding what to do. She came over and hugged me. Didn't say a thing. When she let go, I said, "I'm sorry, Gertie. Don't worry about me."

She looked at me with her gentle eyes. No pity. Nothing but kindness. It was like she understood. Even now, when I think about it, I can still feel the warmth in that look.

GERTIE

I sent a note to Arthur. It said I'd be ready when he asked. I admired him for taking time to respect his sons and their mother. We talked on the phone a few times. His deep voice was so strong. I loved it.

Waiting was hard. Good thing I was used to life being hard.

VELMA

I was home one afternoon while Gertie was working. My car was at the shop and I'd caught a ride from the mechanic. Maddie came home and didn't know I was there. She did this kooky thing I'd seen her do with the phone, where she dialed a combination of numbers then hung up and that somehow made it ring. The phone was in the kitchen and Gertie was there cleaning. Maddie picked up without realizing I'd already picked up, too, and I knew no one was on the line. She proceeded to pretend that her "boyfriend" was calling. The girl didn't have a boyfriend. According to her, all her little junior high friends were finding boyfriends, and she was left out. Her school was about 99 percent White and she said there was only one guy for her—some Black kid named Zeke. She wrote terrible poems in her diary about this boy and how cute he was. From what I read, he'd never even spoken to her. But on this "phone call," she made up a puppy-love conversation. I knew she was doing this to impress Gertie. She wouldn't've pulled that crap in front of me. In this imaginary call, I heard her responding to all the things she wished Zeke would say:

"Oh, you think I'm pretty? Thank you . . . You want to go to the dance, next week? . . . Yeah, we can kiss on the bleachers during 'Stairway to Heaven.' Sounds like fun, Zeke."

Maddie didn't know much of Gertie's situation, except that she wasn't married. She once asked me if Miss Dowd was an "old maid." I felt she was using this fake call to show off. Bragging that she had someone interested in her, while rubbing in Gertie's face that she didn't. I was on the line and told her, "Hang up that damn phone and stay right where you are."

I ran downstairs and she was hiding in the pantry closet. Gertie was cleaning the refrigerator. I pulled Maddie out of the closet, slapped her, and said, "What do you think you're doing?"

"Nothing." She covered her face with her arms. "Leave me alone!"

"You apologize to Miss Dowd."

"*You* should apologize. You're always hitting me."

"And I'm about to hit your ass again if you don't do what I said."

Maddie exhaled and turned to Gertie. "I'm sorry, Miss Dowd."

"Sorry for what?" I said.

"Sorry for having my phone conversation in your presence?"

"That's okay, hon," Gertie said.

Maddie ran up to her room.

I said, "I'm sorry about that, Gertie."

She kept wiping down the refrigerator and said, "She wasn't botherin' me."

"It's her father's fault," I said. "He spoils her."

Gertie shrugged. "I remember that age. It's not easy."

"Humph," I said. "What age *is* easy?"

GERTIE

Arthur took me to a Chinese restaurant on Christmas night. Some friends of his owned it. At the end of our meal, they gave us each a fortune cookie. I cracked mine open and my ring was inside! But a year hadn't passed! I gasped so hard I think I stopped breathing for a bit.

The place was cozy, dark, with red walls, and red paper lanterns hung from the ceiling. It had a full bar, full of loud drunks. When Arthur knelt down on the grimy tile floor, the drunks hooted and clapped. I yelled, "Yes!" before he got the words out. Music played as he stood up. Frank Sinatra. That song about heaven, and dancing cheek to cheek. He pulled me close. It didn't matter that I didn't know how to dance. He led. I followed. It felt like I was gliding through clouds.

VELMA

When Gertie came back to work after the first of the year, she had on a new uniform, her hair had been cut and colored, and she was wearing lipstick and a diamond ring. She shined like a Tiffany chandelier, like she was lit up from the inside. She smiled and hummed a lot. Made me smile, too, to see her so hopeful—the whole relationship in front of her. Made me think of how things were with Phil in the beginning, before they got bad.

At dinner one night I looked across the table, met his eyes, and asked if he remembered the first time we drove up to Monroe together from the Bronx. There was this moment where we both looked at Walton Lake as we passed on the way to our new home, and our new life, and he touched my cheek in a way that kept me hoping we'd be fine long after I should've known we wouldn't.

He looked at me, and I saw something brighten and flit through his eyes fast as a shooting star. For three seconds we were back in that car together, in love. Then he asked Maddie to pass the corn and it was gone.

GERTIE

After we married in the spring, Arthur began to pick me up from work. He met me at the bottom of the driveway the first few weeks. Then one day he pulled up into it, it was steep, and he parked behind the garage. It was a Fri-dee evening, just getting dark, and Velma was taking Maddie down to the diner at Grants. Arthur stepped out of the car when I came through the front door with them.

VELMA

When he saw me and Maddie, the look on that man's face ... He had some nerve.

Velma smiled and said hi, and Arthur stared at her without a word. He blinked. No smile, no greeting. It was so unlike him.

We got in the car. He was quiet. I kissed him and he held my hand. We backed down the steep driveway so slowly I could see Velma getting mad behind the wheel waiting for him to move out of her way. Arthur turned at the waterfall, and then he said, "Schvartzes, Gertie? Why didn't you tell me?"

"What? What does that mean?" I asked. I had an idea of what it meant.

When we stopped at a light, he looked at me. "My sweet love. You don't have to work anymore. We'll be all right. You can help with the boys."

"Are y'unhappy, Arthur?" I asked.

"No, no. I'm fine. I want the best for you."

"You told me only unhappy people call other people names."

It was the first time I saw something in him I didn't like. I turned toward the window so he wouldn't see my tears. He knew they were there. He picked up my hand and kissed my palm.

My Arthur wasn't perfect. But I'd choose him again.

Gertie stopped coming after that. She never called. Never sent a note. Nothing. After a month, I got her on the phone. She told me she didn't know how to say goodbye. I said, "Really? After seven years?"

The line went quiet, but she didn't hang up. I heard her breathing, still there. We both said nothing for a long time. I waited. I'd like to think she wanted to say *something*. Heard her louse of a husband in the background ask who it was. She didn't answer.

I said, "I think I deserved better ... And I wanted you to know that."

She stayed on the line. Didn't speak. When I started sniffling, I finally hung up. Wonder what she was thinking? What she might have said if he wasn't there?

According to Maddie, Phil said, Gertie told him her husband dropped dead just three years after they married. I was sorry to hear that. Hope those few years were happy for her. As hard as losing him must've been, at least she didn't suffer the slow death of a marriage. That crushes the good memories and grinds them down till they're nothing but dust you want to sweep away.

Well, I am glad to know where she is. Maybe I'll get up there and visit her myself one of these days.

got to be real

SUZY

At first Maddie thought I did it on purpose. She thought I was getting back at her 'cause she asked me not to wear my rollers around her friends at her sleepover. She gets on my damn nerves. I am *not* embarrassed by my hair, my rollers, my Ultra Sheen, or my hair net, thank-you-very-much. Told her she could pucker up and kiss my big ol' butt. Still, I swear, what happened was an accident.

Now, I'm not gonna lie, her fourteenth birthday party was *wack.* Me-n-Maddie were the only Black girls outta like fifteen, and my cousin, being raised in the country, isn't exactly the Blackest Black girl herself. Coming from a different world, I was more than a little bit out of place in her crowd. Maybe we have *some* stuff in common, but we don't listen to the same tunes, don't use the same kinda slang, don't eat the same kinda food. We don't use the same hair care or skin care products and we don't even like the same kinda boys.

They all thought I was from "the city." That's code for Harlem, or Bed-Stuy, or someplace where they think they'd get shot. The way those girls looked at me, you woulda thought I was some gangsta bitch from the ghetto streets of one of those movies like *Coffy* or *Super Fly.* I'm from South Floral Park, Long Island. Yeah, it's a mostly Black community, but we aren't pulling guns on anybody. Our houses are pretty, with manicured lawns. Our parents have jobs, and drive nice cars, and send their kids to college. My brother goes to Howard. Those girls never even *heard* of Howard.

They were all sitting around Aunt Velma's antique dining table, eating a nasty-ass Carvel ice cream cake, 'cause Aunt Velma couldn't be bothered to bake Maddie a *real* birthday cake. Couldn't be bothered to supervise either. Auntie made herself a cocktail and holed up in her room.

I was buggin' out when this pretty blond girl, in baby doll pajamas, got up from the table, walked her giraffelike legs across the room to the stereo, and without even asking Maddie, thumbed through the records and put on Barry Manilow.

"Are you for real?" I asked her. And I wasn't just talking about the record.

She sauntered back, swung her long hair to one side, and plopped down.

"We can play disco later," she said. "Don't you think this is a pretty song?"

"No," I said. "And who said anything about disco? I like to dance, but that's not the only thing I'd wanna hear."

Maddie just sat there. She's grown up around these girls and their country manners. And she's in love with Barry-freakin'-Manilow, too.

So, his wack ass was blasting from the stereo, while these snotty girls were sittin' around the table thinking they were hot shit. I'd never seen so much stuck-up-ness in my life. A bunch of 'em were cheerleaders with Maddie last year in junior high, and there was more long hair flinging than this self-respecting, nappy-headed girl in need of a press could take.

Me and my lil ponytail checked out for a few minutes and went downstairs. Didn't think anyone would miss us.

Maddie's house has three levels. The dining room, living room, and kitchen are on the middle, upstairs are the bedrooms, and down on the lower level is my crazy-ass uncle's office and waiting room. But the waiting room has two couches and lots of books, and it just looks like a den when no one's waiting in there. Uncle Phil was in Manhattan, staying at his other office. Overnight. My mom says he's a player. Supposed to be some kinda shrink, but Mom says he's not a real doctor, 'cause he doesn't prescribe medicine. I don't know and don't really care, but what I *do* know is that Uncle Phil is a trip. He talks like a nerd and he's real light skinned, so people could mistake him for White. And he has a wanna-be Afro that *can't*-be because, like Maddie, he's got that fine, almost White-people hair that doesn't have enough kink to keep it standing up on top. So the shit flops in the middle and sags to the sides. He wears an earring, too. A diamond stud. Maddie begs him to take it out when her friends are coming over. And the man is corn-eee but he thinks he's smooth. My mother says he's arrogant. I don't know about all that, but I do know he's a freak. Maddie showed me his sex books. Some of 'em he keeps hidden in his desk drawers, but some of them he leaves right out where anyone can see. And he has this "art" on the walls in his office, these pictures that are totally nasty, like stuff you'd see in a dirty magazine. One picture, near the bookcase, is of this stick-drawn man and a stick-drawn woman, and the man has a big fat boner that looks like a giant pinecone, and the woman has huge fat titties that look like bowling balls. And there's a painting of this White woman with one of her pink nipples hanging all out. My mother would never allow my daddy to put some shit like that up in our house, but Mom says Aunt Velma can't control her man.

Whenever I visit, me and Maddie look at the pictures in the book *The Joy of Sex*, because it's fun, and we learn stuff. I was just sitting down there learning, when the blond chick who put the Barry Manilow single on came through to use the bathroom. I was thinking, *Oh Lord*, but she smiled at me. And she even said "Hi," when she passed, which surprised me, since we hadn't gotten off to the best start upstairs. The other girls didn't smile at me. Some of 'em seemed scared, like I was gonna steal their shit, or beat their ass, or something.

When she came out of the bathroom, she looked down at the book, and her green eyes bugged out.

"What are you doing?" she asked, like she was half scolding me, but like she was into it, too. The page was open to a drawing of this White couple boning. She leaned closer. "Oh my God," she said, kind of squealing. Then she lowered her voice. "Can I look at it with you?"

I almost cracked up. She reminded me of me, the way she seemed to wanna get into some shit.

"I guess," I said. "Why not?"

She plopped down next to me.

"Where the heck did you get this?" she whispered. "Does Madeline know you're down here?"

"My uncle keeps it on the bookshelf," I said. "Maddie doesn't care. Long as my aunt doesn't come down here, it's cool."

She giggled. "That's funny how you and Maddie say, *aahhnt*. We say *ant*. *Aahhnt* sounds so formal. Why do you say it like that?"

"I dunno," I answered. "That's just how we say it."

She looked at me like she wanted to ask something else, but she didn't. She stared back at *The Joy of Sex*. Her baby blue baby doll nightdress made her sunburned pink legs look even longer than they were. She hugged her thighs to her chest, grabbed her long toes, and cracked them, which made me cringe.

"Turn the page," she demanded.

That rubbed me the wrong way. Who the hell was she to be telling me what to do? But I wanted to see the next page anyway, so I kept my cool. Here's where it got funky . . .

I turned the page and there was a drawing of a hippieish-looking White dude with long dark hair, and he had his bearded face deep in the crotch of a brunette White woman with hairy armpits. Her head was tilted back and she looked like she was diggin' it. Me and Maddie looked at the same page a few days earlier and she told me some dirt about some girl I didn't even know, but I figured this chick might be interested since she was from around there. I told her, "See that? Some ho named Krystal Zalinsky did that with a guy named Dave someone-ski."

The girl's whole attitude changed. Her feet hit the floor. Boom! She stood. Her cheeks turned red like apples and she looked like she wanted to slap me. She breathed in, then out with a huff sound, and stomped off.

At first I wasn't sure what the fuck her problem was. I heard her stomps go up the stairs toward the dining room, then past there to the top floor. A door slammed. *Oh shit*, I thought. My nails hit my teeth as my hands flew to my face. I had this sinking feeling that either she was friends with Krystal Zalinsky, or worse: she *was* Krystal Zalinsky.

"Are you a fucking dimwit, Suzy?" Maddie screamed at me a couple of minutes later.

Her eyes were popped open so you could see her entire irises, like chocolate M&M's floating in spoonfuls of milk. Her hair, which she'd straightened for the party, was getting frizzy, because she was sweating.

She looked up at me and shrieked, "Do you have any idea what you've done?"

Her retainer was in. Spit shot out of her mouth and landed on my nose. I wiped it and stood there while she tried to scold me. Please. Maddie's like a foot shorter than I am. And on top of that she was wearing short-sleeved, lavender pajamas with pink bunnies on them and green furry slippers. About as intimidating as a munchkin.

We were in the hallway outside Maddie's room, where Krys had locked herself in and was now sobbing. I could see over the railing to the dining room below where most of Maddie's friends were still spooning up that melted cake. Barry was on repeat, whining like a little bitch, and it made me want to hurl myself off the balcony and end it all. He was singing that tears were in his eyes. Oh, yeah? Tears were in my eyes, too, 'cause that mess was killing me.

A couple other girls were outside the door with us. One of 'em was a very concerned fat girl, Frannie, who was fifteen, like me, but I swear, she looked like an old man. No long-hair flingin' for her with her damn-near crew cut. She also had pockmarks and laugh lines that looked like straight up wrinkles. *And*, she had the nerve to stare me down through glasses that looked like something my seventy-year-old Nana would wear. The other girl, Lisa, a Peppermint Patty-looking, red-haired, freckled chick from next door looked at me like she didn't give a crap what I did to Krys. She just liked the drama. We all tried banging on the door. Krys kept wailing.

"You idiot," Maddie snapped at me, and punched her own leg

like a crazy person. "Why would you open your big mouth without knowing who you were talking to? Fuck!" She stomped her green furry foot. Mad, mad munchkin.

Frannie, with her roly-poly booty, turned to Maddie, all on her high horse, and peered over her old-lady glasses. "Um, excuse me, but where did your cousin hear that gossip in the first place?"

Maddie bit her lip and piped down because she *was* the one who told me, and Frannie knew, because she was standing there when I told Maddie what happened.

"Mm-hmm," Frannie said. "Why don't you worry about apologizing, instead of berating your cousin, who was only repeating the lies you told? Krystal is Catholic, by the way. She's not slutty like you people."

Maddie turned to me and mouthed, "I'm gonna kill you."

"Listen," I said to Frannie, "you didn't just insult me and my cousin, did you? 'Cause if you did, I'ma have to cut you." I stepped closer and stuck my chest out like a dude.

Frannie backed up, sucked in her thick cheeks, and grew paler than she already was. Even Peppermint Patty moved across the hall.

Maddie rolled her eyes and groaned. "Don't listen to her," she said. "Suzy doesn't have a knife. Her father drives a Mercedes." She gritted her teeth at me. "Would you stop it, Suzanne? They can't tell that you're kidding."

"Huh." I stared Frannie down. "Wouldn't be so sure of that if I were you." I could tell Frannie was about to pee on herself. She was scared as shit. I was a tall, lean, mean, brown machine, and I bet she could tell just by looking at me, I could kick her fat ass to the moon. She pushed her glasses back up her oily nose and marched down the hall in her ratty red pajamas that looked like she stole 'em from her daddy.

"Frannie!" Maddie yelled, sounding like she was pleading.

"I'm calling my mother," Frannie squealed, without looking back. "I'm going home!" She hustled her big backside down the stairs with a quickness.

"Great," Maddie snapped at me. "What the hell is wrong with you? I've gotta go to school with these people!"

"What's wrong with *you*?" I asked. "That girl is not your friend. Let her take her ugly behind home. Why do you care?"

Peppermint Patty Lisa snorted and we looked over at her, across the hall. She was trying not to laugh as she tucked some red hair behind her ear. She looked away, pretending she wasn't listening, which was ridiculous because *everyone* was listening. I was wondering where the hell Aunt Velma was. She had to be hearing all the yelling and banging. The girls down at the dining room table could see us up on the balcony. They were watching, like it was a show.

"Frannie really *is* ugly. Inside and out," Peppermint Patty said before finally busting up laughing.

Maddie wasn't laughing. "You don't know who my friends are, Suzy." She sucked up retainer spit and wiped tears. "You don't understand how it is."

"You got that right, girlie," I said. "I don't have a clue. 'Cause where I come from, I don't gossip about people I invite to my house, and I don't hang out with people who think they're better than me. I don't hang out with people *I* think are better than me, either."

She glared at me, and sniffled. "I don't think anyone's better than me, Suzy. Maybe I wanna be more like my friends, but so what?" She smoothed her hair back with both hands, like it bothered her that it was frizzing up.

"Be yourself," I said.

"I *am* myself! I'm *from* here. I'm not you. I don't have to be like you."

I felt sorry for Maddie. She might wanna pretend she's not different from those girls, but listening to Barry Manilow and blow-drying your hair to look like theirs doesn't make you one of 'em.

Frannie grabbed her stuff and headed to the lower level to wait by the front door. Someone finally turned the record off, thank God, and everyone was quiet. Peppermint Patty Lisa wasn't snickering anymore. Even crybaby behind the door stopped bawling.

The door opened. Krys stuck her head out. The whites around her green irises were reddish pink, like the inside of a watermelon.

"I wanna talk to you," she said to Maddie. Her tone was even. Couldn't tell if she was crazy mad or oddly calm.

Maddie swallowed. She hesitated, like she was scared to go inside. Krys tried to close the door. I held it open with my hand and put all my weight behind it so she couldn't. I may not have seen eye to eye with my cousin, but I wasn't letting anyone punk her ass either.

"I didn't know who you were," I told her. "Maybe it seemed like I was messing with you on purpose, but I wasn't. Didn't mean to hurt your feelings." I meant that, but I was also stalling to make sure she wasn't gonna go off on Maddie. Didn't know how those girls fought their battles, but I knew Maddie would do anything to keep a so-called friend; even take a scratch or a punch, and I wasn't having it.

Krys looked at me and wiped her runny nose with the back of her hand.

"*You* didn't hurt my feelings. Would you please let go of the door?" she asked. "I wanna talk to Maddie in private."

"The answer to that would be, no," I said.

"Suzy, it's all right—"

"Be quiet, Maddie," I told her. "The way it works is, and listen real hard, 'cause your clueless ass needs to know this, your *friend* has your back. Your *friend* does not leave you alone in a room with someone who wants to kick your butt. The girl can talk to you, that's fine, but this is your house. *You're* supposed to set the rules, and if you're too much of a kiss-ass to do it, then your *friend* is gonna do it for you."

I saw a flicker of something that looked like understanding spread across Maddie's face.

"That's how we do," I said. "That's how you do, too, whether you know it yet or not." I looked at Krys. "So the door stays open."

Krys seemed pissed, but she didn't put up a fight. I stood in the doorway and she and Maddie moved further inside the purple room. Everything in it—the carpet, the curtains, the walls, the comforter—was lilac, lavender, violet, or grape. Does living around nothing but White folks make you do weird things with color?

Krys slumped down and leaned against the bed with her knees against her chest. Maddie sat opposite her, cross-legged.

"I'm really sorry this happened," Maddie said, lisping on her retainer a little. "I never meant for you to come here and be hurt or embarrassed."

"Where'd you hear that stuff about me and Dave?" Krys asked. She hugged her legs.

Maddie glanced over at me and Peppermint Patty Lisa. We stood right outside the door. Patty Lisa was holding herself and rocking her weight from one foot to the other.

"Who told you that?" Krys said, louder.

Maddie looked at the floor and then shook her head. "No one," she whispered.

"Then why did you say it? Why would you say that about me? I *never* told you that. I told you he kissed me and that he said I was gonna be the prettiest girl in ninth grade, and that I let him feel me up outside of my clothes. That's all!"

"I know. I'm sorry. I shouldn't have said that other stuff."

"Why?" Krys let go of her legs and opened her arms wide. "Just tell me *why* you would start a rumor about me?"

"I didn't! I didn't tell anyone but my cousin," Maddie said, "and she doesn't even know you."

"Well, she was blabbing it. And she heard it from you. So you *did* start a rumor, Madeline. You did. You liar. You told a lie about me, now you're telling another lie. You don't know who she told. She could've told everybody!"

Maddie looked her in the eye. "I'm sorry, Krystal," she said. "Me and Suzy were looking at the book and she was talking about people she knew, saying stuff they did with boys, but I didn't know who any of them were. Then I started talking and . . . made that stuff up because she didn't know who you were, and I never thought anyone else would hear it. I only said it to have something to say, not to start a rumor or be mean. I promise."

Krys scratched an eyebrow. "It sounds to me like you're just a liar for no good reason. So, so fffuck you, Maddie, because it *is* mean. If you were my friend, you wouldn't have brought my name into your smutty little conversation."

Krys got up. Her stuff was on Maddie's bed in a flowery duffel bag that matched a sleeping bag downstairs on the living room floor. She pulled a pair of jeans out of it.

I saw Maddie glance at Peppermint Patty Lisa, who finally stopped rocking, sat down against the wall, and rubbed her temples. Maddie looked up at Krys.

"I really am sorry," she told her. "Sorry for saying it *and* for hurting your feelings. Maybe it seems mean, but in a weird way, it was a compliment."

Krys let out a laugh that was like a grunt at the same time. "In what way, exactly, is telling disgusting lies about me complimentary?"

Maddie chewed her bottom lip for a second. "I could try to explain it," she said, "but I don't know if you could understand."

"Oh, so now I'm stupid, too?" Krys clicked her tongue and tugged her jeans up over her narrow hips. "Why wouldn't I be able to understand it?"

"I didn't mean it like *that*. What I meant was I don't know if I could say it so it makes sense—"

"Then don't bother. Just shut up." She zipped her fly.

Maddie sighed and smoothed the frizz back off her face.

"The compliment part," she said, "is because, the reason I thought of you is because you're like a movie star or something—perfect and famous. You're the girl everyone wishes they were. The one they *would* be if they could."

Maddie stared down at her thumbnails and didn't move. When she finally blinked, tears fell.

She shouldn't have said that stuff, but her situation is hard. As long as she lives here she'll never get to be the girl other girls wish they could be like. She'll never get to feel cute or have the kind of attention from boys that she wants. Around here, she's just some Black girl. Nothing special. If she lived by me, she wouldn't want to be someone else. Guys would like her. Even though Maddie always acts scared of guys. She'd get over that if she had more experience. And some girls would even be jealous because she's light skinned and has good hair. Maddie's pretty. She doesn't feel like she is because her kind of pretty doesn't count here.

Krys wasn't impressed with Maddie's so-called "compliment." She pulled a white sweatshirt on and ran a hand through her hair.

"You have problems," she said. "Where's the phone?"

"In the kitchen," Maddie said, her voice barely above a whisper.

And with that, Krys Zalinsky walked out of the purple room, down the hall, and down the stairs to where everyone was watching. She pushed through the swinging door into the kitchen. Then we couldn't see her anymore. Maddie climbed up slowly and looked at me.

"It's all right," I told her. "You made a mistake. Not everyone's meant to be your friend."

She shook her head. "It's not all right. If *she's* not my friend, no one will be."

"You know *that's* baloney," Peppermint Patty Lisa said, popping up like a jack-in-the-box. I forgot she was even there. She hugged Maddie really tight. "I'm your friend. Krystal's not the queen of everyone."

When Patty Lisa let her go, Maddie smiled, but it was a sad, sad smile.

I said, "What good are friends who only like you 'cause you're friends with some other girl? That's wack, Maddie."

"Yeah," Peppermint Patty said, "whatever 'wack' is. I know you're not friends with me just 'cause of Krystal." She opened the top few buttons on her pajamas like she needed to cool off.

"I know *you* know," Maddie said. There was an edge in her voice.

"You're a cool girl," Peppermint Patty said. "I don't think it'll be that bad."

"Lisa. If Krys hates me, you know there'll be a lot of people who *won't* think I'm cool and won't hang out with me anymore."

"Okay, that's fake," I told her. "People like that are fake-ass friends and you need to check yourself, 'cause you sound fake, too. Is that what you want, Maddie?"

Peppermint Patty turned and looked at me. "Oh, she's not fake. If a real friend has your back, trust me, Maddie's no phony."

"I didn't do anything, Lisa. I shouldn't have told anyone," Maddie said.

"Shhh," Peppermint Patty whispered and stared Maddie in the eye. Something was up with them.

Then Maddie screwed up her face at me and said, "Of course I don't want my friends to be fake, Suzy." She wiped her fingers under both eyes. "I want them to be real. I wanna be real, too."

"You *are* real," Peppermint Patty said. And she shocked me, because she rolled her neck like a sista. Took me forever to teach Maddie how to do that.

"Now let's party," Peppermint Patty yelled.

Maddie followed her down the stairs.

Hazel-eyed Julia, who looked like a flower child in a long, tie-dyed T-shirt, put on the Bee Gees' *Saturday Night Fever* record, *without asking*, and most of the other girls got up and started doing the bus stop. They did it different than we do in So Flo, but not too bad and close enough that I could join in. I saw 'em checkin' me out, thinkin' I was cool, 'cause my version had a lil more oomph to it.

And turn, turn, turn, clap! Get down, theotherway, spinaround-clap! I gotta admit, that part was kinda fun.

Maddie was headed into the kitchen, when Krys walked out right past her, snatched up her sleeping bag, and went down to the front door to stand with Frannie. Instead of going into the kitchen, Maddie turned and stared at their backs. After a minute, she came over and did the bus stop with me, Julia, Peppermint Patty Lisa, and the rest of the girls. She had no rhythm, and no one cared. I think everyone was glad to see her trying to have a good time with the friends who were staying.

When Krys and Frannie got picked up, Aunt Velma finally poked her head out of her room. Guess she heard the cars.

"Everything all right down there?" she asked, sounding *toasted*.

Nobody answered. We kept dancing and she disappeared again.

A little later, when we were getting ready to go to bed, I went up to the bathroom and put my pink foam rollers in even though Maddie asked me not to. When I came downstairs, I thought she was gonna have an attitude about it and I was ready if she did, but she just smiled at me and said goodnight. I laid down thinking, *cool*.

Then Peppermint Patty Lisa asked, "Do all colored girls wear curlers to bed?"

And the kinks of the hairs on the back of my neck rose into fists. I clenched my teeth and looked over at Maddie. It was dark, but I could tell her hands were covering her face, cringing. I took a breath and let it out s l o w l y.

"The proper term is *Black*," I said. "*Black* girls, and no, we don't all wear rollers to bed."

"Oh yeah, *Black*," Peppermint Patty said. "Right. Sorry."

I rested my elbow on the floor and propped my head up with my hand. "So, did Maddie hear that mess about Krys from *you*?"

"Uh . . . what?" she asked, sounding too surprised. "No idea what you're talking about."

She wasn't very smooth. Flower Child Julia said, "Everyone could tell you had something to do with it, the way you ran up the stairs right away."

Peppermint Patty Lisa sighed. "Fine. My brother told me. He heard it from Dave Marini, the guy she's dating."

I looked at Maddie. She was quiet, staring at the ceiling. "Do you really wish you could be Krys? Or were you just covering?"

"Why?" Maddie asked without looking at me.

Julia said, "*Everyone* wishes they could be Krys. All the boys like her."

"Okay?" Maddie said to me, in a way that meant *leave me alone*.

So I did. I talked to Patty Lisa. "You think what you heard was true? Don't know about the boys around here, but where I live, they're always lying about messing with girls."

"Yeah, they lie about it here, too," Patty Lisa said. Then she looked at Maddie. "You ever wear curlers to bed?"

"Uuugh," Maddie groaned. She looked at me. "I told you this would happen!"

I said, "Black girls have all kinds of hair. Maddie's is different from mine, so she doesn't *have* to wear rollers. But she could wear them, to keep her hair from getting frizzy." I fingered the nappy new growth on the nape of my neck.

"Oh. How come *you* have to wear them?" she asked.

"Lisa," Maddie whined.

I wondered, was Peppermint Patty *trying* to work my nerves or just really curious? "Because I'll wake up looking crazy if I don't. Do all White girls ask so many questions?"

"*Sorry,*" Peppermint Patty Lisa said. Then sounding like a cross between Scooby-Doo and Yogi Bear she said, "But if I don't ask, how'm I supposed to know?"

Guess she had a point.

Everyone started laughing. Even me and Maddie. Kinda hard not to when they all started giggling their butts off.

Wasn't as funny to me as it was to them. I didn't like having to explain shit about my hair, but maybe it is better if people ask instead of thinking stupid stuff that turns out to be wrong. I laughed with them. I figured that's what you gotta do where Maddie lives, if you wanna get along.

make a space

Monroe, New York, 1978

Phil is shirtless, sitting at the old oak table in the new kitchen. His Afro is puffed out on the right side, flat on the left. He's leaning on one elbow, his other in the air behind him as he scratches the back of his head. He looks contorted, Maddie thinks, like in a game of Twister.

"Hey Dad," she says as she walks in. She knew he was in here because she heard him clanging stuff on the counter. Her new bedroom is right down the hall.

A cup of English breakfast tea steeps in front of him, a bottle of Dewar's beside that. The kettle, still hot, hisses on the stove. He's grouchy in the morning. Usually best not to say much. This is important, though. "Will you drive me to Julia's soon?" she asks.

Her butt bumps against a chair as she squeezes between it and the counter to get to the fridge. "Ugh," she grouses. Their round table is too wide for this long, skinny kitchen. The retro white cabinets, glossy appliances, and Formica countertops are jazzy, but they just moved in a few weeks ago and some of the furniture, like this antique table, doesn't fit right in the new space.

Maddie grabs half a grapefruit and a spoon and sits across from him in her mother's chair. Velma left to open her shop already.

"Huh, Daddy? You said you'd drive me, remember?"

"You need to eat more than that," he grumbles.

"Did you forget I'm on a diet?" She stabs the pink grapefruit with her spoon and tries some. Cool on her teeth, bitter on her tongue.

His chair has room to move. More than half the white-tiled room stretches behind it. Velma gets the other side, the shorter half of the kitchen, but there's still plenty of space. When they're all at the table,

Maddie's stuck on the side where the chair is crammed against the counter.

Phil wears white tennis shorts. Nothing else. At least he's not beer-bellied and hairy like Julia's dad. Her father looks good for his age. Maybe too good. Yesterday he took her to the city to see her voice teacher in *The Best Little Whorehouse in Texas*, and some White lady on line for the bathroom saw him waiting. She said he was handsome. Then she asked Maddie if he was her boyfriend. The lady had gray hair and Maddie didn't want to be rude to an old person, but *boyfriend?* Why would she think that? Gross.

He's using the fancy china with the gold rims. A pack of Vantage cigarettes sits next to his saucer, and a leftover lamb chop beside that on a plate. Her mom says they're not supposed to use those dishes except for special occasions.

"Have some of this meat." He holds out a piece.

"Daddy. Ew."

"You crazy?" He raises his eyebrows. "This is good."

"I don't eat baby animals."

He lets out a sigh. A scotch-smelling cloud sails across the table toward her. It's medicinal, in a good way, she thinks, like it can kill germs and scary thoughts. When she was little and he used to tip-toe into her room to kiss her goodnight before he went to bed, his breath was often scotch scented. She'd wake up but sleep better after.

He pops the piece of lamb into his mouth. Smacks his lips. "Lamb with mint jelly is my favorite dish."

Maddie looks up at the ceiling. "I know, Dad. You said that last night. You say it *every* time Mom makes it for you. 'Lamb with mint jelly is my favorite dish.'"

He slurps his spiked tea and clanks his cup on the gold-rimmed saucer he's not supposed to be using. He narrows his black eyes at her.

"What?" She smiles.

"Don't mock your father." He smiles.

"But you say the same thing over and over. It's annoying."

He lowers his chin and tilts his head toward her. "If I complained every time you were annoying, I'd lose my voice." His laughter is silent at first, a breathy squeak puffing up from his chest into his throat. It swells into a cackle that goes on until he coughs.

Maddie doesn't think that was funny. "It was nice of her to make your favorite," she says. "Especially after we got home late. She never makes anything special for me."

Phil takes another bite and speaks with his mouth full. "Who the hell can keep up with what you eat, Maddie? One week, it's nothing but tuna. The next, it's all tomatoes." His eyes sweep over her. "You *have* lost weight though. Looks good. Your mother could stand to give that diet a try." He snorts.

That wasn't funny either. She's glad he can tell she's thinner, though. She looks down at herself in her pink bikini top and jean shorts. She hopes she's skinny enough for Julia's party. Oh! That reminds her to scootch her butt forward to the wooden edge of the seat. Velma recaned these antique chairs herself and they carve mini octagons into the backs of Maddie's thighs if she sits on them too long.

"Planning to swim today?" Phil asks, cutting another piece of lamb.

"Yeah, Dad. I'm going to Julia's pool party. You said you'd drive me, remember?"

"You eating enough protein, kiddo?"

"I'm supposed to be there by eleven."

"Have some eggs, at least."

"Dad. I already told you, on Dr. Stillman's quick *inches*-off diet, as opposed to his quick *weight*-loss diet, you can't *have* protein. And my stomach has to be flat." She smacks her bare belly. "Zeke Odom is supposed to be at this party."

"No protein?" His eyebrows slide together like dominoes. "Sixteen is too young for that kind of diet."

"I'm about to be *fifteen*. You don't even know how old I am?"

He slurps more alcoholic tea. "Wanna be thin for the boys, Maddie?" He winks as if she's up to something.

She's *so* not. She wishes she were. Last year, a junior who said she was cute told her that if he brought home a Black girl, even one as light as Maddie, his parents would kick him out, disown him, and move back to the old country.

"*Boy*. There's only one to choose from," she says, shoving grapefruit into her mouth.

"Well, which boys *have* you dated? You never tell me about them."
Does he need a hearing aid?

"Oh, you don't want to talk about that with your father?" He chuckles. Yawns. "I see."

"Which boys *could* I date? There are like three Black guys in the whole school. Only one of them is cute. Ezekiel Odom."

Her dad frowns. Hard. A frown squared. He gave her an IQ test when she was nine and when she took too long on one puzzle, it was that exact look: *You're too stupid to be mine.*

"Date *other* boys, Maddie," he says with the tone of *du-uh*.

"Like who? I've been in school with the same hick-town butt-heads since kindergarten. There're the boys who call me *colored*, and the ones who've called me n-i-g-g-e-r. Then there're the ones who haven't called me either but think Black people are trash, and say so. And finally, there are the ones who *don't* say those kinds of things but who have siblings, parents, or grandparents who *do*. And that's about it in this stupid town."

"Oh, everything's *so* terrible for you," he says, throwing his bed-head back. "Woe is Maddie." He busts out a laugh so enormous it riles up phlegm again and he draws it up his throat. "Just awful the way you've had to live in beautiful homes, travel the world, go to the theater and concerts, take voice lessons, tennis lessons . . . Terrible life. Poor you."

She eats her grapefruit and stares at the table's dark lines of wood grain running through light amber, which reminds her of cake. She misses cake. She wonders if he really thinks things have been nothing but great for her. *Really?* If he knew all the things she's never told him, what would he think then?

"Did you know your father grew up poor?"

Her eyes snap up to meet his. "Are you kidding? You've only told me about a billion times."

"The life you live." He shakes his head. "You have no idea."

"Dad, can you *please* give me a ride to Julia's in an hour?"

He lights a filtered cigarette. Inhales. Exhales. The smoke is in her face.

"We talked about this." She waves her hand batting the cloud away. It stings her eyes and makes her nose itch. "The pool party? Remember?" She coughs. "It's why I've been dieting? You said you'd give me a ride."

"Pool party?"

"*Yes!*"

He drops the match on the teacup saucer, swings his long legs sideways and crosses them. They're deep brown from the sun, but his feet are light tan and there's a line at his ankle where his socks would be. "No. I don't remember anything about that. You can swim here."

Rising to her bare feet, she feels her face getting hot. She's simmering, like the kettle still hissing on the stove. "I starved myself for two months. Zeke Odom is going to be there. I *have* to go to this party!"

"Don't you shake your fists and raise your voice at me. Sit your ass down."

She paces across from him. "If I'm ever gonna have a boyfriend here, Zeke is my only chance."

Phil yawns and scratches the flattened curls on his head. He takes a drag on his cigarette.

"Daddy . . . Pleeeease." She bounces on the balls of her feet.

He belches. "Maddie, there'll be other parties. I have plans today. I'm not driving you anywhere."

"Oh-my-God." She feels a panicked sweat break out on her lower back as she stomps in a circle on the linoleum behind her mother's chair. Smoke is in her face and in her lungs. "Can I have money for a taxi, then? Please?" She coughs.

"Didn't I take you to the city yesterday? To that play you've been pestering me about?"

She looks at him. "But you never said I'd be waiving my chance to go to this party."

"You had your day. Today, *I'm* having friends over to play tennis and swim at *our* house and I need your help."

"Help? With *what*?"

"My friend Flynn is bringing her little girl. I need you to look after her while the adults play tennis."

"That's not fair. You didn't tell me anything about babysitting. I've been prepping for this party for *months*."

"Maddie. All the things I do for you. You can't do this *one* thing for your father?"

"Fuuuuuck!" She flops face down onto her bed, like a knocked-out boxer. Then she slides onto her knees and punches her pillows with both fists until she's breathless. This is foul. She's embarrassed to tell Julia. Julia's been itching to introduce her to Zeke. He's friends with one of her friends who's bringing him. Maddie's dream guy: tall, muscular, athletic, golden brown, curly 'fro, like hers, and he's *fine*. She's had her eye on him since he first moved to Monroe and she saw him play Pop Warner football in Smith Clove Park when she was twelve. She'd never seen a boy in this town as fo-*ine* as Zeke. He ignored her. Julia's mother was there and she told Maddie he was more into sports than girls, but to give him time. She has been patient. She's also done calisthenics and starved herself skinny for this party. She's trained like a fucking athlete and now her father decides to forfeit so she doesn't even get to play!

Julia's outside prepping for the party when Maddie calls. "I'm not allowed to leave my house today," she tells Julia's mom.

The woman gasps. In a Brooklyn accent she says, "Are ya kidding? Julia's gonna be so disappointed. How can ya do this to her?"

"It's not me, Mrs. Romano. It's my dad." Maddie's voice quavers. "You wanna talk to him for me? Maybe you could change his mind?"

No, she doesn't wanna talk to him. She prefers to be mad at Maddie for disappointing her daughter. Must be nice to have parents who care when you're disappointed.

Lucinda is chubby and four. Maddie used to see her toddling around the tennis club down near their old house in town. She has aquamarine eyes and fat rosy cheeks like a doll. Her blond curls are Slinkys, bouncing and dangling around her head. She wears yellow shorts and a white T-shirt with chocolate milk splattered on it. Too snug, it rides up her round belly. If Maddie weren't in the mood to kill someone, she might think the kid was cute.

They end up in the ivy-covered stone cottage adjacent to the house. Maddie's father sees his kooky patients in here during the week. Under the ceiling fan, she sits, and Lucinda squats on the braided rug on the wood floor in the waiting room.

Maddie shows her the therapy dollhouse Phil uses when he treats kids. It's portable and folds into a gray wooden box with a brass handle and latches. When you open it, it's one floor and only the interior. Looks more like her grandparents' apartment in New York City than a house. There's a bunch of dollhouse furniture and a few little dolls.

"This is the mommy," Lucinda says, cross-eyed as she holds a lady doll in front of her nose, inspecting it. The doll's black hair, red blouse, and black skirt are painted on a flesh-colored (*white*) rubbery body with long gummy arms and legs that bend any way you please. The tennis game echoes faintly through the window—multiple voices, laughter, the ball bouncing, *clokt—ting—clokt—ting.*

Something stinky emanates from Lucinda. Maddie hopes it's only a fart. At four, she's got to be potty trained, right?

"Lucinda, what's that smell?"

The kid looks up from the doll with egg-sized eyes, and shrugs. "Could be *you*," she says.

Damn. Touché.

Lucinda smiles a you-know-that-shit-was-funny smile. Maddie smiles back, because it was. Butt bombs served with a side of wit. Impressive.

The little girl turns back to the box, lays the mommy doll on a bed beside what looks like a daddy doll, with brown hair and a blue shirt, and she sticks a little kid doll outside the door.

"Let me in," she shouts. She sits the mother doll up and says, "Go back to sleep, Cinda!"

The little kid doll bangs on the door. Lucinda drops the kid, crosses her pudgy arms, and pouts.

"That your mommy and daddy?" Maddie asks. "They locked you out?"

"Not *my* daddy," she says in a tone Maddie hears as *you dummy*.

Lucinda picks up the male doll from the bed and flings it out of the dollhouse onto the floor. On her belly, she slides to where it's landed. She picks up the gummy doll again, rises to a squat, and this time she hurls that sucker against the wall. Bang! Maddie thinks she means to kill the doll. They look at it, laid out, on the hardwood floor.

Maddie's about to tell her that's not nice when Lucinda turns to her with icy eyes. "Could be *your* daddy," she says.

Maddie is frozen for a moment. Holy shit. But she's only a baby. She doesn't know what she's saying. *Does she?*

Lucinda straightens her chubby legs, stands, and announces, "I'm hungry," as she waddles toward the door. Maddie looks back at the dead doll, then gets up and follows the little girl out of Phil's office cottage. She feels kind of dazed like she's been knocked upside her skull and her brain is jiggling.

"Mommy!" Lucinda yells from the stone walkway. She looks around. Her mother is nowhere in sight. Her round face turns lollipop red, and her eyes glisten with tears.

"Shh," Maddie says. "It's okay. I'll take you to your mommy."

She holds Lucinda's hand. It's sticky and kind of gross, but the grass is a soothing carpet under her feet once they get around the pool, past the stone wall, and onto the lawn that stretches down to the tennis court at the bottom of the hill.

As they approach, Maddie sees a White couple she recognizes, Morty and Muriel, playing tennis, and her father and Lucinda's mother, Flynn, sitting on the grass beside each other, watching. Their legs are stretched out in front of them, touching.

Yes, touching.

His dark thigh is pressed against her light one. His hand rests on the back of her white tennis dress, below her dirty-blond hair.

Maddie stares.

What does this mean? Okay, she can guess what it means. She doesn't want to, so she thinks, maybe . . . he's like a big brother to her? She's sad, and he's consoling her?

Before they moved to this house, her parents showed her around the property: two cottages, a main house, a pool, tennis court, a

grape arbor, apple trees, flowerbeds, and lawn sculptures. It's an es-
tate and much grander than their old house in town, which was no
shack. Amazed, Maddie said, "Wow, we're rich."

Her mother said, "No, honey. Rich is when you don't have to work
or touch your principal."

As they were leaving, Phil stopped to speak to the groundskeeper.
Velma and Maddie got into the station wagon. Velma looked into
the rearview mirror, patted her pressed hair, and said, "Your father's
gonna prance around here with his chest puffed out like he's some
kind of aristocrat, but I want you to know, Maddie, he didn't accomplish this on his own. When I met your father he didn't know *anything*
about money. *I'm* the one who taught him about saving and investing.
And money from my business contributed to the down payment on
this place. He wouldn't be where he is without my help."

Maddie thought it was weird of Velma to tell her all that. Then.
If her mother were here right *now*, she'd probably grab this lady by
her long hair, connect a fist to her face, and fling her ass off their
property.

On the court, the couple enjoys a long volley. Back and forth,
bounce, hit. *Clokt—ting*. Bearded Morty compliments thin-haired
Muriel on her forehand. Neither of them is trying to beat the
other; they're playing gently, for the fun of it. They got married in
the Arringtons' living room when Maddie was seven. Phil was the
best man. They visited them a few times, and once Muriel played
guitar and sang a Buffy Sainte-Marie song, "Until It's Time for You
to Go."

Lucinda skips ahead and lands in her mother's lap. Seconds later
Maddie is standing in front of them. Flynn is smiling. Not sad. Phil
lifts his Ray-Bans and eyes Lucinda like she's a gnat he'd like to swat
away. He doesn't bother to put any distance between himself and
Lucinda's mother. His thigh remains against hers. His hand stays
on her back.

Maddie thinks, *I can see you, y'know?* But he knows. He can see
her, too.

She wants to throw a doll against a wall.

"She said she's hungry," Maddie tells Lucinda's mother, before staring down at her feet. Her toenails are painted pink to match the bikini she'd hoped Zeke would see.

"We'll all eat in an hour," Phil snaps. "I ordered Chinese. She can wait till then."

Flynn tilts her head and eyes him sideways. "She's four years old, Phil."

"I—uh, I don't think parents should let their children run things."

"That may work for you and your kid, but when my kid is hungry, I feed her."

His jaw clenches and his lips press together, annoyed. Knowing him, Maddie bets he's thinking, *That fat little girl could stand to miss a meal.*

Flynn squeezes Lucinda to her chest. Then she shakes her head back so her hair almost touches the grass. It's silky, long, and super straight. The kind Maddie tried to get with a blow dryer for years until she gave up.

Silky Locks looks down at Lucinda and strokes her cheek. "There's a bag on the patio with a sandwich and a banana in it. Would you give her that, please?"

Wait. Is she talking to me? Maddie wonders. Flynn doesn't even look at her. She lifts the kid out of her lap and stands her on her feet.

"Go with Maddie, Cinda," she says. "Be a good girl." She kisses her nose.

The kid pouts but doesn't refuse. Maddie stares at her and only her, because she hates where her father's thigh is right now and where his hand is. She can't stand this lady and her long fucking hair, and that she's on their lawn with her dad.

She takes Lucinda's grubby little hand and they climb the hill. She wants to be doing this about as much as she wants to eat a steaming turd. But it's not Lucinda's fault she's missing Julia's party, *and* the chance to meet Zeke Odom, because she's here being the fucking help so her father can flirt with stuck-up Flynn, who doesn't even look at her while she's telling Maddie to mind her kid.

Maddie feeds the girl. Reads her Dr. Seuss books. Lucinda is long-faced, pink bottom lip poked out. Maddie feels the same way. They try watching TV. Nothing but bullshit—old movies, golf. The little girl takes a nap on Maddie's bed. While she lies beside her, Maddie's eyes are on the blank ceiling; however, she's seeing her father down the hill touching that woman who's not her mom. He tried to play that shit off like it was appropriate. Please. Even this baby knows better. It's why she's so mopey. Maddie wishes Lucinda were her age so they could talk about it.

When the old folks come up the hill to swim and eat their Chinese food by the pool, Lucinda scurries outside to be with her mommy. Maddie sips a glass of Tab and watches from her window. Flynn pulls her tennis dress over her head and flaunts her bikini. Ugh. She's thin, but so what? Her backside's as flat as Maddie's abdominals. Maddie could diet from now until the new millennium and she'd still have a booty. When she was younger and that douchebag Tobias called her "bubble-butt" and made her cry, her mother thought it was funny. She called her the same thing. Her father taught her the word *steatopygia*, the scientific name for the genetic characteristic, and he explained that it was due to her sub-Saharan ancestry. "Be proud of it, Maddie," he said. Right. How's she supposed to do that when she lives in a place where *no one* appreciates it?

No Booty plays with Lucinda in the shallow end while Maddie's father stands near the edge, *staring*, along with his friend Morty, whose facial hair's so thick you can't see his lips. Poor mousy Muriel sits alone, upright on a lounge chair. She doesn't take off her tennis dress. She doesn't smile either. Maddie remembers her singing, "You're not a dream, you're not an angel, you're a man . . ." She got that right.

Maddie stays in her air-conditioned room even though her stomach is growling and the food is poolside. When Flynn and Lucinda get out and wrap up in the big green towels Maddie's mother bought at Bloomingdale's, she watches her father sit beside them at the table with the yellow shade umbrella. His eyes are fixed on Flat Ass the way their dog Brutus (rest in peace) used to gape at steak bones. Drooling.

Maddie yanks her window shade down so hard the damn thing snaps back up. Her stomach rumbles like a subway train. Her appetite, however, has hurled itself onto the tracks.

She calls Julia. No answer. She wonders if Zeke showed up.

Lucinda comes back into her room when the adults finish eating. Damn. She'd hoped they'd leave, but it's back to tennis. And Maddie's back to being mammy.

Lucinda kneels on the rust-colored carpet and plays with Maddie's Toot-a-loop Radio, twisting it into different shapes. When she returns it to its original donut, she wears it like a bracelet. Until she drops it; then she's scared to touch the thing again. Maddie's dying to ask her: sooo . . . *was my daddy in your mommy's bedroom?* But she doesn't want to know as much as she does want to know. And she can't press that conversation with a little kid.

Maddie plays a recent voice lesson for Lucinda on her tape recorder. She coaxes her into practicing warm-up scales with her. La-la-la-la-la-la-la. That lasts about a minute, before Lucinda screws up her face and says, "What kinda song is *this*?"

She takes a seat in Maddie's white wicker rocker. She rocks. Then she jumps out, her blond Slinkys stretching and retracting, and she hops over to the collage decorating Maddie's closet's sliding doors. Maddie has taped pictures of things she likes or wants (like Zeke Odom), and singers and actors she admires, places she wants to go, or live (like New York City). Lucinda fingers the pictures of Donna Summer and Diana Ross, asks who they are, and if she knows them. When Maddie tells her they're famous performers, she doesn't know them, the kid loses interest and wants to play a game. The only one Maddie has that a little girl can play is Perfection. It has a bunch of shapes and as many holes to match them. There's a timer and you have to fit the pieces into the right holes before it goes off and they all pop out.

It says ages four and up on the box, but Lucinda is stunningly horrible at this game. Curls falling in her face, she tries to stick a hexagon into a circle, a diamond into a square. Her chubby little fingers slam pieces onto the board violently, as if that'll make them fit. Maybe she doesn't care if they do. Maddie doesn't ask. Lucinda occupies herself for a long while.

She tries calling Julia; the phone just rings and rings.

Later, when his company and the kid are finally gone, Phil taps on Maddie's door and opens it without waiting for her to say it's okay.

"Hey, kiddo. How'd you enjoy playing with the little girl?"

Is he for real?

Reclining on her bed, Maddie thinks *screw you* as she stares across the room at the pictures on her closet. Soon, she'll be old enough to get out of this house, out of this town, and stick herself somewhere inside those pictures of New York City, where she can have her own apartment and not be the only Black girl for miles.

After a long silence, he says, "Okay. Well, thanks for watching her. It was helpful. I'm gonna shower, then how about we go to dinner?"

She is starving. And ready to end her diet. No Zeke, no point.

"With just you?" she asks, staring at the Washington Square Arch stuck next to a picture of Frankie Crocker from an ad for WBLS, the Black radio station Suzy turned her onto.

"Yeah," he says, like, *of course.*

"What about Mom?" She looks at him.

He shrugs. "All right. Call her if you want to. We can meet at the Duck Cedar. Forty-five minutes." He walks off, down the hall.

Maddie puts on mascara, lip gloss, a halter, and her Calvin's, because you never know. Zeke could be there.

On the drive over to dinner in Phil's new Mazda RX-7, he wears a white polo shirt and his Ray-Bans. He smokes, brags about his tennis playing, and listens to Beethoven on an 8-track tape that's big as a brick. Maddie opens the window to breathe.

They meet Velma at the family-style restaurant across the road from her shop. Surrounded by leafy trees, the Duck Cedar Inn and Velma Arrington Antiques are the only buildings on this stretch of Route 17.

The lobby is homey and it smells like buttery garlic bread baking. Maddie begins to salivate. God, I'm hungry, she thinks. Velma, who's there waiting for them, stands and smiles at Phil. Maddie sees that she's freshened her lipstick and powder. Her mother is pretty, but she wears too much perfume and way too much makeup caked on her face. There's a line where the foundation (that doesn't match her skin tone) meets her neck. The short dark hair she takes out of pink rollers every morning is styled in stiff, curled waves. It doesn't shake and flow the way Flynn's does. It's more like the hair of the dolls in the therapy dollhouse.

She has on white pants and a light blue knit top with three-quarter sleeves and a white collar. She's not skinny. Her body's curvy, with hips and a backside—womanly. She says hi to Maddie and kisses Phil on the lips.

Maddie watches him the way a tennis player eyes the ball. He's indifferent. Asks about her day as the three of them wait to be seated, but he doesn't look at her, and Maddie can tell he doesn't give two shits when her mother talks with pride about a couple of sales she made that day.

The smell of grilled steak wafts by and she breathes it in. Deeply. Maddie plans to eat every food group. Twice. Dr. Stillman *and* his diet can kiss her high-yellow bubble-butt. She probably won't see Zeke until school starts anyway. Still, she can't help looking around for him. Wishing. Of course there's nothing but White folks in here aside from them.

They sit toward the back near a window overlooking the scenic parking lot. Maddie and her mother across from her father. It's not that bright in here, but he keeps his Ray-Bans on. He orders the salad bar, and when he gets up, Velma turns to Maddie.

"What'd you do today?"

Maddie sighs. "I was *supposed* to go to Julia's pool party, but Dad had friends over to play tennis and swim, and he made me babysit, because that lady Flynn from the tennis club brought her daughter."

"*What?*" Velma's voice shoots up an octave. Rage blazes across her face.

Shit, Maddie thinks. She hasn't even said a word about the touching thighs or where she saw her father's hand, or how he was ogling Flynn's nonexistent ass.

"He made you babysit for that bitch?" Velma's face turns *really* red, even through the mask of makeup.

Maddie's afraid to say another thing.

"You know that's your father's *girlfriend*, right?"

Her mouth falls open. *She knows?*

"Yes, Maddie. And guess what else? She's not the only one."

Whoa. *What?* Maddie can't speak or breathe.

"I know you think he's so great—he takes you to the city, buys you things, spends *all* that time with you—but your father is a player, and I'm not talking about tennis. He's been running around with these bitches for *years*." She breathes in, then out slowly. "I haven't said anything to you, because as far as I knew, he was keeping that crap out of our house, but this . . ." She stabs a finger at the air, clinking the row of gold bracelets on her wrist. "He thinks he's gonna bring his cunts to *my* fucking house? And have you babysitting?"

The C-word? Maddie realizes this is *really* bad.

Velma's eyes stretch way open, her irises looking like marbles. She's breathing funny and Maddie worries she'll have a stroke.

Her father approaches the table with a mountain of greens blanketed with ranch dressing.

"Motherfucker." Velma jumps up, jabbing her fork toward his face with each syllable, her bracelets jingling. "You . . . are nothin' but a nigger!" she screams.

Oh-my-God. This is beyond bad. Maddie's never heard her mother say *that* word. Her stomach plummets. Her pulse throbs in her neck. She feels people staring. How could they not? Her parents, her *Black* parents are out of their seats and her mother is shrieking. It's a spectacle and she's part of it.

"Sit down and be quiet," Phil hisses.

"Go to hell."

The redheaded hostess who knows Maddie's mother by name is heading over. Velma's hand rises to stop her. "Don't worry, Jacqui. I'm leaving." She glowers at Maddie's father. "Think you're so sophisticated, *Dr.* Arrington," she says with a scoff. "But you're just a low-class, selfish—"

"This is not the place—"

"sorry, son of a bitch."

"for your stupid mouth, Velma. Shut up," he barks through gritted teeth. "You're only embarrassing yourself."

"Fuck you, nigger." She flings the fork at his chest and walks away.

Maddie doesn't know what to do. Her mother's leaving. She looks up at her father standing there in his ridiculous Ray-Bans holding his salad plate. Is he scowling? At *me*?

"What did you tell her?" he asks.

She wants to throw a doll against a wall and stomp the fuck out of it. She follows her mother.

Velma's hands grip the wheel of her yacht-sized Chevy station wagon. Her cloying perfume makes Maddie's nose run.

"I'm sorry," Velma says, sniffling. "I don't mean to damage your relationship with your father."

Ha, Maddie thinks. Hugging herself, she stares through the windshield at the winding road as water begins splattering the glass.

"But he's out of control bringing that woman to my house."

"It's raining, Mom."

"Tired of him shitting on me."

"You wanna put the windshield wipers on?"

"Don't ever let a man disrespect you. Always know your worth, Maddie." She looks straight ahead.

Maddie leans over and lifts the lever engaging the wipers. Velma slaps her hand, hard.

"Ow!"

"Don't do that while I'm driving!"

"I'd like to stay alive."

"Jesus, can you think of anyone but yourself?" Velma lets out a wailing sob.

A car comes toward them. Maddie winces as it passes. "Sorry," she says. "I'm sorry he did this to you." She looks at her mother and sees that tears are cutting grooves into her makeup.

"Me, too." Velma sucks in air through her sniffles.

"If he's done it before . . . why have you stayed?"

"What?" she snaps, turning to glare at Maddie. She looks back at the road, quiet for a while. "I thought he would stop. I hoped so, anyway. It's what men do," she says. "Your grandfather's no different. And why the hell should *I* leave? If anyone's leaving it's gonna be him. In a pine box, if he doesn't stop fucking with me."

When they get home, Velma runs into the guest room across the hall from Maddie's room. She slams the door and locks it. With the air-conditioning off, her scent lingers in the humidity, thick and oppressive, like cigarette smoke. Maddie hears her crying, and she knocks. "Leave me alone!" her mother shouts.

Julia calls. Zeke *was* there. He looked good, she tells Maddie. What a bod, she says. A bunch of girls in teeny bikinis sat around talking to him. She tells her who. Maddie knows them all—skinny, long-haired, pretty White girls. He definitely enjoyed the company, Julia says, rubbing it in. Her voice is tight. Clipped. She's angry Maddie didn't come. Maddie would tell her what happened if she could. She hangs up, because she can't.

Her parents have fought since she can remember. And she's pretty sure her father cheated with that horrible painter lady, Flora Goldberg's mother, but it's never been this in her face. Her mother can be mean, and she's always angry, but she has tried to please her father. She used to bring him breakfast in bed. She sewed tight, low-cut dresses to be appealing for him. She still decorates the house and cooks him special meals. What she can't do is be a skinny White woman with long hair and no ass.

Maddie prowls into the kitchen down the hall from her room. She snatches the leftover cartons of Chinese. Every single one. Egg rolls, fried rice, beef with broccoli, sweet-and-sour chicken. The fortune cookies, too. Arms stuffed, she tiptoes back to her room, locks the door, and shovels forkfuls into her mouth.

The garage door creaks open and there's the growl of her father's RX-7 pulling in. Shit. Soon the basement door to the kitchen slams, shaking the walls. His heavy steps thump through the foyer and up the stairs to her parents' bedroom, and then back down again. Next they thud into Maddie's hallway. Her heart is galloping. *Please don't fight anymore.* She sets the sweet-and-sour chicken down and grips the edge of her mattress so tight her fingernails hurt. She stops breathing to listen to him across the hall.

"Velma," he yells, jiggling the guest room knob. He bangs on the door. She doesn't answer. "You wanted Maddie to know so much, huh?" he says. "Bet you didn't her tell everything, did you? . . . Oh, now you got nothing to say? Good. Keep your big mouth and your big ass in there and out of my sight." He hits the door once more and walks away.

Her ass *isn't* fucking big and at least she *has* one. Prick.

Maddie hears the suction peel-pop from the kitchen as he opens the freezer. There's the crack of,the lever on the ice tray, then the plop of cubes into a glass. The generous pour of Dewar's isn't loud enough, but she does hear the tinkle of ice hitting the glass as he carries it through the foyer and thuds up the stairs.

She breathes.

After only one bite of an eggroll and a few more forkfuls of chicken, barely enough to mess up Dr. Stillman's diet, the cartons go back to the kitchen. She eyes the bottle of scotch. Killer of scary thoughts. She could use some help with that so she pours a glass.

Back in her room, she inhales the strong smell and then guzzles some. It burns her throat. Last time she drank scotch was a couple of years ago at On Luck, the local Chinese spot. It's notorious for serving alcohol to minors and yet, she, Julia, Lisa, and some other thirteen-year-old friends were allowed to go. Velma dropped Maddie and Lisa off and gave them money. Maddie ordered egg foo young and a dry Rob Roy—her father's drink; it's the only cocktail she knew.

She sips some more scotch, instead of guzzling. She knows she'll have to go slow. She sets the glass down and curls around a pillow that she pretends is Zeke, loving her, and promising that things will be okay. While she waits for the scotch to numb her scary thoughts, "Zeke" gets mucky with tears and snot.

As much as Maddie wants a boyfriend, when she's honest with herself, she fears she'll never have one. Not just because there's nearly no one for her in Monroe. But because when she imagines being with someone, anyone, even if she hopes it will feel good, she knows she'll panic. Her cousin Suzy's already done it. She loves sex. Maddie would rather touch herself than be pinned down under a guy. Zeke would probably dump her if she ever did get to date him. Maybe she'll always be alone.

In the morning, her father stands outside her closed door before going to the cottage to see his Monday morning patients. He reminds Maddie they have a tennis lesson in the Catskills later.

"I'm not going," she yells.

"Your lesson was paid for in advance."

"I don't care."

He's quiet in the hall for a moment. Then he says, "Happy, Velma?" His footsteps head back down the hall. The screen door snaps shut with a twang. Through her window, Maddie sees him disappear into his office.

Seconds later she hears her mother emerge from the guest room. Velma tries her doorknob without knocking.

"Open up, Maddie."

"Please leave me alone."

"Who the hell do you think you're talking to? Open this goddamn door."

Fuck. There's still scotch sitting on her nightstand. She sticks the glass way under her bed and hopes her mother won't smell it.

When she lets her in, Velma leans against the doorframe and says, "I think you should give your father a chance to apologize."

"Not interested." Maddie sits down cross-legged on the carpet in her underwear.

Her mother's hair is a wreck—random pieces sticking straight up. She didn't wear her rollers last night. She's still in yesterday's clothes and she doesn't have her face on. She hands Maddie a tiny black velvet box from her shop. In it, a pair of diamond earrings.

"Wow. They're pretty."

"Aren't they?" Velma brightens. "They're Art Deco, from the 1920s, and that setting is platinum, Maddie." Her voice sparkles as she points with her fingernail. "Just look at the detail, the workmanship.

God, I *love* them. They're supposed to be for your birthday, but I want you to have them now."

Maddie looks up at her. "Thanks, Mom."

Velma's face is puffy, her eyes swollen. She pats at her hair. "I know I'm not a warm and fuzzy mother, Maddie, but you're my baby, and I want you to know you're a princess. You have class and you don't need to take crap from anybody. Remember that."

"Okay." She nods.

"I'm sorry about yesterday," she says. "That stuff is between me and your father. Give him a chance to talk with you."

"I don't wanna talk to him."

"Maddie, take a bath and get dressed. I know you're upset, but he's still your father, and I don't want this on my conscience."

She used to like her father's RX-7. Now she agrees with her mother. "We're not a two-person family," she'd said when Phil bought the two-seater. "We don't all fit."

As he drives, he asks, "So, how are you feeling?"

Maddie stares out the window at random cars. Zeke could be in one.

Phil pushes the cigarette lighter in. "I can understand it if you're angry," he says.

She clicks her tongue and wishes he would shut the fuck up.

"Your father's not perfect. Sometimes adults . . . do things their children won't understand until they're grown. But y'know, your mother and I haven't been getting along for a while. I told her I wanted a divorce years ago and then again last year, and she refuses to discuss it."

Is this supposed to be his apology?

He lights a cigarette. "New York State, Maddie, is one of the only states where people can't get divorced simply because they want to. You have to prove the other person has violated the marital contract. Did you know that?"

The car fills with smoke. Maddie's eyes water. She rolls down her window. "I've never even been on a date," she says. "Why the hell would I know that?"

"I don't expect you to understand." He takes a drag, exhales. "But I feel trapped in this marriage."

"I don't wanna hear this."

"Yeah, of course you don't. You sound just like her."

She slices him up with her eyes. "Who *should* I sound like? Your *girlfriend*?"

He stares at the road.

She wants to curse him out so bad. "Why did you buy the new house?"

He looks at her. "Good question." He nods, eyes back on the road. "It was a life goal. Something I wanted. Can't have everything I want. Can't get out of this mess of a marriage, but I can keep moving forward . . . in the ways I'm able to."

Maddie goes back to looking out the window. "It'll never be a happy house."

He smokes. "Not as long as your mother's in it, no."

During one of their fights years ago, before they moved, her mother ran downstairs into his office one night. Maddie heard everything. He was on the phone. Velma pulled it out of the wall and threw it at him. "I'm not interesting enough? Is that it?" she yelled. "Why? Because I don't have a PhD? Your educated hussy got something between her legs that I don't?"

It scared Maddie, but no one talked about it. When she had her suspicions about that Goldberg woman it was never talked about either. When you don't talk about things you can almost pretend they're not real.

"We have an open relationship, Maddie. I know your mother's not going to tell you that, because she wants to play the victim, but that's the truth."

Open relationship? Maddie doesn't ask if that means what she thinks it means. She doesn't want to know.

Phil puts on a classical 8-track. Dvořák. Maddie sees that he looks deep in thought. And he starts picking his nose. Seriously. He's *really* digging the hell up in it. Like she's not even there.

The car pulls onto the blacktop parking lot at the tennis school. He turns the engine off, opens the door, and climbs out. Maddie stares through the windshield at the long green clubhouse that looks like a trailer. The courts are behind the building. Phil leans down to look at her. "Get out of the car."

She doesn't move.

"Dammit, Maddie." He slams the door, muttering, and heads into the school.

She sits there, knowing he'll be gone for an hour. There's no shade and it's getting hot already. With her window down the heat is still oppressive. Her thighs sweat on the leather seats. She gets out and leans against the door. That's burning up, too, but she doesn't let her skin touch, just her shorts and T-shirt. She crosses her arms and waits. That Buffy Sainte-Marie song she remembers mousy Muriel singing has been on her mind. Maybe she can find the sheet music and practice it with her teacher.

"You're not a dream, you're not an angel, you're a man. I'm not a queen, I'm a woman, take my hand. We'll make a space in the lives that we've planned. And here we'll stay, until it's time for you to go."

A car pulls into the space beside Maddie. A Mercedes 450SL. Her dream car. Wow. One day she wants to ride in a car like that with Zeke Odom.

A guy gets out in tennis whites. Blond, twenty-something, dashing. A Ken doll.

She smiles. "Beautiful car."

He closes his door and eyes her sternly. "What are you doing?" he asks.

"Nothing . . . just waiting for my dad."

He scoffs. "Sure you are. Get out of here. Get away from that car. *Scram.*"

She fingers one of the Deco diamond studs in her earlobe and says, "My father's inside taking a lesson. He's a psychologist. This is his car." Hot tears splash her cheeks. Shit. She didn't want to do that in front of him.

The Ken doll squints at her a second. Then he turns around, locks his car, and walks away.

She looks down at the blacktop and wipes her face with the bottom of her T-shirt.

On the ride home Maddie tells her father how that man spoke to her. "Why do we have to live where there's no one like us?"

"You should've come inside and taken your lesson, and that wouldn't have happened," he snaps.

"*You* should've let me go to that party," she screams. "And I wouldn't have to know you're a dick."

"Want me to put you out of this car? You will not talk to your father that way. What happened is between your mother and me. It's got nothing to do with you."

"I was there! If you wanted it to have nothing to do with me, you shouldn't have made me babysit your *girlfriend's* daughter!"

"Y'know, Maddie, most fathers don't spend this kind of time with their kids. You realize that? I didn't get any lessons when I was a boy. My father died when I was ten. I grew up in the ghetto. Think you'd rather live there?"

Maddie stares out the window at the sun pouring through the trees on I-84. "Your choices hurt, Dad," she says.

He doesn't respond.

And she doesn't tell him that they leave scars, too.

They pull into the driveway. Maddie gets out and walks toward the stone wall and the steps that lead up to the patio.

"Come get your racket," Phil shouts.

She turns. He's standing beside the rear glass hatch. Maddie goes back. She lifts the racket out. He walks away and up the steps. She hears the screen door open and twang shut. She slams the hatch and flings the racket against the stone wall. She picks it up and backhands it against the rocks. Over and over and over.

She's ordered to sit with her parents at dinner. The chair is crammed tight against the counter behind her, pinning her ribs into the oak table in front of her.

Her mother wears a fresh mask of makeup. Her parents stare at their plates in silence and chew the veal Velma has broiled.

Maddie refuses to eat it.

Not that she's still dieting. She knows there *is* no diet or anything else to be done to her body or soul that will make her fit into this place.

She's done trying.

One day, as soon as she can, Maddie will move from this asylum and into her future. She can hardly wait until it's time for her to go.

time travel

Hoboken, New Jersey, 1989

MADDIE

Twenty-one years later I'll run into you outside the PATH station in Hoboken in front of the wide green awning that leads down to the trains. Sounds of rumbling below and the din of chatter swirling, you'll yell my name above the noise, saying it like a question, as if you could actually be unsure that it's me.

I'll turn and totter on the top step. Just in time. Seconds later and I'd be swept into the stream of bodies flowing to the tracks.

It'll be shortly after five p.m. on a late September weekday, humid and sunny, with air that smells of commuters caught in unexpected high heat. Perspiration will roll down my back and leak between the butt cheeks you used to make fun of.

I'll squint against the sun and stare at you. You'll smile with closed lips and brown eyes that will be gentler than I remember. Several seconds will pass before you'll say, "Wow. First time I've ever seen you away from home. Where're you living these days?"

"Manhattan," I'll say.

"Oh. The big city," you'll say, like it's a truly good thing.

I'll nod. I won't ask you anything. I'll look at you and wait.

Suits of blue, black, gray, and tan will dodge and whoosh past us in both directions. Heels clicking on concrete, huffs and impatient scoffs, we'll be in the way.

I'll shield my eyes with one hand and be silent for so long it'll feel impolite. You'll hold a cheap gray suit jacket over one shoulder, your white collared shirt bearing sweat marks under the arms.

You'll smell of Obsession for Men, alluring and more sophisticated than the Old Spice I used to notice at the bus stop during high school, when you rarely spoke to me. Your chest will be broad and you'll be slim, like me, which will mean something, because twenty-one years earlier we were chubby six year olds foraging together for Ding Dongs and Oreos my mother hid deep in the pantry so we wouldn't overeat. We'd find them and eat them all, and that thrill was a bond we shared.

But being connoisseurs of Nabisco cookies and Hostess snack cakes, and being buddies from the time we could crawl, never made our bond as strong as the one you shared with every kid in the neighborhood but me.

Someone will bump into you and you'll fall into me and grab my arm before I lose my balance on the top step.

"Sorry. You all right?" you'll ask.

I'll say, "Fine, thanks." And take my arm back.

That day, twenty-one years after I lost you, I'll be wearing a tomato-red kufi atop unapologetically kinky hair—wild kinks I tamed the soul out of when I lived across the street from you, hoping straight hair would make me pretty, and more like everyone else. But you called me an ugly, bubble-butted nigger at the bus stop. Elementary school became junior high, which turned into high school, and I barely existed. You had all those years to speak to me. That day I'll wonder, why now?

I'll have on black chunky boots and a dress that's lime-green, like LifeSavers candies. Red, black, and green are Pan-African colors, and I'll wear them because, at the time, I'll be mad and militant, saying fuck you to you and everyone else from home who said my color, my hair, and my big butt made me ugly. That day at the PATH station it won't matter to me that you were only a boy when you said those things.

I won't smile. I won't be warm. I'll forget any mean things I may have said back at the bus stop. I probably said some, because I *will* remember how you winced at the mention of your fat mom, crippled father, and port-wine stain birthmarked baby sister. My tongue, sharpened on figurative and literal sticks and stones hurled at me by neighborhood bullies, must have pierced your soft spots sometimes, too. Yet you'll look at me that day with a tenderness that insists cruel words never passed between us.

Your dark hair will be short. Your skin clean-shaven, clear, the spots of adolescence healed and faded. Your face will flush and your eyes will brighten the way they used to shine when you were my round-cheeked running buddy. You'll look deep into me with such warmth that against my will you'll begin to melt the icicles that numbed me inside.

My name, when you say it, will sound like songs from playtimes past. In your eyes I'll catch a glimpse of us singing on swings, flying above the grass where we found four-leaf clovers. You'll invite me into a little chamber of your heart where you saved us. But I won't go. I won't be ready to remember how to get there.

There will be no mention of what happened to us, or what didn't happen that should have. You'll sing my name again, a young boy's sweetness shining out of your grown man's face, and you'll say, "You were my first best friend."

I'll know you're telling me you're sorry. You didn't mean to hurt me. You were just a kid.

I'll nod politely and shrug off your words of apology. I'll carry my bubble-butt and my baggage down the stairs, catch my train, and move on with my life.

In another twenty-one years, I'll be middle-aged and softer inside and out, the rough edges of resentment worn down with experience. I'll remember how you said my name that day and the way you looked at me with affection. I'll transport myself back to the PATH station, in front of the stairs, trains rumbling below, bodies whooshing by, and I'll be kinder to you. I will. Because by then I'll know that love is the only feeling left once enough time has passed.

The End

acknowledgments

Many thanks to Roxane Gay, and to the University of Georgia Press's
Beth Snead and Jon Davies. I'm immensely grateful for this opportunity.

Thanks to Dara Hyde for encouraging me to develop these stories.

To my mentors and colleagues at Antioch University Los Angeles who
critiqued early drafts of these stories: Alma Luz Villanueva, Steve Heller,
Tara Ison, Susan Taylor Chehak, Dana Johnson, Lisa Ruiz, Seth Fisher,
Antonia Crane, Gordon Johnson, Tisha Marie Reichle-Aguilera, Nate Hansen,
Meghan McCord, Tina Rubin, Aya de Leon, and my love, Leonard Chang—
thank you.

Thanks to the print and online journals that published a number of these
stories: the *Phoenix Soul*, formerly *Sprout Magazine* online, *Red Fez*, *Arlijo
Journal*, the *Emerson Review*, *Elohi Gadugi Journal*, *Hunger Mountain*,
Callaloo, *Xavier Review*, and *Soundings Review*.

Thanks to the wonderful LA literary friends who've provided opportunities
to read these stories publicly: David Rocklin, Chiwan Choi, Natashia Deon,
Ashely Perez, and Patrick O'Neil.

Love and thanks to the fabulous organization Women Who Submit.

To my childhood friends and former teachers: Andrew Fetherolf,
Carol Meyerdirks-Tsao, Tracy Stora, David Konis, Brenda Polsky,

Beverly Green, Frazier Prince, Annie Rudden, Joe Landi, Jane Warshaw-Radix, Harold Moroknek, Esther Schrager McInnes and her daughter Hannah McInnes, Jonathan Klug, Robin Perrin Nowicki, Marty and Reena Manson, Wally MacGuire, Don Johnson, and Ron Johnson—I appreciate you and your support very much.

Thanks to my mentors and colleagues at Callaloo Writing Workshop at Brown University who workshopped two stories: Jacinda Townsend, Ravi Howard, Marame Bàlla, Kiietti Walker-Parker, and Nafissa Thompson-Spires.

Thanks to mentors and colleagues at the Prague Summer Program for Writers who workshopped multiple stories: Robert Eversz, Richard Katrovas, Valerie Burns, Kimberly Reyes, Caleb Klitzke, Allen Jones, Jaimy Gordon, Mary B. Sellers, Jennifer Shuk Lan Crooks, Patricia Hampl, Stuart Dybek, and Grace Daley Bydalek.

Thanks to my former writing group members who read early drafts: Ann Marsh, Lisa Richardson, Reyna Grande, Lara Bazelon, Jessica Garrison, Sonia Nazario, and Barbara Thomas.

I'm grateful to friends and family who've read and critiqued the stories and/or who've shown up to events to hear me read them: Vera Johnson, Hillary Johnson, William L. Johnson, Elle Johnson, Marissa Lee, Jesse Rhines, Nicole Sconiers, Cheryl Lane-Lewis, Katrina Reid, Eriq La Salle, Jeff Stetson, Frances Sackett, Nana-Ama Danquah, Richard Torres, Michael X. Ferraro, Patricia Kaufman, Adrienne Crew, Virginie Dangales, Heather Hamilton, Debralyn Press, Robert Morgan Fisher, Doug and Susan Segal, Rena Hecht, Dara Gray, Audrey Schmedes, Kristen Johnson, Candace Culp, Eric Hetzel, Ernest Brawley, Gregory Vahanian, Cyd Gold, Claudia Gold, Kevin Rock, Pamela Mshana, Mariva Mshana Dawes, Dena Crowder, Robin McKee, Jan Ford, Brandi Collins, Elyce Strong-Mann, Cynthia Bond, and a special thanks to Kate Maruyama, a brilliant writer, a great friend, and my trusted first reader.

The Flannery O'Connor Award for Short Fiction

David Walton, *Evening Out*
Leigh Allison Wilson, *From the Bottom Up*
Sandra Thompson, *Close-Ups*
Susan Neville, *The Invention of Flight*
Mary Hood, *How Far She Went*
François Camoin, *Why Men Are Afraid of Women*
Molly Giles, *Rough Translations*
Daniel Curley, *Living with Snakes*
Peter Meinke, *The Piano Tuner*
Tony Ardizzone, *The Evening News*
Salvatore La Puma, *The Boys of Bensonhurst*
Melissa Pritchard, *Spirit Seizures*
Philip F. Deaver, *Silent Retreats*
Gail Galloway Adams, *The Purchase of Order*
Carole L. Glickfeld, *Useful Gifts*
Antonya Nelson, *The Expendables*
Nancy Zafris, *The People I Know*
Robert Abel, *Ghost Traps*
T. M. McNally, *Low Flying Aircraft*
Alfred DePew, *The Melancholy of Departure*
Dennis Hathaway, *The Consequences of Desire*
Rita Ciresi, *Mother Rocket*
Dianne Nelson Oberhansly, *A Brief History of Male Nudes in America*
Christopher McIlroy, *All My Relations*
Carol Lee Lorenzo, *Nervous Dancer*
C. M. Mayo, *Sky over El Nido*
Wendy Brenner, *Large Animals in Everyday Life*
Paul Rawlins, *No Lie Like Love*
Harvey Grossinger, *The Quarry*
Ha Jin, *Under the Red Flag*
Andy Plattner, *Winter Money*
Frank Soos, *Unified Field Theory*
Mary Clyde, *Survival Rates*
Hester Kaplan, *The Edge of Marriage*
Darrell Spencer, *CAUTION Men in Trees*
Robert Anderson, *Ice Age*
Bill Roorbach, *Big Bend*

Dana Johnson, *Break Any Woman Down*

Gina Ochsner, *The Necessary Grace to Fall*

Kellie Wells, *Compression Scars*

Eric Shade, *Eyesores*

Catherine Brady, *Curled in the Bed of Love*

Ed Allen, *Ate It Anyway*

Gary Fincke, *Sorry I Worried You*

Barbara Sutton, *The Send-Away Girl*

David Crouse, *Copy Cats*

Randy F. Nelson, *The Imaginary Lives of Mechanical Men*

Greg Downs, *Spit Baths*

Peter LaSalle, *Tell Borges If You See Him: Tales of Contemporary Somnambulism*

Anne Panning, *Super America*

Margot Singer, *The Pale of Settlement*

Andrew Porter, *The Theory of Light and Matter*

Peter Selgin, *Drowning Lessons*

Geoffrey Becker, *Black Elvis*

Lori Ostlund, *The Bigness of the World*

Linda LeGarde Grover, *The Dance Boots*

Jessica Treadway, *Please Come Back to Me*

Amina Gautier, *At-Risk*

Melinda Moustakis, *Bear Down, Bear North*

E. J. Levy, *Love, in Theory*

Hugh Sheehy, *The Invisibles*

Jacquelin Gorman, *The Viewing Room*

Tom Kealey, *Thieves I've Known*

Karin Lin-Greenberg, *Faulty Predictions*

Monica McFawn, *Bright Shards of Someplace Else*

Toni Graham, *The Suicide Club*

Siamak Vossoughi, *Better Than War*

Lisa Graley, *The Current That Carries*

Anne Raeff, *The Jungle Around Us*

Becky Mandelbaum, *Bad Kansas*

Kirsten Sundberg Lunstrum, *What We Do with the Wreckage*

Colette Sartor, *Once Removed*

Patrick Earl Ryan, *If We Were Electric*

Kate McIntyre, *Mad Prairie*

Toni Ann Johnson, *Light Skin Gone to Waste*

Anniversary Anthologies